Praise for **CHARLES C**
& **KENNEDY 3**

"An intricate espionage thriller that's both timely and convincing."
— **KIRKUS**

"Enthralling, haunting … Cumming is often compared to John le Carré, but he is his own man—taking the spy thriller to a new level of storytelling, one that illuminates the darkest corners of our modern world."
— **FINANCIAL TIMES**

"Cumming masterfully orchestrates suspense as the characters' pasts come to bear on their present … This espionage tale grips from the get-go."
— **PUBLISHERS WEEKLY**

"Atmospheric and packed with threat, it thrills on every single page."
— **DAILY MAIL**

"A compelling exploration of the consequences of realpolitik and the intermingling of the personal with the political."
— **THE GUARDIAN**

"Cumming marshals his twin time frames expertly and illuminates an awful chapter in recent history. A first-rate spy thriller."
— **THE MAIL ON SUNDAY**

"Enlightening and satisfying."
— **LA TIMES**

"[A] haunting, masterful work."
— a **FINANCIAL TIMES** "Best Thriller of 2023"

"This remains one of the finest espionage series going, and *Kennedy 35* never disappoints. Charles Cumming has a great eye for historical detail, which he mixes in seamlessly with all the action to create outstanding thrillers that are not to be missed."

— BOOKREPORTER

"As is true in real life, time is not linear and Kite carries the past with him into the present not as history but as living fact ... *Kennedy 35* is an engrossing glimpse into a future where we all may have to come to terms with what we have done."

— REVIEWING THE EVIDENCE

"Charles Cumming is up there with the very best spy writers."

—IAN RANKIN

KENNEDY
35

By Charles Cumming

KENNEDY 35

CHARLES CUMMING

THE MYSTERIOUS PRESS
NEW YORK, NY

KENNEDY 35

Mysterious Press
An Imprint of Penzler Publishers
58 Warren Street
New York, N.Y. 10007

First Mysterious Press paperback edition

First published in the UK by HarperCollins*Publishers* Ltd.

Library of Congress Control Number: 2023908390

Paperback ISBN: 978-1-61316-592-8
ebook ISBN: 978-1-61316-456-3

10 9 8 7 6 5 4 3 2 1

Printed in the United States of America
Distributed by W. W. Norton & Company

for Cassius and Hamish

*and to the memory of my sister, Alexandra Nielsen
(1968–2023)*

Index of Characters

The Kite family:

Lachlan Kite ('Lockie'), intelligence officer
Isobel Paulsen, Lachlan's wife, a doctor
Cheryl Kite (née Chapman), Lachlan's mother
Ingrid Kite, Lachlan's daughter (b.2020)

BOX 88:

Michael Strawson, veteran CIA officer and co-founder of BOX 88 (d.2005)
Azhar Masood, Kite's No2 at 'The Cathedral', BOX 88 headquarters in London
Cara Jannaway, former MI5 officer
Robert Vosse, senior MI5 officer
Freddie Lane, computer analyst (a 'Turing')
Jerry Walters, a Turing
Ricky Ackerman, former CIA officer
Omar Gueye, Senegalese operative in Dakar
Naby Gueye, Omar's brother

Other Characters:

Martha Raine, Kite's girlfriend in 1995

Eric Appiah, Senegalese schoolfriend of Kite
Philippe Vauban, French war reporter
Grace Mavinga, Congolese Hutu businesswoman
Augustin Bagaza, Rwandan Hutu *genocidaire*
Demba Diatta, hotelier in Dakar
Lucian Michael Cablean, American writer and podcaster
Jean-François Fournier, French intelligence officer (DGSE)
Yves Duval, businessman (retired DGSE officer)
Maurice Lagarde, disgruntled DGSE officer and memoirist
Lindsey Berida, associate of Yves Duval
Mohammed Suidani, associate of Grace Mavinga
Graham Platt, financial lawyer with the London firm Rycroft Maule

A Note on the Rwandan Genocide

In 1990, Tutsi fighters with the Rwandan Patriotic Front (RPF), operating under the leadership of Paul Kagame, attempted to overthrow the country's Hutu-led government. In the ensuing civil war, French president François Mitterand armed and supported Rwanda's Hutu leader Juvénal Habyarimana. A ceasefire was declared in 1993 and a power-sharing agreement reached. Hardline Hutu extremists who opposed the deal formed the Interahamwe.

On 6 April 1994, a plane carrying Habyarimana was shot down near the capital, Kigali. In the days which followed, Hutu soldiers, police and militia murdered key Tutsi and moderate Hutu military and political leaders. The Interahamwe used the assassination as a pretext for launching a genocidal campaign against the minority Tutsi population. In a period of just over 100 days, an estimated 600,000 Tutsis were hunted down and murdered, often by neighbours armed with machetes and other crude weapons. Sexual violence was rife. As many as half a million women were raped during the Rwandan genocide.

Radio Télévision Libre des Milles Collines (RLTM) was a Rwandan radio station which played a key role in propagating hate speech and inciting violence against the Tutsis. RLTM broadcasts had a particular impact in rural areas where radio was the prime source of news. Presenters gave advice to listeners on how to identify Tutsis and frequently provided detailed information on their where-abouts, leading to targeted killings.

UN peacekeepers under the command of General Roméo Dallaire did not intervene to stop the genocide. The mass killings ended only when the RPF gained control of Rwanda in July, forcing Hutu war criminals (*genocidaires*) to flee into neighbouring Zaire (now the Democratic Republic of the Congo). The International Criminal Tribunal for Rwanda later held individuals associated with Radio Milles Collines responsible for their role in the genocide. The station's founder, Félicien Kabuga, was arrested in Paris in 2020 after more than twenty-five years on the run. He pleaded not guilty to charges of genocide, incitement to commit genocide, persecution, extermination and murder. In August 2023, United Nations judges in the Hague declared Kabuga, 90, unfit to stand trial because of dementia.

C.C. London 2023

'To beguile the time
Look like the time; bear welcome in your eye,
Your hand, your tongue: look like the innocent flower,
But be the serpent under't.'
William Shakespeare, *Macbeth*

'The memory of Rwanda sits like a tumour leaking
poison into the back of my head.'
Aidan Hartley, *The Zanzibar Chest*

Dakar, Senegal
1995

'You will not like what I am about to tell you.'

The man was in his early thirties, scruffily dressed in a stained T-shirt and torn denim jeans. There were scars on the backs of his hands. He looked tired and hadn't shaved for several days. He was seated in a wicker chair smoking a filterless French cigarette, sunlight on his clothes cut by a Venetian blind.

'You'd be surprised,' Michael Strawson replied. 'I've seen a lot. I've heard a lot. Just tell me.'

'You won't want to hear it because you will never have heard anything like it before.' It was as though the man had not listened to what the American had told him. 'This was a new savagery. Even you, Mike, with everything that you and my father experienced – in El Salvador, in Cambodia – you still won't believe it. People deny that it happened. You will want to tell yourself that I have got my facts wrong, that I am making it up. How else to explain something like this?'

'Like I said, Philippe, just tell me.'

A black mood of sorrow emanated from Philippe Vauban like the sudden rain in Dakar which had left the room feeling cloistered and damp.

'Once I have described what I saw and what I learned,

your instinct will be to walk away, to think that there is some alternative version of history and I am just some crazy, burned-out hack. You will want to believe in your soul that human beings are not capable of something like this. But I am here to tell you that they can sink this low. It all happened. I saw it happen.'

'Tell me what you saw.'

A band of sunlight struck Vauban's eyes through the slats of the blind. There was the sudden blast of a truck far below on Rue Parchappe.

'You know who I am.' He gave an exhausted shrug. 'But do you know how I got there, how I came to be in Rwanda?'

'I can guess.'

The Frenchman drew deeply on the cigarette, holding in the smoke as he gathered his thoughts.

'The crazy thing is I started out wanting adventure. Adrenaline. I was young and unafraid. So I joined the Legion. I wanted to discover the world, make an impact on it. I guess I wanted to be more like my father. Then you realise the world is not changed by you being in it. You become interested only in truth.' Strawson nodded solemnly. 'So I became a journalist who wanted to write truthful stories. Then I discover that there is no such thing as truth. Only interpretation. So, finally, I wanted justice. This is what I want. Everything else is meaningless, *éphémère*.'

'What kind of justice? This is not a court of law, Philippe. I am not a judge.'

'Why don't I start with some facts?' Vauban had again ignored what Strawson was trying to tell him. 'In a period of six weeks, no more, in the spring of last year, at least eight hundred thousand men, women and children were murdered. Butchered. Some people put the number closer to a million. That's less than one hundred days to erase seventy per cent of the entire Tutsi population of Rwanda.'

'We know this. It's been widely reported.'

A look of impatience.

'Has the butchery been widely reported? The speed and brutality, the ruthlessness of it?' Vauban took a final drag on the cigarette. Flakes of ash dropped onto the back of his hand. He did not seem to notice. 'I met a reporter in Kigali. He told me: "It takes ten thousand dead Africans to furrow the brow of even one left-leaning white." How many whites is that? Less than a hundred people world-wide who really care about what happened. You would get more attention if the Rwandans had been starving. You can show swollen stomachs on CNN, you can show children on the BBC with bodies like skeletons, kids with eyes the size of dinner plates. Then white Europeans, white Americans, suddenly they will care. Bob Geldof will get his friends together and everybody will feel better for having tried to do something. But you cannot show mass murder. Apparently you cannot show what happened in Rwanda. No television station in the world would broad-cast what happened last year. Not the real truth of it. The edges and the details maybe, but not the whole truth.'

Vauban stubbed out the cigarette, immediately lighting another. Strawson was studying him as he might have studied his own son, fearing that he was at the edge of a breakdown.

'People would be sick,' the Frenchman continued. 'They would ring the station to complain. You can't show streets running with blood on the evening news. You cannot show girls as young as twelve or thirteen being raped and then opened up with machetes on 60 Minutes. Young Tutsi boys with their feet sliced off so that they can never become soldiers. Imagine that on *France Soir*. They didn't show what the Hutus had scrawled on the doors of the huts which belonged to their Tutsi neighbours: "Death to Cockroaches". They didn't show the bodies buzzing with maggots and flies, the wild dogs eating human corpses. They didn't show the blood dripping off the clubs and the machetes, the vultures circling and settling on the dead.'

5

'Try not to become upset.' Strawson knew that there was nothing he could do to console Vauban. The memories were locked in his mind; there would be no removing them. 'Try not to be emotional,' he said, maintaining a professional tone. 'Just tell me about Augustin Bagaza. What you know about him. Where you saw him. Why you think my organisation can help you.'

Vauban suppressed a look of dismay; for so long he had wanted someone to bear witness to his revulsion and pain. How could a person who had been through what he had been through not 'become upset'? How could they not be 'emotional'? He took another deep drag on the new cigarette, looking for a moment as though he was questioning the good sense of continuing. In the street below, the same truck blasted the same horn.

'You know it's not so much the bodies I remember as the smell. Blood and faeces and rotting flesh like animal manure on a hot summer day.' He looked towards the window, speaking in a kind of daze to the slats in the blind. 'There was very little food and water in those first few weeks after we were allowed in. Just what we brought with us and what Dallaire told his people they could hand out to the press corps. Day after day we ate the same UN rations: tinned cassoulet, tinned potatoes, tinned cheese. I knew that I must have vitamins so I ate guavas off the trees in Kigali. Now if somebody puts a guava in front of me, or if I taste or smell the brine of tinned food, I throw up.' In French he added: 'It's like an inversion of Proust's fucking *madeleines*. A taste to transport me back to hell.'

'Bagaza,' the American repeated quietly.

There was a knock at the door. Vauban shouted: '*Pas maintenant!*' and footsteps moved back along the corridor.

'Bagaza is being protected.' Vauban was staring at Strawson, exhausted eyes looking directly into his. 'Some kind of deal with the French. Paris still pulls the strings here, yes? Mitterand gave the Interahamwe guns and machetes;

6

he gave every Hutu the tools to commit mass murder. So French intelligence officers keep Augustin Bagaza safe in his bed. You probably know the local guy. Yves Duval. He is under instructions to get Bagaza out of Senegal. He knows too many of their secrets.'

'I don't know about that. If what you say is true, Paris would have flown him out by now.'

'Even so. The clock is ticking. It is only a matter of time. Duval is here. His team are watching him. Bagaza will be like Habyarimana's wife. You heard about her? Her entire extended family, many of them organisers of the genocide, are living in the Marais. Mitterand even gave them money when they arrived – 200,000 francs at the airport!'

'We know,' Strawson replied. He was wearing a pale linen suit and had taken off his shoes so that his feet could breathe a little. All the time his mind was turning over the good sense of doing what he knew Vauban was going to ask him to do.

'You're sure it's him?' he asked. 'You're sure it was Bagaza?'

'I am certain.'

'This is the same man you met in Rwanda last year?'

'The same man.' There was a paperback on the table beside Vauban's chair, a French translation of *The Secret History*. The back cover had come away in the heat. The Frenchman held it up. 'As sure as I am looking at this book, but I am also looking at you.' It was an overcomplication of his normally faultless English. 'He is living at number 35 Rue Kennedy in an apartment on the fourth floor. With his Congolese whore, the woman who encourages and celebrates his evil. I have seen them come out. I have seen them go in.'

'And did Bagaza see you? Did he recognise you?'

A defiant shake of the head. 'No chance. I was in my car. Maybe on the street as a white man he would notice me, but not inside a rental car. Do you know what it's like to sit there, knowing what this man did to people I knew and cared about? Knowing that Bagaza personally instructed tens of thousands of people to commit mass murder, knowing that he showed many of them how to do it with his bare hands?' Vauban paused for a moment, running a hand through his hair. 'I can't work. I can't sleep while this monster walks the streets of Dakar. You owe me, Mike. You owe my father.'

'Daytime or night?'

'What?'

'When did you see him?'

'Daytime. Bright sunshine. No hat. No sunglasses. The fucking Eichmann of the Rwandan genocide walking around Dakar like he owns the place.'

'What makes you think he's being protected by Yves Duval? You have any evidence?'

Vauban shrugged. For the first time there was a hesitancy in his manner. Strawson noticed that one of the scabs on the knuckle of his right hand had started to bleed.

'How else could he get an apartment in Plateau, how else can he walk the streets as a free man? Either he is being protected or he is preparing to leave. Somebody gets him a new passport, suddenly he is an Ivorian diplomat flying to Washington with a new identity. He gets a new life, a fresh start, while naked girls lie dead in the long grass. Do you want him to be able to do that, Mike? If it was Eichmann himself, would you allow that to happen?'

'Of course not.' Michael Strawson didn't go in for emotional arguments; he was interested only in facts and outcomes. 'The diplomatic passport,' he continued. 'Tell me more about that.'

'It's a ratline for the Hutus. They come here, they go to Côte d'Ivoire, to Lagos, they pay enough money to the right people, they get a new identity.'

It was the first time Strawson had heard about it. He wondered if it was something Vauban was making up in order to convince him.

'Maybe I'm wrong,' the Frenchman continued, sensing this. 'Maybe he's thinking about starting another radio station here. Not Radio Mille Collines. Perhaps Radio Corniche or Radio Dakar? Fill Senegalese minds with the same poison he used on the Hutus in Kigali. "Do your work!" he screamed at them. And, wow, did they work hard, Mike. Have you any idea how difficult, how exhausting it is to kill a man with a machete, how many blows it takes? Those things are heavy. Your adrenaline is running, you quickly get tired.'

'Stay with the facts. Describe him. Describe what you saw. Did you see him again? Are you sure he's still here in Dakar, still on Rue Kennedy?'

'I have seen him three times. He is still here, believe me! The devil walks among us.'

'Who else have you told about this?'

'Nobody.' This with a note of defiant pride. 'Just you. You're the only person I know who has the power to do something about it. I don't trust anybody else.'

'And what is it exactly that you want me to do?'

'I want the world to know that the French government protected a *genocidaire*. I want Augustin Bagaza to pay for his crimes. And I want him dead.'

Paris, France
2022

'Follow the money.'

Jean-François Fournier is an officer with the General Directorate for External Security, more commonly known as the DGSE. He has been working for France's overseas intelligence service for almost eight years and is recognised as one of the new breed of spies with a reformist zeal inspired in part by the republic's youthful, ambitious president, embarking now on his second term in office.

'You recognise this line of course,' Fournier continues. 'One of the great American films of the 1970s, *All the President's Men*. A suggestion to the journalists Bob Woodward and Carl Bernstein that they should pursue the financial links between the Watergate burglars and Richard Nixon's White House.'

Fournier wonders if he is striking the right note. He is speaking to a small Paris conference room of six men and one woman, all of whom outrank him in age and seniority. He is trying to convince them to investigate one of their own, a former DGSE officer whose criminal activities will provoke a political firestorm if left unchecked. The faces of his colleagues are composed but attentive; Fournier knows that he is well-respected within the Service but that what he is proposing is likely to prove deeply unpopular with the old guard.

'Let's be honest,' he says, taking a slightly different tack. 'What we might choose to call Yves Duval's second career has been an open secret in this organisation for at least fifteen years. You all know the story. He left the Service in 2002, borrowed over 13 million euros from an Angolan government minister under investigation by the DGSE, used the money to buy numerous small businesses and properties in sub-Saharan Africa, linked his burgeoning portfolio of interests to a network of phantom shareholders, phoney investors and so-called "company directors", then reintroduced himself to the drug dealers, weapons smugglers and crooked politicians whose acquaintance he had made while carrying out legitimate business on behalf of the French government. Yves Duval offered these men a tailored money laundering service for a 20 per cent cut of what our British friends like to call their "ill-gotten gains". In simple terms he has become a fixer, a middleman, moving dirty money through a network of brass plate companies, offshore bank accounts and phantom investment portfolios until that money emerges squeaky clean at the end of a long spin cycle.'

Fournier pauses to take a sip of water. He had rehearsed that section of his presentation several times and is pleased with how it came off. He knows that he has the room's attention, but it is not yet clear if his plea for action will be greeted with approval or contempt.

'We allowed Yves Duval to carry on,' he continues. 'We had larger matters to contend with. Afghanistan. Iraq. The financial crisis. The activities of al-Qaeda and Islamic State. Duval was permitted to re-enter civilian life and to set himself up as a criminal mastermind.' A momentary pause. 'Take a look at this man. His name is Pierre Eglise.'

Fournier clicks a laptop on the low table in front of him and turns to see that a Powerpoint image of a young French soldier in full military uniform has appeared on the large white screen.

'Corporal Eglise lost his life seven months ago at the hands of Boko Haram. You are all familiar with the circumstances. Four other French soldiers were killed in the same attack in northern Nigeria. Three French aid workers were also injured, one of them critically. Today I will demonstrate that this soldier, this married man and father of two young children, would still be alive today were it not for our former colleague, Yves Duval.'

Now a first indication of possible dissent: the head of the Strategy Directorate makes a clicking noise in the back of his throat and adjusts the position of his chair. Fournier ignores this.

'We turned the other cheek. We *enabled* Duval's criminality. We lacked both the desire and the resources to bring this man to justice. We knew that it would be all but impossible to prove that he was guilty. All of us accept this, no? But now something has changed. Yves Duval is no longer laundering money for political elites, for South African drug smugglers, for Nigerian warlords. No. He is laundering money for Islamic State. By his actions, he has endangered French lives. By putting money into the pockets of religious fanatics, he has brought about the deaths of French soldiers and citizens. For this, I believe, our former colleague must pay a heavy price. Duval must be brought to justice.'

Fournier turns briefly to check that the photograph of Eglise is still visible behind him. He feels that the slain soldier is watching over him, encouraging him, willing him to succeed. Now he clicks the Powerpoint to a subsequent slide which shows a slim, bearded East African of about forty walking along a street in Mogadishu speaking into a mobile phone.

'Most of you know this man. Ousmane Ahmed Zein, chief financier for the Allied Democratic Forces, or "ADF" for short. Terrorist groups of all types will use kidnapping and ransom to extort funds from their victims. What happens to this money? To whom does a man like Zein turn in order to conceal that money's origin and to facilitate the purchase of weapons and ammunition? He turns to Yves Duval, a man with more than twenty years of experience in receiving cash, disguising its origin and redistributing the funds into the legitimate global banking system. On Zein's behalf, Duval's operation created a charity, "Beyond Aleppo", to which unsuspecting housewives in Stuttgart made cash donations in the mistaken belief that the money would go towards helping Syrian refugees in Germany. Duval also orchestrated the creation of "Red Sea Relief", a charitable foundation promising humanitarian aid to the suffering people of Yemen. The cash donations and wire transfers instead went towards supporting the activities of ADF. Follow the money.'

'Monsieur Fournier.' A sudden interruption from the chief of the Strategy Directorate, the same click at the back of his throat. 'What is it exactly that you propose to do? We arrest Duval, there is a very public trial, it emerges that he is a former French spy, there is a scandal. We are already dealing with the fallout from Maurice Lagarde's leaked memoir which accuses Duval not only of forming a longstanding relationship with a key figure from the Rwandan genocide but also of providing refuge to a known *genocidaire* in Senegal. Are you really suggesting that we dig all this up, spend hundreds of thousands of euros during a budgetary crisis, just to give ourselves and the French government a headache it does not need nor deserve? The President – wisely or not – recently apologised for France's role in the genocide. He acknowledged that François Mitterand enjoyed a close personal friendship with the Hutu government of Juvénal Habyarimana, providing his administration with financial and military support in their fight against the Tutsis. France stood aside as the slaughter began; indeed, on occasion, we facilitated the escape of perpetrators of the genocide. This is something of which our country should be ashamed. We were on the wrong side of history. All this would come out in a trial, Jean-François. Why put the nation through it?'

Fournier is silent for a moment. He takes time to look at each of the officers in front of him, studying their reactions one by one.

'The key figure in the Rwandan genocide you refer to is a woman who is already being investigated by one of my associates. Analysis reveals that she owns a complex network of import and export companies operating in free trade zones and countries with weak regulatory oversight. She and many of Duval's other associates and family members are the directors of brass plate companies with bank accounts in Turkey, Cyprus and Kenya, many of which have triggered Suspicious Activity Reports. Why? Because they are used by Duval to clean cash on behalf of whatever gangster, terrorist or politician is prepared to pay his 20 per cent commission. The woman in question's assets include hotels and restaurants in Nairobi, Entebbe, Kinshasa and Dar Es Salaam, some of them real, many of them fictitious. If you want to stay the night at "Opal Residences" in Brazzaville, for example, I say good luck to you. The hotel does not exist.' A small exertion of laughter from the room's only woman, not much more than an ironic sniff. 'Most of these so-called hotels and restaurants, nightclubs and cocktail bars have a track record of fake invoices and unexplained cash deposits. They are part of Duval's vast international network of legitimate and illegitimate businesses, all of which are designed to confuse and to obscure.'

Fournier takes another sip of water, just as the Director of Political Intelligence leans forward in his chair.

'I must have missed this report,' he says. 'Who is this woman you are referring to?'

Fournier steps away from the desk, closing the lid of the laptop.

'MI6 has a nickname for her,' he replies. 'They call her Lady Macbeth.'

The present day

1

Robin Whitaker was drinking a cup of milkless *lapsang souchong* in the dusty, semi-chaotic basement of his art gallery in the heart of Piccadilly when he heard the welcome jingle of the doorbell. He looked up and ascertained from the foggy CCTV screen that a tall, smartly dressed black man of about forty had entered the premises. Ordinarily one of the girls on the desk would have been there to welcome him, but Jasmine and Ayesha were both off sick – the former with asymptomatic Covid, the latter with mental health problems – so Whitaker himself had to climb the short flight of spiralling metal stairs to greet his customer.

On an ordinary day he was lucky if more than half a dozen members of the public set foot in the gallery. Usually there would be a couple of tourists, a grifter looking to offload a third-rate watercolour, pedestrians sheltering from the inevitable London rain or a genuine collector making an enquiry about one of the works on display. Whitaker's days were slow, particularly in the aftermath of the pandemic, and sales were rare. Yet the markup on his pieces was so substantial that he needed only to shift one or two paintings every month to keep his head above water.

He reached the top of the stairs. On closer inspection, the customer was even taller than Whitaker had anticipated and closer to fifty than forty. He was too well-dressed to be British and not corporate enough for an American. There was definitely money about him – it was there in the loafers and the signet ring, in the Hermès scarf and the tailored cashmere overcoat – but it was not yet possible to tell if he was browser or buyer. The man was carrying a cup of takeaway coffee. That was often a bad sign; collectors who intended to drop £25,000 on a piece of contemporary British art didn't wander in off the street with a flat white from Pret.

'Good morning,' said Whitaker, making a mental note to turn on the air conditioning. Summer was on the way and the gallery was getting stuffy.

'Hello there.'

To Whitaker's surprise, the accent was English public school, smooth as polished stone. Perhaps he was a well-heeled Nigerian diplomat or, better still, an Angolan with pockets as deep as an oil well. Whitaker glanced at the cup of coffee.

'How can I help you?'

A pursing of the lips, a nervous exhalation, a sorry-to-waste-your-time smile. He was a well-built man, just on the right side of overweight, with a gentle giant quality that made Whitaker warm to him.

'Am I speaking to Mr Robin Whitaker?'

'You are.'

'You're still the owner of this gallery? You have worked here for some time?'

Whitaker was surprised by the line of questioning but conceded that, yes, he had bought the gallery in 1997 – moving from a different site in Fulham – and worked there ever since. Who was asking? The stranger's hair was neatly clipped, his jaw closely shaved. A strong but not unpleasant smell of citrus had filled the room. Perhaps he had come from an early morning appointment at Truefitt & Hill.

'So, Mister Whitaker, if I may. What I am about to say may sound very strange, very unusual to you, but I hope you will understand why it is that I am asking.'

Maybe he was just a conman; Whitaker had met the sort a hundred times. There would be photographs of a sumptuous Home Counties country house stuffed with priceless works of art; tales of a sudden, unexpected inheritance from an uncle in Abuja; perhaps a watercolour that had recently come into his possession attributed to Monet or Renoir; something, at least, to whet the mark's appetite.

'Go on,' he said evenly.

'This is the Lawrence Gallery? There are no other Lawrence Galleries in the area, no other Robin Whitakers?'

'None that I am aware of.'

'Then allow me to introduce myself.' In order to grasp Whitaker in a firm handshake, the man switched the Pret coffee to his left hand and strode forward. 'Eric Appiah. Very good to meet you, sir. A long time ago I was educated here in England. I had a friend, Lachlan Kite. Does that name mean anything to you?'

There were few things Whitaker prized more than his gift for discretion. Of course, he recognised the name – Kite was one of his most loyal and valued customers – but he wasn't about to reveal that to a perfect stranger.

'Why don't you tell me what the name means to you and we can take it from there?'

Appiah liked that reply very much. He understood it to contain both loyalty to his client but also prudence in the face of a stranger. With an amused grin and a reverent nod he communicated to Whitaker that he had won his enduring respect.

'As I said, he is an old friend of mine from thirty years ago. We spent some time together in my country – I'm originally from Senegal. I saw him as recently as 2007.' To Whitaker, 2007 was not recent; it felt as distant as the moon landings. 'Then I had a robbery. My phones, my laptop, every last record of every person I've ever met wiped from memory. Even the Cloud couldn't save me, whatever the Cloud is. We rely too much on computers these days for everything, wouldn't you say?'

Appiah appeared to want Whitaker to agree with his rather mundane observation, so he nodded briskly, encouraging his mysterious customer to continue.

'Now with everybody else there was a way of tracking them down. Facebook. Twitter. Instagram. Friends of friends. But I've lost touch with 90 per cent of the boys who were at Alford and the remaining 10 per cent haven't seen Lockie since 1989.'

Lockie. Whitaker had never heard the nickname. Nor had he known that Kite had been a student at Alford College; somehow it made him think less of him. Appiah must be the son of a well-heeled Senegalese politician or diplomat, a potentate with the ambition and wherewithal to send his firstborn to the most famous school in the world so that he might be transformed into the impeccably polite English gentleman who now stood before him.

'And you think I might be able to help.'

'I do!' An explosively enthusiastic response, packed with hope and expectation. 'I know that he's always bought paintings from you. Even in his twenties Lockie was something of an amateur collector, yes? He always used to talk about this place.' Appiah gestured at the walls of the gallery as though he was standing on sacred ground. 'So I found myself passing your door with my cup of coffee and suddenly I thought – "Eureka! Robin Whitaker is the man to ask".'

It was the least convincing thing that Appiah had said. Whitaker sensed that there was something desperate in his search for Kite; this large man's enveloping, caffeinated ebullience spoke of a personal crisis which only 'Lockie' could resolve. Whitaker had long suspected that Kite worked in some unknown dimension of the secret world;

he too had struggled to track him down online, finding only sporadic references to a mysterious oil company named 'Grechis Petroleum'. Whenever Kite came into the gallery he had almost always recently returned from working overseas. Natural gas had been mentioned in passing as one of his 'concerns', but down the years so had journalism and finance. Ever discreet, Whitaker had never shared with anyone his pet theory that Kite was an MI6 officer, nor had he ever found the courage to enquire too deeply into Kite's working life. He was very obviously a private man, wealthy and withheld. Whitaker prized Kite as a client and wouldn't risk the relationship by asking too many personal questions.

'I've also forgotten his email,' Appiah exclaimed as though committing email addresses to memory was something at which he usually excelled. 'I even tried Alford, but they have no record of where Lockie works or lives these days. He's certainly never turned up at any of our reunions. So I thought perhaps you might be in a position to put me in touch with him? You see, it's rather urgent. It's very important that I speak to him. When I lost my phone, my address book – well, I lost everything.'

A cyclist passed on the street shouting angrily into a mobile phone. Appiah stared at Whitaker, waiting for a response.

'What an unusual request,' he said finally. 'You want me to connect you to an individual who may or may not have once bought a painting from me?'

'That's right. I'm aware that it's slightly crazy.' He laughed in the way that public schoolboys laugh when they fully expect you to go along with exactly what they want. 'I couldn't think of anything else. Lockie had a girlfriend for a long time, Martha, but that all ended badly. I can't just call her up and ask her to put us back in touch, even if I knew how to find her. For all I know she no longer has anything to do with him.'

Martha Raine. Whitaker remembered the name. Kite had bought a painting for her as an engagement present at least twenty years ago. The wedding had never happened, for reasons unknown. Kite had got married much later, to a Swedish-American doctor called Isobel.

'Why don't I leave you my card?' Appiah was saying, sensing Whitaker's reluctance to cooperate. 'If you can reach him in any way, please tell him that Eric Appiah was passing through London. It really is vital that I see him. Vital that we chat. Tell him I'm staying at Claridge's for another week and after that back to Paris.'

'Claridge's?' Whitaker wondered if Mr Appiah might be a potential buyer after all. The *quid pro quo* of a modest watercolour in exchange for contacting Kite might suit them both very well. 'You couldn't be staying in a better hotel.' He reached for the Pret, offering to set it down. 'Why don't I show you one or two paintings and we can chat a little more about Lockie?'

2

Over more than three decades as an intelligence officer, Lachlan Kite had given a lot of thought to what might constitute personal happiness. In 1989, on his first assignment as an untested eighteen-year-old, he saw the man who had recruited him into the secret world – his teacher and friend Billy Peele – gunned down in the street. In Russia, three years later, a woman with whom Kite had been romantically involved was assaulted and raped by FSB thugs. In his thirties he had lost the woman he loved, Martha Raine, to another man; now Kite, an only child, was watching his mother slowly waste away from Alzheimer's disease. Within the past two years he had been kidnapped by an Iranian gang who had also seized his wife, Isobel, a trauma which had almost ended their marriage. These were not experiences that a man easily forgot or from which he quickly recovered.

And yet Lachlan Kite was suddenly, continuously, unequivocally happy. In the midst of the global pandemic Isobel had given birth to a baby girl, Ingrid, and moved back home to Sweden to live with her mother. Kite, who had been estranged from her for the best part of six months, had flown to Stockholm to repair the marriage and to meet his daughter for the first time. BOX 88, the Anglo-American intelligence service to which he had dedicated his working life, did not have a human resources department, nor any official policy regarding parental leave. Nevertheless, as the man in charge of global operations, Kite had given himself three months off to spend time with his new family.

He had rented a small house at the edge of a lake in Djursholm, built a nursery for Ingrid on the first floor, bought two yards of paperbacks from the English Bookshop in Uppsala and acquired a plug-in hybrid Volvo complete with rear-facing child seat. Day after day Lachlan and Isobel did little else but attend to their daughter's every need. They bathed and fed her, bought her too many clothes and too many soft toys in the shops of Stockholm, comforted her when she woke up crying in the small hours of the morning and changed a never-ending succession of nappies. The experience of becoming a father for the first time on the eve of his fiftieth birthday had changed Kite in ways that he fully acknowledged only after Isobel had pointed them out.

'You're much calmer,' she told him. 'Less distracted. Before it was always as though a part of you was at work, lost in the past, figuring things out. This is the first time in our relationship when I've felt that you are entirely present.'

'I'm sorry it was like that,' he replied. 'When I was with you, we were happy, weren't we?'

'Of course we were.'

'You had your shifts at the hospital, I had London . . .'

They were eating dinner at Caliban, a slick new restaurant in Vasastan serving what was described as 'progressive Swedish cuisine': cured fish, acidified vegetables, various genres of mollusc and seaweed. Malin, Isobel's mother, was babysitting. Isobel touched her husband's hand across the table.

'It's fine.' She waved her earlier remark away; it had sounded more critical than she had intended. 'I think both of us feel the same thing. A kind of pure selflessness. Until

28

Ingrid came along, I didn't know what it was to surrender my own concerns, my own needs, my ego so completely.'

Was this also how Kite felt? The master spy, a man who had killed in cold blood, was nowadays to be found cooing and singing, dancing and giggling, reduced to a cliché of besotted fatherly adoration as he blew raspberries on Ingrid's stomach. To touch his daughter's blond hair, to witness her delighted smile when he or Isobel walked into a room, to kiss her soft neck and cheeks, was a pleasure such as he had never known. Before Ingrid, a parent's love for their child had been theoretical to him; he had even used it for leverage. Now at last Kite understood a father's fierce, primal protectiveness. He was not softer nor more sentimental as a consequence of Ingrid's birth, yet her laughter was a sound sweeter to him than anything in music or nature. The smell of her skin, her hopeless attempts at crawling, the Jackson Pollock smears of pureed food on her face after every meal – to this tough, uncompromising man it was magical.

Yet Kite knew that it could not last. He would not be able to remain in Sweden indefinitely; work would call him back, and he would gladly go, leaving behind the simple family life he had built in Stockholm and returning only when his professional obligations allowed him to.

'You're more selfless than I am,' he said. 'I know what you mean about setting your own needs to one side, but I won't be able to do this forever. I'll have to go back.'

'I understand,' Isobel replied.

'Apart from anything else I need to earn a living.'

'We both do.' She pointed at one of the plates. 'How else will we pay for our fermented celeriac?'

Kite laughed, took a sip of wine and held onto the stem of the glass as he spoke.

'I'm old enough and wise enough to know that work will never provide me with anything other than momentary satisfaction.' He was recently back from a successful operation in Dubai, but the buzz of scoring a significant victory over the FSB had been ephemeral. 'You know as well as I do that my father looked for happiness at the bottom of a bottle. Mum extracted a strange kind of contentment from making other people feel that they had disappointed her. The last few weeks have been the closest I've come to a sense of peace for a long time.'

'We're lucky that she sleeps,' Isobel replied, not wanting to spoil the night with talk of Kite's sabbatical coming to its inevitable end. 'When you're tired, when they're sick, that's when the fun stops.'

'True. Meanwhile I'm turning into Pop Larkin.'

Isobel had spent her formative years in America and Kite had to explain the reference. In his twenties he had watched a handful of episodes of *The Darling Buds of May* purely for the opportunity to gawp at Catherine Zeta-Jones.

'Surely Bryan Mills,' she responded. 'You have a particular set of skills, acquired over a long period of time.' She was two Negronis down and mimicked Liam Neeson's low Irish drawl in *Taken*. 'You went to an English boarding school. You work for British intelligence. Pay for my dinner and that'll be the end of it.'

Even as she joked, Kite's mind was halfway out of the restaurant, on a plane somewhere over the North Sea, heading back to London to deal with whatever crisis MI6 and CIA lacked the bandwidth or desire to confront. And then, just like that, as if perfectly to illustrate his predicament, WhatsApp pinged inside his jacket. Kite took out the phone, opened the message and felt the old familiar bump of operational adrenaline coursing through his veins.

'Who's it from?'

'Just a guy I buy paintings from in London,' Kite replied. 'He's got something he wants me to look at.'

3

Later, when they were back at the house relaxing in the living room with glasses of single malt and Chet Baker on Spotify, Isobel pointed at Kite's phone and said: 'Who texted you in the restaurant? It felt like it was about more than just a painting.'

There was a new understanding between them: when it came to BOX 88, Isobel could ask about anything and everything. For her own peace of mind, as wife and mother, she needed to know more about Kite's work. He had promised to be as open with her as official secrecy allowed, though he would never tell her anything which might compromise her safety.

'You're right,' he said. 'And as perceptive as ever. It was about more than just a painting.'

'So it wasn't from the man who sells pictures to you? What's his name, Robin Whitaker?'

'It was from Robin, yes. Someone has been in touch with him, looking for me. Somebody from the old days.'

There was a faint cry on the baby monitor, Ingrid in the midst of a dream. They were both momentarily silenced. Kite hit pause on Spotify and glanced at the screen. The blurred, infra-red image showed Ingrid lying peacefully on her back. Isobel was halfway out of her chair, listening intently, but when there was no further sound she sat back and returned to the conversation.

'Who from the old days?'

Secrecy was so ingrained in Kite's behaviour that his first instinct was to lie. He restarted the music, Chet purring the chorus of 'Almost Blue', poignant and heartbreaking. Should he risk telling Isobel about Eric Appiah or hide behind protocol?

'Somebody I was at school with.'

'A spook?'

That didn't really cover Eric Appiah in all his complexity. He was businessman and part-time spy, womaniser and father of six, a cherished friend whom Kite trusted like a brother. That he should have chosen to make contact so eccentrically, using Whitaker as a cut-out, suggested that Appiah had stumbled on something important which could only be entrusted to BOX 88. What that might be, Kite could not be sure. Appiah had fingers in innumerable African pies: government ministers and captains of industry crowded his address book. Those of a more sensitive persuasion – the spies and mercenaries, the diamond smugglers and Mandarin-speaking lawyers – preferred that he keep their relationships secret.

'He's not really a spook. Not formally, anyway. He's Senegalese, the son of a big hitter out there. His name is Eric.'

'And he knows that you buy paintings from Whitaker?'

'Evidently.'

'Almost Blue' was coming to an end. Kite hated it that the song always made him think about Martha. He wondered if Isobel had been listening to the lyrics and would somehow intuit this.

'He doesn't have your contact details?' she asked. 'Or he's afraid that his phone is bugged, that somebody's reading his emails?'

A year earlier Appiah had found evidence of Pegasus

on his Android, an Israeli-designed zero-click spyware capable of accessing the phone's messaging apps, camera, microphone and passwords. Since then, he had been understandably paranoid about technical surveillance. Kite explained this to Isobel, reassuring her that London regularly monitored his own phones for similar viruses.

'So he wants to see you?'

According to Whitaker's message, Appiah was staying at Claridge's, a codeword for a less salubrious hotel in Chiswick which Appiah regularly used as a base.

'He wants me to give him a call. If it's important, I'm afraid I'll have to go to London.'

A discreet nod, not quite of assent but certainly of understanding. Isobel had acknowledged that they were embarking on the next stage of their reconciliation: Kite would go back to BOX 88 and make the marriage work by travelling regularly between London and Stockholm.

'So he was at Alford with you?' she asked, taking a wary sip of whisky.

Kite knew that his wife wanted to have a deeper understanding of the man who had punctured their evening. Whenever he thought of Appiah, it was the younger man he remembered, principally the friend who had helped him through the violence and upheaval of 1995.

'We played cricket together,' he began. 'First eleven. Eric bowled, I batted. We were in different houses, but he knew people like Xav. When we were fifteen or sixteen, the three of us almost got caught climbing on the roof of School Hall at three o'clock in the morning. We drank a lot, smoked hash in Slough, went to the same parties.'

'And he was from a rich family, like Xavier?'

'Very rich,' Kite confirmed. 'Construction.'

Details of the 1995 operation were coming back to him, regret and frustration still pecking at his heart after all these years. When he recalled that time, Kite didn't picture the lavish Appiah villa in Fann, the beach at Toubab Dialaw or the blood-orange sunrise over the Faidherbe Bridge. No, he recalled only the nature of his own shame, remembering Dakar as the moment when his life began to unravel.

'Eric has helped us on and off down the years,' he said, wondering how to explain the arrangement between Appiah and BOX 88 without breaching security. 'It's a long story.'

'One of those stories you're allowed to tell me or one of those stories you're not allowed to tell me?'

Kite looked at their glasses, both now empty. There was half a bottle of Glen Scotia in the kitchen. Ingrid would be awake at six, the day starting all over again. What had happened in Senegal was a tragedy, as close as Kite had come to a professional debacle, an operation beset by problems of shoddy organisation, second-rate personnel and sheer rotten bad luck.

'I can tell you this one,' he said.

4

Lachlan Kite had graduated from Edinburgh University in the summer of 1994, a year after the operation in Russia which had made him a star at BOX 88. His boss, Michael Strawson, had given him some well-earned leave then sent him to New York for six months to learn his trade at the agency's US headquarters in lower Manhattan. There had been courses in weaponry and encrypted communications, seminars on geopolitics, long days at a desk overlooking the Hudson River listening to surveillance recordings of Iraqi intelligence officers formulating a plan to assassinate former President George Bush. From time to time, employees would gather around the television to catch a glimpse of the O.J. Simpson trial, which was being broadcast to a transfixed nation: all were of the belief that Simpson was guilty and would likely go to prison for the rest of his life. Kite's girlfriend, Martha, had regularly flown over from London to see him. They had explored New York together, visited friends at Brown University, enjoyed a drunken weekend in Atlantic City gambling at Trump Taj Mahal and eating saltwater taffy on the Boardwalk. Kite had shown Martha around a snow-covered Ellis Island, bought her a necklace at Tiffany's and taken her to hear Woody Allen playing clarinet at Michael's Pub. He felt invincible, superior, chosen: he had money in the bank, an enviable job and was living in what was then the most exciting city in the world. His heroes were Fitzroy MacLean and T.E. Lawrence, men who had reshaped the world in their twenties. Little did Kite know that so much of what he had begun to take for granted would be stripped away from him in less than two years.

He had returned home on Good Friday, 14 April 1995, with a carton of Winston Lights, a bottle of Jim Beam and a fascination for America which lasted for the next two decades. He had just turned twenty-four. Martha had found them a one-bedroom flat in Battersea and they moved in over the Easter weekend, putting up bookshelves, painting their bedroom and fixing a leaking tap in the kitchen. For security reasons Strawson wanted to keep Kite at arm's length from 'The Cathedral' – the nickname for BOX 88's London headquarters – and encouraged him to keep up his cover as a slightly dissolute graduate with no clear idea what he wanted to do with his life. To that end Kite found work as a waiter and signed up for an Arabic course at SOAS. He knew that at any moment he might be called upon to leave the country at short notice with no clear indication when he would return; equally, he was aware that it might be many months before Strawson found him an operation 'worthy of your talents but suited to your experience'. The remark, part of a letter Strawson had written to Kite shortly after his return from New York, was typical of the American: it contained both flattery and a tacit reminder that Kite was still a fledgling spy with much to learn about the secret world.

The Senegal operation came just at a point when Kite was becoming frustrated with the direction of his days and the sameness of London life. His contemporaries from Alford and Edinburgh had mostly found jobs in television and advertising: two of them had gone into the music business, another into sports marketing. Often bored and unfulfilled, Kite spent his free time at the cinema, played five-a-side football under the Westway and took Martha to Brighton and Paris for dirty weekends. His drug-taking days were behind him: Strawson had always been wary of Kite's fondness for a night out and BOX 88 officers could be subjected to testing at any time. So while his friends were clubbing in the redevelopment at King's Cross, rubbing shoulders with Bjork and Goldie on a Sunday night at the Blue Note, Kite was waiting tables for five pounds an hour in Battersea, his only bad habit an occasional game of poker after hours at the restaurant.

The order to make contact arrived out of the blue. A package was dropped through Kite's letterbox on a September morning shortly after Martha had left the flat to go for a run. Kite could still remember the giddy feeling of opening the padded envelope to find a British Telecom pager inside and a tourist postcard of a black London taxi. He had waited impatiently for the first message to come through, an instruction to make his way to Chelsea, to wait at the Limerston Street bus stop shortly after 2 p.m. and to watch for a black cab, number plate to follow. The taxi would be under the control of BOX 88; Kite did not know who he was going to meet nor what might be asked of him.

Even at a distance of almost thirty years, Kite's near-photographic memory did not fail him as he related these events to Isobel. He could still picture the wide chicane of World's End, feel the buzz of the pager vibrating in his hip pocket as the number plate came through. Across King's Road, half a dozen tables outside an Italian restaurant had edged nervously into the late summer sun. A middle-aged couple were sharing a bowl of *spaghetti pomodoro*, laughing as they twirled the strands onto their forks, kissing like the dogs in *Lady and the Tramp*. At a neighbouring table a bald businessman was testing out a pair of reading glasses, moving them up and down on his nose as he scanned the menu. Kite turned to see a taxi approaching the bus stop, but the number plate didn't match. He settled next to a woman with greying hair who was intently reading the front page of the *Independent*. Moments later the correct taxi approached from the west. Kite stepped away from the bus stop and raised his hand to hail it.

Michael Strawson was waiting in the back seat. The American's Hemingway beard seemed longer and whiter than usual and he was wearing an unseasonably thick Aran jumper; Kite wanted to tell him that he looked like a fisherman who had come ashore for supplies, but the boss didn't seem in the mood for jokes. The driver of the cab was wearing a Queens Park Rangers football shirt and listening to Debbie Thrower on Radio 2.

'What are you reading?' Strawson asked, indicating the book in Kite's hand. There was something about hearing his low Virginian drawl which made Kite feel eighteen again.

'*Fever Pitch*,' he replied, holding it up. 'Memoir about an Arsenal . . .'

'I know what it's about.' Strawson always gave the impression of having seen every play, watched every film and read every novel in the cultural conversation. Kite wondered when he found the time. 'For an American who doesn't watch soccer and thinks you guys are all hooligans, I thought it was pretty good. How's the love nest?'

Kite's relationship had long been a subject of fascination for Strawson. He liked Martha, he knew that she had been brave and resourceful in Russia two years earlier, but Kite was sure that he saw her as a threat to his career at BOX 88.

'It's great,' he replied carefully. 'Small, expensive. The neighbours have a baby who screams all hours of the day and night, but we're very happy.'

'You two must be hitting the six-year mark by now, no?'

Strawson already knew the answer to his own question:

he had been present in France in 1989 when Kite and Martha had first got together.

'Just passed it,' he replied. Then, mischievously: 'How's your marriage, Michael?'

That stopped the conversation in its tracks. The taxi passed a pub on the corner of Beaufort Street where, at the age of fifteen, Kite's closest friend, Xavier Bonnard, had thrown up in the toilets after getting drunk on Guinness and tequila. Strawson narrowed his slate-grey eyes.

'Last I heard Martha was at a loose end. Quit her job in TV.'

'That's right.' Kite wondered how Strawson knew this but didn't ask how he had come by the information. 'She's thinking of doing a law conversion.'

'And your Arabic course has, well . . . run its course?'

'I can dip in and out.' He wondered if Strawson was clearing the way for an operation which might involve Martha. Were BOX thinking of formally bringing her into the fold? 'There are exams next spring,' he added, 'but a lot of the work I can do on my own.'

'So you're ready?'

Intrigued, Kite was about to say: 'Of course I'm ready', but didn't want to sound impatient. Instead, he said simply: 'Always.'

The ghost of a smile moved the whiskers of Strawson's unkempt beard.

'Need you to take a vacation,' he began. 'You might be back home in a week, might take more than that. Hard to say until you get there.'

'Where am I going?'

'Dakar.'

Kite ran a list of African capital cities through his mind and matched Dakar to Senegal. Outside Picasso's, a restaurant on King's Road, he saw somebody he recognised from Alford. Chelsea was the playground of the privately educated

39

Sloane Ranger and King's Road its main artery. The parents of his former schoolmates bought their groceries at Partridges, their bed linen at Peter Jones, their jewellery at Butler and Wilson. Xavier's mother, Lady Rosamund Penley, lived less than a mile away in a five-storey house on Hereford Square.

'You had a Senegalese friend at Alford, am I correct?' Strawson asked.

'Eric Appiah?'

'That's the guy. Father is some big shot industrialist if I recall correctly.'

'You recall correctly.' Kite assumed Strawson had heard about him via Billy Peele, the history teacher at Alford who had recruited him into BOX 88 in 1989. 'Is Eric one of us?'

The American seemed to find the question amusing.

'No, no,' he replied. 'Just somebody you might want to look up when you're there. He lives in Dakar, right?'

'Last I heard.'

Kite had played cricket with Appiah, who regularly terrified the opposition batsmen with his 80mph yorkers. 'He went to Brown. I haven't seen him since I left school.'

From the look on his face, Strawson already knew this.

'Sure,' he said. 'So if the opportunity arises, maybe let him know you're coming out. Good to have a friendly face on the ground. Natural cover, too.'

The cab made a left turn at Peter Jones, 'Hotel California' on Radio 2.

'What's the job?' Kite asked.

'We're watching somebody of interest in Senegal. You will be part of the team involved in that effort. I need you to take some money out there. A package. Very simple, very straightforward. How's your Wolof?'

'My what?'

'Local language. They also speak French. That up to speed or is your head full of Arabic?'

'I'll be fine.' Kite resolved to buy a copy of *Le Monde*

when he got off the bus and to rent some French movies at his local video shop. 'I can practise for the next few days.'

'You'll also need injections for yellow fever and your tetanus up to date. A dog bites you out there, you're in a world of pain. Lot of AIDS, too, but with Martha around she'll keep that wandering pecker of yours zipped up.'

'Martha is coming with me?'

'That going to be a problem?'

Though he had sensed that Strawson wanted her to be involved, Kite was nevertheless surprised at the decision.

'I'll need to run it past her but it shouldn't be a problem. In what capacity?'

'You're a couple. Backpacking. Travelling together. Martha knows who you are, she knows what you do. We're happy to pay for her to have a free holiday if it means you don't attract the wrong kind of attention.'

Kite didn't know what sort of 'attention' Strawson might be referring to; he knew nothing about the political situation in Senegal, even less about the potential dangers to backpacking British tourists on its coast.

'Will it be safe for her?'

'Perfectly safe. You sit on the beach for a couple of days and wait for instructions. Swim. Grab a beer with Eric. Eat some fish. Think you can do that?'

'Of course we can do that.' Kite assumed that Strawson was busily pulling together the disparate threads of a complex operation of which he was only one tiny part.

'Good.' Strawson checked the time. 'But she flies home on my instruction. You might be leaving with her, you might be staying in Senegal. We don't yet have a clear picture of what's happening on the ground. It's what you might call a fluid situation.'

Kite wondered if there was another angle to Martha being involved: was Strawson thinking of recruiting her on a formal basis – or hoping to break them up?

41

'Who are you looking at out there?'

Strawson touched the chaotic strands of his unkempt beard. It was his habit never to divulge sensitive information unless it was absolutely necessary.

'Hutu. A *genocidaire*. Got out of Rwanda via Tanzania late last year, managed to make his way into Senegal. Killed a lot of people. Langley not interested, same goes for London. That's where BOX comes in. We get him out, put him on trial, put him away for the rest of his days. But a lot of ground to cover before we can make that happen.'

The taxi came to a halt in a queue of traffic on Sloane Avenue. Debbie Thrower was excitedly anticipating the imminent arrival of the Bee Gees in the Radio 2 studio. She played 'Staying Alive' to set the mood.

'What do I tell Martha?'

'You tell her the truth.' Strawson seemed surprised that Kite had seen fit to ask the question. 'She's just a tourist. You might have to stay on for a while, you might both be coming home inside a week. If she's happy to take some hard currency through Customs, we would welcome that. Either take it all or split it with your girl. Your contact will meet you in Toubab Dialaw and take it from you.'

'Toubab Dialaw? That's where we're going?'

'Beach resort about an hour south of Dakar. You'll be staying in a guest house. Small place, secluded, bohemian. Guy that owns it is some kind of eccentric Haitian émigré. Clam shells everywhere, mosaic tiles, a voodoo vibe, like Gaudí helped with the décor. You'll like it. A few tourists, mostly Americans and Europeans. You and Martha take it easy there, wait for us to come calling. Contact phrase is nothing complicated. You'll be asked if you know somebody in England named Miles Feaver. If you have no concerns about security, you say that you knew him at university. If there's a problem, if for any reason you think you might be compromised, you say you've never heard of him.'

'Simple enough.' Kite wondered why a straightforward

meeting at an off-the-beaten-track guest house on the coast of Senegal would require a contact phrase. Who else would know Kite was there? 'Are there other services looking at this guy, this *genocidaire*? French? African? Is he protected?'

Strawson hesitated. Perhaps he was at the edge of what he knew about the situation.

'We're looking at that. We'll know soon enough. I just need feet on the ground. Eyes and ears. It's a tough environment. Right now, you and Martha are just a young couple backpacking around West Africa. I've got you a street map. Familiarise yourself with Dakar, particularly the area around Rue Kennedy. Anybody asks, you have plans to travel north by road to St Louis which is an old French colonial town on the border with Mauritania. Then maybe southern Morocco, maybe Ivory Coast, who knows? Take this.' Strawson passed Kite a bulky manila envelope which he was told contained the map, $5000 in traveller's cheques and 40,000 French francs. 'It's going to be hotter than Krakatoa at Christmas. Temperature drops below 90, count yourself lucky. You'll need anti-malarials. Don't take Lariam, that shit screws up your mind. Talk to Martha tonight, clear it with her, go to Trailfinders in the morning. You fly out Monday. That sound possible?'

'Very possible.' With grudging frustration Kite realised that spending more than two weeks in Africa would likely mean missing his mother's fiftieth birthday. He had been organising the party for the best part of a month. 'If I have to stay out there for any length of time, it means I'll miss my mother's fiftieth.'

'Too bad,' Strawson replied. 'You can go to her sixtieth.'

5

They left London four days later.

The heat. That was what Kite remembered most vividly from those first chaotic hours in Dakar. Not the confusion of the dilapidated airport or the clamour of the taxi drivers or the long wait for luggage and the fear that Customs had gone through their rucksacks and found the money. No, just the cloak of debilitating heat which enveloped them as soon as they emerged from the plane. As a child, Kite had been taken on holiday to a Scottish seaside hotel which boasted an indoor swimming pool and sauna. He had sat in the tight confines of the little wooden hutch with his father but could stand it for no more than five minutes; the humidity became too much to bear and he had to run outside to dive into the pool. This was Senegal in late September; a relentless, enervating sauna from which there was no respite.

Then the people. Kite had never been further south than a tourist resort in Turkey. In his imagination, Africa had always been a vast, stricken continent of famines and Live Aid, of costume dramas about seedy British aristocrats living it up in colonial Kenya. After meeting Strawson he had read *West Africa on a Shoestring* and bought a coffee table book about Senegal in a second-hand shop on Gloucester Road.

The book had interesting photographs of Dakar and St Louis in the 1960s and 70s. But nothing had prepared him for the colour and energy and noise of this place, the bark of Wolof, the sense from the first moments of moving without control inside a steaming pot with the lid about to blow off. Kite loved it. He was entirely out of his element, away from stagnant London and happily operational again. Those first moments in Africa amazed him. He had to check his own surprise at suddenly being surrounded by black faces, black bodies, as if somehow all the world was run by white Europeans and they had taken the afternoon off just as his plane touched down.

It took Kite and Martha a long time to convey to the driver of their dented, creaking Peugeot taxi that they wanted to leave the city and go south-east to Toubab Dialaw. He was a cheerful middle-aged man with crooked, yellowed teeth who could not read the piece of paper on which Kite had written the name of the town. Kite tried showing him a map of the coast with the guest house circled, but it became clear that the driver did not understand what he was being shown. Instead, pulling to the side of the busy road beside a stucco colonial building bursting with bougainvillea, he engaged in a lengthy conversation with another driver in a nearby car who seemed equally baffled by Kite's request. Eventually Martha tried a different pronunciation of 'Toubab Dialaw', mimicking the harsh, guttural sounds of the Wolof spoken by the men, and by some miracle of enunciation the driver suddenly understood and they restarted their journey.

The taxi had no discernible suspension and an engine which growled like a tractor. The interior smelled of old mosquito repellent. Kite was in the front seat with the rucksack between his legs. He opened it up and felt inside for the outline of the package; it was exactly where he had placed it. Martha had checked her bag as soon as it came off the carousel; her money was also safe. Kite assumed it was for paying local agents and had told her as much in London. At no point had Martha shown any hesitation about coming out to Senegal. She knew that she would be going home after a week; she was aware that Kite would likely have to stay behind. She was glad that he had been honest with her and flattered that Strawson considered her a safe pair of hands. Kite did not share with her his suspicion that Strawson was trying to come between them; at the same time, he wondered again if the trip to Senegal was a way of testing her. If Martha passed, would they recruit her? It was impossible to know. He was not even sure how he might react. Would he be excited for her, or would it somehow strip away some of the rarefied appeal of working for BOX 88?

The taxi driver was wearing cheap plastic sunglasses and beaded bracelets on his wrists. He kept pushing buttons on the radio, happily skipping stations playing local music and American hits, bursts of Wolof and Bob Marley. Even with the four windows fully down the wind offered no respite from the clogging humidity. Kite wondered how long it would take him to adjust to the climate; being operational in this place – on a stakeout, for example, or tailing someone on the streets of Dakar – would be debilitating. There was a box of tissues glued to the dashboard. He took one, wiping the sweat from his nose and cheeks. Within seconds the tissue had disintegrated into a warm, damp ball. He had never felt more white, more Scottish.

'Any idea how far away we are?' Martha asked from the back seat. She put her hand on his neck. Sweat formed instantly with the contact.

'An hour? Maybe two? Guidebook said the guest house is about sixty kilometres from the airport.'

A sandstorm had blown through the city, settling on everything in its path so that the streets were edged with pale red dust. For some time they drove slowly behind a horse and cart, a smell of animal flank and dung through the open windows. Whenever the taxi ground to a halt the enveloping heat of the late afternoon thickened around them like an opened oven door. Kite saw minibuses plastered with the faces of Sufi holy men, half-finished concrete buildings fissured with cracks. Women walked among the traffic in colourful, patterned dresses which flared at the bottom so that they seemed to float through the din and chaos; some had baskets balanced on their heads just like in the photographs Kite had seen back in London. He never had any thought in his mind that they might stumble and the baskets would fall. They were serene.

Eventually the taxi passed through the city and came out into a greener open country of pylons and baobab trees. They drove for some time on a potholed, two-lane highway. Kite had tried to engage the driver in conversation, but he spoke no French, only Wolof and a few cheerful words of English which he had already used to enquire after the wellbeing of 'Lady Diana' and Paul Gascoigne. For another half-hour they continued across the open country on bumpy tarmac roads, occasionally coming to a halt to allow livestock to cross or to buy bottled water and packets of French crisps at roadside shacks. Under a beige sky they passed through a small township bordered by grey breezeblock walls, coming to a halt at a police check. Barefoot boys in shorts and torn T-shirts were playing happily at the side of the road, jumping in and out of old tyres, climbing on the bonnets of abandoned cars. One of them kicked a punctured football into an eruption of thick, tangled grass; Kite thought of snakes and wondered if the boys would risk trying to retrieve it. The policeman manning the checkpoint showed no interest in the taxi and waved it through, pausing only to lean down and stare at Martha.

'Just like Russia,' she said, remembering their escape from Voronezh. Again she touched Kite's neck and again the contact made a bead of sweat form on his skin.

The township was a smaller but no less chaotic version of the section of northern Dakar through which they had driven from the airport. It was a place without tarmac or road markings. The centre was a dusty, loosely arranged market of wooden stalls, many protected by coloured awnings which had been ripped by winds and stained with the ubiquitous red Saharan dust. Cars and motorbikes and belching trucks moved in all directions. There were low wooden tables at the side of the road occupied by women in vibrantly coloured dresses and men in the same ripped T-shirts as their younger brothers and cousins playing football at the edge of town. Brooms, caged birds, counterfeit trainers, coils of wire: everything was for sale. Kite saw vast piles of bananas, fresh mangoes, cashews, melons; he thought of the feeble grocery section at his local Sainsbury's in Clapham, everything wrapped in polystyrene and cling film. At one shack there were cuts of butchered meat attracting flies in ninety-degree heat. Beside another, a man with torn trousers was fixing a motorbike with no more than a screwdriver and a rusty can of oil.

They drove away from the marketplace in the direction of the sea, heat haze on the long straight road. Homes were visible down potholed side roads, shacks for entire families constructed of mud bricks and corrugated iron. Never had Kite seen so many people with nothing to occupy them: hundreds of men were walking around without apparent aim or purpose, some of them crouched by the side of the road, others leaning on motorbikes or the severed trunks of trees. The leaves of the trees were coated in dust; goats and stray dogs sheltered from the heat beneath them. Just as Kite stared at the men they passed, they also stared back at him.

'This place is extraordinary,' he muttered.

'Say again?' said Martha. It was difficult to hear above the din of the engine and the clatter of the taxi as it dropped into the potholes. Even the heat seemed to possess its own noise.

'Not what I expected,' he replied.

'What did you expect?'

Kite wasn't sure. Ever since the meeting with Strawson, most of his thoughts had been operational; all that mattered was getting to Toubab and waiting for his contact. But there was a part of him that was just a backpacking traveller of twenty-four, living his cover, exploring the world with a girlfriend. Knowing that he was heading to Senegal, Kite had realised how little he understood about Africa. He had celebrated the release of Nelson Mandela in 1990. He knew that more than a dozen American Marines had been slaughtered in Mogadishu in 1993. He had watched news reports on the genocide in Rwanda without understanding why it had come about or asking what the West might have done to prevent it. To his shame, before he had looked it up, he had not been able to remember if the Hutus had massacred the Tutsis or if the Tutsis had massacred the Hutus. He knew that there was now an appalling humanitarian crisis in Burundi and Zaire but could not recall ever talking about this with his friends or even hearing the problem discussed on *Question Time* or *Newsnight*. Why had he ignored these stories? London was Oasis and Blur. It was *Friends* and *Don't Forget Your Toothbrush*. It was games of poker with the chefs and kitchen porters at the restaurant, not conversations about political instability in sub-Saharan Africa. He felt these two sides of his existence – the frivolous and the serious – as opposites without any discernible connection. Most people thought of Lachlan Kite as a happy-go-lucky twenty-something graduate making ends meet as a waiter; Kite knew that every aspect of his life – the Arabic course, the part-time job, even his relationship with Martha – was being controlled by BOX 88. It was how Strawson wanted it.

A car pulled up alongside the taxi. Two children were

49

sitting on the lap of a woman in the passenger seat; there were at least four others crammed in behind her. Kite was thinking of seat belts and crash test dummies when a motorbike buzzed past him on the inside with a small boy – no older than four or five – riding pillion. He was clinging to the driver's naked chest.

'That's really disgusting,' said Martha.

'What is?'

Kite saw that she was reading the guidebook.

'They have a thing called mangoworm here.'

'What's that?' Trailfinders had arranged for them to have shots for yellow fever, hepatitis and typhoid. Nobody had said anything about mangoworm.

'A disease of contact with the eggs of flies laid in sand or grass.' She made a noise of comic disgust. 'You can even catch it from clothes left out to dry in the sun. Touch the eggs for long enough and they seep under your skin, eventually forming a boil which hatches baby maggots.'

'Reminds me,' said Kite. 'Did you take your malaria pill?'

'Yes, doctor.'

The driver was asking a gap-toothed passer-by for directions. They were pointed down a long, straight road where goats wandered in the dust and the sun. Pulling away they passed the remnants of a rusted Citroën 2CV, the engine stripped for parts. Moments later, skirting the edge of Toubab Dialaw, Kite glimpsed the sea for the first time. They bumped down towards the glittering ocean and at last reached the guest house.

'This is place!' the driver exclaimed triumphantly, suddenly finding enough English to wish Kite a 'happy vacation'. As he switched off the engine a cooling sea breeze came in off the water. 'You want I stay?'

Kite said it would not be necessary. He had no need of a driver and thanked the man for bringing them safely from Dakar. It was almost six o'clock. The sun was setting over the quiet, haphazard alleyways which criss-crossed the hill. Kite's bones were stiff as he climbed out of the Peugeot.

'Swim,' said Martha, looking sapped from the long journey. 'Let's check in and swim.'

He looked around, half-expecting to see Strawson's contact waiting for him in the shade of the vast baobab tree at the entrance to the guest house. But there was just a young Senegalese woman wearing a denim skirt and T-shirt clearing cups from a table. Nearby an old man was smoking a filterless cigarette, staring at them intently. In that moment, as Kite looked up at the neat rows of clam shells and scuffed tiles decorating the entrance to the guest house, a strange, unsettling feeling came over him. It was unlike anything he had experienced before in his career. It was not stress or anxiety, more a sense of foreboding. He knew with a kind of sinister conviction that something was going to go wrong in this place.

'You OK, Lockie?'

Martha had seen the look on his face. Kite thought that he had covered up his disquiet, but she saw that something was bothering him. As he was brushing it off, blaming the heat and the long journey, they were distracted by a figure emerging from the guest house. He was six foot six, wearing loose cotton trousers and a Lacoste polo shirt. His face was as familiar as the genial, booming voice.

'Welcome, welcome, welcome!' said Eric Appiah. 'Great to see you, Lockie! So tell me. How was your journey?'

6

'Eric!' Kite had telephoned Appiah from London, told him what flight they were on and the name of the guest house in Toubab, but never imagined for a second that his old school friend would be there to welcome them. 'What are you doing here?'

'I wanted to surprise you!'

Kite was flooded with memories: of Appiah buying bottles of Smirnoff with a fake ID in the back street off-licences of Slough; being chased across the rooftops of the ancient school by an irate security guard at three o'clock in the morning; comforting his friend when he learned that his Senegalese grandfather had died suddenly in a car accident. It was the first time Kite had ever seen a boy at Alford in tears.

'Amazing to see you,' he said as Appiah slapped him hard on the back.

'You too, man.' Kite's shirt was soaked in sweat; Appiah's was as dry as paper and smelled of his signature Kouros aftershave. Kite remembered him spraying it around a cricket pavilion after taking six wickets against Charterhouse. 'I'm on my way to Saly for a party tonight. Thought I'd grab a beer en route and wait for you guys to show. You must be Martha?'

Kite introduced them, noting that Martha reacted to Appiah the way everyone did: warming to him instantly, sensing his compassion and kindness. His friend had filled out in the six years since they had left school and was now a clean-cut, sophisticated man plainly enjoying his wealth and status in Senegal. At Alford Appiah had been one of only three black boys in a school of more than 1,200, always unfailingly cheerful and polite but unquestionably isolated. He now had a liberated spring in his step; four years at an American university had flushed out the toxins of boarding school life.

'How was your journey?' he asked.

'Hot,' they replied in unison.

Kite carried his rucksack into the dark interior of the guest house, Appiah shouldering Martha's bags. The young Senegalese woman who had been clearing the cups took their passport numbers and gave them a key. Only then did it occur to Kite that Appiah might be part of Strawson's team. Had he been sent to collect the money? Surely that was too far-fetched. Had Billy Peele talent-spotted dozens of Alfordians during his time at the school? Perhaps there had been nothing particularly exceptional about Kite's own recruitment in 1989.

'Your first time here, right?' Appiah asked.

'First time,' Martha confirmed.

'So what the hell made you guys come to Senegal in the hottest month of the year? You should be staying at my house in Dakar. At least we have air-conditioning!'

Kite explained that they had wanted a break from London and the chance to do some travelling. Remembering Strawson's advice, he mentioned St Louis and Morocco as potential destinations. If there was the possibility of coming to Dakar later in the trip, they would love to have dinner with him and look around the city.

'Nonsense!' Appiah exclaimed. 'Screw all that British politeness. This place is beautiful, but you'll be bored after three days.' At Alford his accent had been deliberately posh; just like Kite, Appiah was an outsider who had changed the way he spoke in order to fit in. Now his voice had an easy transatlantic swing. 'I insist you come and stay for at least one night. We have incredible clubs here, amazing music. I'll take you to all the best places.'

Kite wondered what the angle was. If Appiah was part of the team watching the *genocidaire*, maybe he needed to find an excuse for Kite to visit Dakar.

'Sounds great,' Martha replied. 'We were going to go for a swim before the sun sets. Join us?'

Appiah indicated that he was dressed for the party in Saly and didn't want to change out of his clothes.

'Why don't you come with me?' he suggested. 'Have your swim, take a shower, I can sit here and wait. Saly is great, you'll love it.'

Kite looked at Martha, trying to gauge her mood. It was like a moment between an old married couple who both secretly want to stay in and watch television.

'Let's go another time,' Kite replied, sensing her reluctance. If Appiah was BOX, there was no need to go to Saly. He could pass him the money in their room without anybody noticing.

'As you wish!'

So they had a drink on the terrace – a Coke for Appiah, thirst-slaking Flag lagers for Kite and Martha – as the sun went down and the sea darkened and the possibility of a refreshing swim receded. Sitting on the warm terrace listening to the pull and draw of waves on the beach, the cry of huge birds soaring above them in the evening sky, Kite felt that he had passed through some kind of portal into a world with which he was altogether unfamiliar. Just twelve hours earlier he had been sitting on his rucksack at a damp Heathrow eating a ham-and-cheese sandwich from Marks & Spencer; he was suddenly at the western-most tip of Africa waiting for word of an operation that

54

might already have begun. He kept expecting Appiah to ask the question – 'Do you know someone in England called Miles Feaver?' – but the enquiry never came. Instead, they talked about Alford and Brown University, discovering that Appiah had run a club night in Providence and was going into business as a music producer. Kite remembered how much they had liked one another. His father had a phrase he had been fond of repeating: 'You can make new friends, but you can't make old ones.' This was how he felt about Eric Appiah. The longer the conversation went on, the more unlikely it seemed that this genial, easy-going entrepreneur could have anything to do with BOX 88.

'Time for me to go to Saly,' Eric announced as he drained his second bottle of Coke. There were now other guests on the terrace: a couple of British hippies with dreadlocks and a crumpled pack of playing cards; a middle-aged Belgian with nothing to say to his much younger African girlfriend; two bearded Canadian backpackers playing back-gammon for loose change. 'Really great seeing you guys. And so lovely to meet you, Martha. Lockie is a lucky man.'

Appiah kissed Martha's cheek as she stood up. Kite decided to give him one final chance to show his hand and offered to walk him out to his car; if there was something clandestine to be shared between them, this would be the moment. Yet nothing came of it. Appiah embraced him, his shirt still crisp and dry, expressed his regret that they were not coming to Saly for the party and again extended the invitation to come and stay at his house in Dakar.

'Anything you need, Lockie, just call me,' he said. 'You have any problems, you need any advice on where to go, places to eat, places to stay, I'm your man. While you are in my country you are my guest. I'll do anything for you.'

Kite thought nothing of these words at the time; it was the kind of thing people said when they had no expecta-tion of the offer being taken up. He was to discover that

Senegalese *teranga* was very different to empty British platitudes of non-existent hospitality. Appiah had meant every word. And within a few days Kite would be testing his friend's patience in ways that neither man could possibly have imagined.

7

Nobody came for the money.

Kite and Martha spent three days shuttling between the guest house and the long, wide beach below, swimming in the Atlantic, playing football and frisbee with the local children, hunting for shade in the afternoons when the fierce heat became too much to bear. From the sea cliff they could watch women older than Kite's mother walking on the beach arm in arm with muscled local boys. Fishermen would land their catches in the late morning, snapper, tuna and *thiof* silvering against the brightly coloured hulls of the *pirogues*. On the second day Martha bought two tilapia and some langoustines and carried them back to the guest house in a flimsy plastic bag; they were gutted and grilled and served to them at lunch within twenty minutes. There was very little to do except read and talk and smoke. They could not leave Toubab Dialaw in case someone from BOX arrived for the money. There were no restaurants in town, only a shack bar at the top of a dusty hill serving *bissap* and *ndambé*. Their spartan room, a thatched dome perched on a low cliff overlooking the sea, had space only for a double bed encased in a flimsy mosquito net and a torn wicker chair on which they piled their clothes. They played backgammon on a board

Martha had bought on a family trip to Istanbul and chatted to the staff, who taught them some basic words and phrases in Wolof. At night, full of Flag and cheap whisky, they opened the windows and made love as the ocean breeze cooled their naked bodies. To the north Kite could see the distant lights of Dakar, glowing like some promise of a more exciting future.

It should all have been intensely relaxing, a welcome break from the damp grey skies and sameness of London, yet Kite was never able to shake off the sense of imbalance, of imminent bad luck, which had settled on him as soon as he had arrived at the guest house. It was not a pessimism directly connected to the operation, more a general sense that something was going to go wrong in Senegal. When on their second afternoon he heard screaming on the beach, Kite's first thought was that a shark had attacked a swimmer; upon closer investigation he discovered that a local boy was simply enjoying himself in the surf. The following day Martha failed to come back from a short walk. Kite became concerned that she had been mugged or had an accident; she eventually returned to the guest house safe and sound, explaining that she had stopped to look at some local artwork. It was utterly unlike Kite to be so fatalistic. He hid his anxiety from Martha. There was nothing cheerless or solemn in his day-to-day mood; it was more like a curse which had been laid on him, a premonition of ills to come. They were living in a paradise of crystal-clear sunlight and laughter which, at any moment, was going to be torn away from him with the suddenness of a violent storm.

Perhaps the nature of their bogus holiday was playing on Kite's nerves. Perhaps it was the long wait for contact from BOX. There was also the relentless, sapping heat which made everything feel heavier, slower, unfamiliar. Prior to the operation at Xavier's villa in 1989, Kite had received weeks of training. In 1993, he had been a last-minute replacement for an injured BOX 88 officer but had nevertheless been given two days of intense preparation before departing for Voronezh. This time, he had received nothing but a few traveller's cheques from Michael Strawson, a street map of Dakar and a tip to avoid taking Lariam. 'We're watching somebody of interest in Senegal,' was all that the American had said. 'You will be part of the team involved in that effort.' But how? In what way? And why hadn't anybody come for the money? Their bedroom at the guest house was hardly Fort Knox. Kite and Martha were often on the beach; anybody with a skeleton key could pick the simple lock and steal the packages. Kite had hidden them in the rafters of the thatched roof, but someone looking would easily find them.

On the third day in Toubab it occurred to him that perhaps Senegal was a training operation. Kite's patience, his ability to wait and to improvise, was being tested. But why this voodoo sensation in his bones that he was on the brink of catastrophe? All the waiting around – the swimming and the reading, the backgammon and the beach football – with no contact from BOX seemed pointless. If Strawson was to be believed, there was a mass murderer hiding out in a city less than 100km to the north. He had told Kite that there was 'a lot of ground to cover' before the *genocidaire* could be arrested. Why? Kite longed to put Martha on a plane back to London, to get into Dakar and to play a more active role in the arrest. Waiting around in a remote seaside guesthouse with so little information to go on was not only frustrating, it was oddly humiliating. Had he not already proved himself in Mougins and Voronezh? Why, then, had Strawson seen fit to demote him to the role of a bit-part player?

It was in this frustrated, resigned mood that he first encountered Philippe Vauban. Kite had been having a siesta, woken at around seven o'clock, taken a shower and walked down to the terrace to look for Martha. She was sitting with a man at a table near the bar, touching the necklace Kite had given her as a Christmas present, adjusting her hair as she listened intently, occasionally smiling at something the man said. According to Kite's training, these were all unconscious signs of sexual attraction. The bile of his jealousy stirred. He watched them for some time, spying on the woman he loved. Oumy, a member of staff who worked the lunch shift, walked past him and said 'Hello, Mister Lockie' in her clear, sing-song voice, loud enough to cause Martha to look up. There was an immediate change in her demeanour, almost as though she had been caught out. He heard her say:

'There you are!'

The man who had been seated with his back to Kite now turned. He was in his early thirties with a tanned, weathered face, unkempt brown hair bleached by the African sun and broad, muscular shoulders. He was wearing cotton trousers and a dirty white T-shirt, no logo, a pair of Ray-Bans on the table in front of him, doubtless so that Martha could see his sharp blue eyes. Kite thought of the male models with whom his mother sometimes appeared in adverts for Debenhams and Thomas Cook, but there was nothing primped about this guy, no trace of the hairdresser or tanning salon. He looked tough, experienced. It would have been no surprise at all to Kite if he was BOX.

'Found you,' he said to Martha. 'I fell asleep.'

'This is Philippe,' she replied. 'He just checked in.'

Kite shook the man's hand and said: 'Lachlan.' There was so much in the eye contact – rivalry, self-confidence, an undertow of menace – that Kite wondered if he was slightly drunk.

'Philippe Vauban.' He did not get up from his chair. 'You are English?'

'Scottish.' There was a small tattoo on Vauban's forearm of the type associated with the French Foreign Legion. 'My girlfriend is English.'

'Your girlfriend.' Vauban let the word hang in the stifling air like the justification for a duel. 'Good to know.'

They sat down. Mamadou, the rotund Senegalese who ran the bar and never seemed to sleep, knew without asking that Kite would want a Flag. It appeared in front of him within sixty seconds, condensation pulling the label off, the bottle ice-cold to the touch.

'They know you well,' Vauban observed. He wasn't drunk, just unusually self-possessed. 'You've stayed here before?'

'First time.' Kite raised his Flag in a wordless toast. Martha and the Frenchman were drinking mint teas.

'Best place on this stretch of coast,' Vauban announced, making it sound as though he had written a guidebook detailing every hotel and guest house from Accra to Nouakchott. 'You know the history of the hotel? Guy who owns it is Haitian. That's why you're getting all the shells, the balustrades, the little tiles in the decoration. Senegal is a crossroads of French, Arab, Christian, Muslim. They're lucky not to have found oil here, no cocoa or rubber either. That's why everybody gets along. *Teranga*. The people of Senegal believe that giving is better than receiving. Not like the Nigerians, the Angolans; they are greedy. Selfish and corrupt. But this place' – he pointed at a conch shell glued to the ceiling – 'this is not from Senegalese culture. It's pure Haiti. The owner is originally from Port-au-Prince.'

'Yes, we know,' Kite replied, thinking about the Tonton Macoute. In New York a colleague had bought him a copy of *The Comedians* in the Strand bookshop. It had occurred to him that the sense of foreboding he was carrying around in the guest house was as a direct result of having read Greene's novel. 'You ever been?'

'I was there in '91,' Vauban replied. 'Coup d'état.'

It was an ace of spades remark to which there was no obvious response. Seeing the surprised look on their faces, Vauban invited himself to explain.

61

'Aristide was sent into exile. Military revolution. Small story, didn't see much western coverage. Too many other things going on. Soviet Union collapse. Balkans and Gulf War.'

He had laid his professional cards on the table.

'Philippe is a journalist, sweetheart,' said Martha.

'You don't say.'

'*Photojournaliste*, to be exact,' he replied, using his native tongue. The accent was dry and low, a smoker's voice. 'I work for AFP, Agence France Presse. Not right now but a lot in the past.'

There was an old 35mm Nikon camera on the table lying next to a notebook and a soft pack of Gitanes Blanc. Vauban extracted one, produced a Zippo lighter from the pocket of his cotton trousers, cupped the flame and lit the cigarette with a dexterity which would have drawn the admiration of Jean-Paul Belmondo. *This guy is building his own myth,* thought Kite, swigging the Flag. *He wants the world to know how special he is.* He looked at Martha and saw her as all men must have seen her: luminously beautiful, as unattainable as a priceless jewel, a prize to be won. It occurred to him that everything about Vauban's appearance and demeanour, right down to the worn leather bracelets on his tanned wrists and the gold chain nestling in his chest hair, was machine-tooled to attract women.

'So what are you two doing here?'

Vauban seemed bored by his own question, as though he had asked it only out of politeness. He showed very little interest in Kite's answer, spending most of the time trying to catch Mamadou's attention so that he could order a cold Flag of his own. Kite went through the usual routine – 'We're on a break from life in London, between jobs, travelling up to Morocco' – wondering how much Vauban already knew. If he was Strawson's man, no doubt the American had already filled him in.

'Philippe has just got back from Saly,' Martha said,

seemingly straining for conversation. 'You know, the place where Eric was going the night we arrived.'

'What's it like?'

'It's not much.' Vauban's tone suggested that he had an international database of party towns at his fingertips with which to compare it. 'Small place, normal bars. Busy at the weekend. A lot of tourists, a lot of girls. Not much to see unless you like eating fish and sitting on a beach.'

'We like eating fish and sitting on a beach,' said Martha, rather too cheerily for Kite's liking.

'So you no longer work for AFP?' he asked. 'You're on a break?'

'I'm always working.' Vauban nodded respectfully at the Nikon and the notebook. 'In Africa there is always a story.'

Martha took the bait.

'So what are you writing about at the moment?'

The Flag came. Mamadou set it down in front of Vauban, a fly fighting against the breeze trying to reach it. A small bird darted from the kitchen towards the open sea. Mamadou touched Kite very lightly on the shoulder as he walked back to the bar.

'Right now I work on something private, something close to my heart.' Vauban paused, cultivating an atmosphere of mystery as he took a sip of the lager. He set it down and said: 'No match for a Tusker on a hot day.'

'A Tusker?'

'Local beer in Nairobi.' A car was coming down the hill. Vauban left his seat to take a look. It was evident he was waiting for someone. 'The man who invented it was gored by an elephant, so they gave it this name.' He returned to his chair. 'Nothing like it after a long hot day in the field. This Flag' – he held the bottle up and frowned disdainfully – 'is OK but not the same effect.'

Kite laid a bet with himself that in a blind tasting Vauban wouldn't be able to tell the difference between a Flag, a Tusker and a can of Carling Black Label. He said: 'Well, we're a long way from Nairobi,' in a way that made Martha shift uncomfortably in her chair.

'Where did you two meet?' the Frenchman asked. Martha was about to reply but he cut her off. 'No, let me guess.' Vauban looked at them in the way that he might have looked at a particularly unappetising dish on a buffet. 'University. Am I right?'

'Not quite,' Martha replied. Kite hoped that she was as irritated by Vauban as he was. 'Actually we met in France. Before university. Then I went to Oxford, Lockie was in Edinburgh.'

'Cold there,' Vauban observed. 'I prefer the west coast of Scotland. They have the water from the Caribbean . . .'

'The Gulf Stream,' said Kite.

'That's correct. Although of course in France we call it *le Gulf Stream*.' This appeared to be Vauban's idea of a joke though neither Kite nor Martha laughed. Undeterred, he passed a hand through the locks of his thick, unkempt hair and smiled to himself. There was at least three days' stubble on his jaw and a red mark on his neck where an insect had got the better of him. 'Makes everything warmer. The weather, the people. You British can sometimes be a little cold, a little calculating, know what I mean? I have never been to Oxford, but I had a girlfriend who studied there. Very beautiful, very smart. Not English. She was from Brazil actually. Kind of crazy.'

They had reached another of the Frenchman's conversational cul-de-sacs; he had managed to boast of sexual conquest, to insult the British and to tutor Kite, a Scot, on the meteorological merits of the Gulf Stream, yet had left no obvious path on which the discussion could continue. Martha had long since finished smoking her cigarette and decided to take herself off for a shower. As she left, she commented on the enveloping, ceaseless humidity, unwittingly giving Vauban another chance to show off about his globe-trotting lifestyle.

'At the start of my career I lived in Tanzania,' he said. 'You don't know humidity until you've experienced the heat in Dar es Salaam. My apartment had a chest freezer, you know the ones the size of a small car?' He stretched his arms out, making a box with his hands. 'You could climb inside. With my roommates we used to take turns going in, to close the door and cool off. But then of course as soon as you climbed out the benefit was lost.'

'We need one here,' Martha replied, catching Kite's eye as she walked away. 'The sweltering sky.'

'You get used to the heat,' Vauban replied, oblivious to the play on words. He raised his voice slightly so that he could be sure Martha would be able to hear him over the noise of the ocean. 'It is just a question of adjustment.'

Kite wanted nothing more than to go back to the room with her, but duty kept him at the table. If Vauban was BOX, he would surely soon reveal his hand, though his personality – vain, self-absorbed, charmless – did not fit Kite's idea of an effective intelligence officer. Perhaps he was a courier or cut-out, a useful source of information about the world's trouble spots. Then again, maybe he was just a self-important hack taking a holiday on the coast of Senegal.

'Tell me about yourself, Locklang,' he said, studying Kite over the rim of his Flag. 'What do you do for a living?'

Kite longed to tell the truth, just to see the look on Vauban's face, but had to stick to the script. Mamadou put his favourite bootleg cassette of Sade on the hi-fi and they were treated to the opening bars of 'Your Love Is King'.

'I'm studying Arabic at the moment, working as a waiter at a restaurant to make ends meet.'

'Arabic?' For the first time Vauban appeared to take an interest in him. 'Good for you. So you study at school for ten years. You study at university in Edinburgh. Now you take more classes in Arabic. How old are you?'

'I'm twenty-four.'

'What is your life experience?'

Kite wondered if Vauban had intended to be so direct; it sounded like a question which had been mistranslated from French.

'Evidently not as wide nor as varied as yours, Philippe.'

'I upset you?'

'Not at all. My life experience is just like everybody else's life experience. I'm still young.'

Suddenly the music stopped and all the lights on the deck went out. They were seated in almost total darkness; only the glow from a distant hurricane lamp provided any illumination. In the distance the white crests of the waves were lit by the moon.

'Power cut,' said Vauban, stating the obvious. 'Very normal in Africa.' He clicked his Zippo and set it down on the table so that the flame flickered in the wind. 'Happened in Saly all the time.'

Kite hadn't been in one for several years. He remembered Strawson deliberately switching off the electricity at his mother's hotel during one of his first training exercises in 1989. He could smell the solvent from the Zippo, a memory of camping trips with his father. Just as he was wondering if Martha would be able to find her way in the dark, the lights returned.

'Just like that,' he said, enjoying the hum of the guest house as each room was revived.

'Faster than usual,' Vauban observed.

Mamadou, who had been on his way out to the terrace with two lamps, returned to the bar and reset the hi-fi. Sade was halfway through 'Is It a Crime?'; Mamadou started to sing along. Kite heard another car coming down the hill. This time Vauban sensed that his guest had at last arrived.

'Who are you waiting for?' Kite asked as he stood up from his chair, almost knocking over a Flag. Kite caught it before it fell.

'Just a friend,' the Frenchman replied, seeming to admire the speed of Kite's reflexes.

The 'friend' appeared moments later, a beautiful black woman, no older than twenty or twenty-one, wearing tight denim jeans and a cropped top which showed off her flat, smooth stomach. She brought with her a smell of peach shower gel and was shouldering a small overnight bag. A pair of cheap plastic sunglasses were pushed up over her head.

'*Chérie*,' said Vauban, kissing her on the mouth and placing a proprietorial hand around her waist. 'How was your journey?'

Instead of taking a chair, the girl curled into Vauban's lap like a kitten, eyes on Kite, slipping her hand down the Frenchman's shirt and kissing his neck. For some time they ignored him as they whispered sweet nothings to one another in French. It was apparent that the girl had taken a taxi from Saly to join him at the guest house; she had used some money Vauban had given her two days earlier to pay for the fare. Vauban told her that there was 'another present' waiting for her in his room and the girl giggled. Kite thought of Strawson's warning about AIDS. In the background he could hear Mamadou's quiet falsetto singing along to 'The Sweetest Taboo'.

'I'll leave you to it,' he told them, realising that he had been wasting his time thinking that Vauban was BOX. He was just a war reporter enjoying some coastal R'n'R. 'Looks like you have some catching up to do.'

'This is Fatou,' Vauban explained. It was a name she presumably adopted for the benefit of Western tourists. Kite thought of the woman he had seen at the bar of the Hotel Brno in Voronezh and assumed that Vauban's friend was also for sale.

'Hello,' he said in Wolof. 'Nice to meet you.'

She nodded but said nothing. Instead she took a swig of Kite's abandoned Flag and knocked her heels against the leg of Vauban's chair. A strangely triumphant look appeared on the Frenchman's face.

'Before you go,' he said, looking up at Kite as he stood over them. 'There was something I meant to ask you.'

'Go ahead.'

Kite was pushing his chair back in front of the table. One of the legs caught on a crack in the tiled floor.

'In England, did you ever know a man called Miles Feaver?'

8

Kite had given up on hearing the contact phrase.

'I did,' he said, taken aback by Vauban's timing. 'I knew Miles very well. He was at university with me.'

'Good,' the Frenchman replied. He had hailed Mamadou and was giving him a drinks order. 'Maybe later we can talk about him.'

'Sure.' Kite glanced at Fatou. 'When you're finished.'

The remark sounded haughty, but Kite was in a sour mood. What was more important: the operation in Dakar or a night with a bar girl from Saly? He climbed the steps to his room; at least he could now give Martha the good news that BOX had made contact, even if it meant that he would have to work alongside Vauban. He turned the handle and walked inside.

Both windows were open, a bottle of Boots suntan lotion toppled over on the floor. The pages of a paperback book were flapping in the wind and an empty water bottle had rolled off the bedside table. Somebody had opened a drawer and scattered items onto the bed.

'Martha?'

For an awful moment, Kite feared that she had been kidnapped. Then, over the noise of the ocean, he heard retching. Opening the bathroom door, he saw Martha naked on her knees, holding her hair back with a shaking hand. She was covered in sweat. There was a smell of stagnant seawater overlaid with vomit.

'I'm fine,' she said breathlessly, waving him away. 'Fine.'

Immediately she was sick again. Kite backed out of the room. Making an instant deduction of which he was slightly ashamed, he realised that Martha's condition could impact the start of the operation. If Vauban's instructions were to leave the guest house in the morning, Kite would be caught between his duty to BOX and his duty to Martha.

How had this happened? They had eaten the same food, drunk the same water. Kite pictured the glasses of mint tea on the table in the bar. Christ, had Vauban dosed her? Had that been Strawson's plan all along – to force Kite to choose between his private life and his job? Surely he would not be that callous.

Martha retched again. Her throat sounded bone dry, nothing left in the stomach to come up. He heard her pulling herself up, the click of the plastic toilet seat as she sat down.

'Can I do anything?'

'Give me five minutes, will you?' Her voice was almost a whisper.

Kite left the room. His dread that something would go wrong had come to pass. As he walked down the rickety wooden steps he could hear Martha gasping in pain and wanted to go back to help her. Vauban and Fatou were still on the terrace, drinking whisky and pawing one another. He went in search of Oumy and told her in French that Martha was sick. Oumy said that they could fetch a doctor, but in her experience there was rarely any cure for food poisoning. The patient had to wait for the virus to pass through their system, to drink lots of bottled water, to rest and eat only simple foods. Kite agreed that it was better to wait, not entirely trusting the prospect of a village doctor coming to treat Martha. Back in the room he read

70

about malaria symptoms in the guidebook while his girl-friend lay in the foetal position beside him. She said that she didn't have a fever, just a constant nausea and intense stomach cramps.

As the night wore on, laughter could be heard in the next room. Vauban was in the hut with his girl. The contrast between Martha's misery and Fatou's occasional gasps of sexual pleasure was stark. The girl would frequently yelp or laugh drunkenly. As night fell and the guest house became quiet, it proved impossible to get to sleep. Martha often dozed off only to wake suddenly and rush to the bathroom. In the moonlight her face looked deathly pale. She kept apologising for her condition: it was unlike her to be ill and she hated being a burden to him. Back in bed, Kite mopped her brow with a T-shirt he had soaked in water, increasingly convinced that she had contracted malaria. Yet she had not been bitten; they had been careful with sprays and creams and always draped the mosquito net over the bed when they were sleeping. Between visits to the bathroom, Martha told him that she had eaten some nuts before talking to Vauban on the terrace. She wondered if these had caused her illness. Through all this Kite kept wondering what he would do if Martha's condition did not improve. He had an earworm from the bar and kept hearing the chorus to 'Sweetest Taboo' on a loop in his mind. Leaving Martha in bed, he crept outside, intending to go for a short, head-clearing walk on the beach.

As soon as he was at the bottom of the steps, he heard Vauban coming out of the neighbouring hut. Kite looked up. The Frenchman was naked but for a pair of tight white underpants that gave off a fluorescent glow in the moonlight.

'Hello there,' he said, lighting a cigarette. The sound of the Zippo clicking and snapping shut was like the scuttle of a small animal in the rafters. 'Can't sleep?'

'Sick,' Kite replied, pointing towards Martha.

71

'*Merde*,' said Vauban, indicating that Kite should walk up the steps so that they could talk privately.

'*Malade?*' he asked when Kite had reached the top. He had left the door of his hut open. Kite could see Fatou naked on the bed, fast asleep beneath a mosquito net. To his surprise he saw that her hair was cropped short; there was a black wig on the bedside table like a prop from a school play. Kite wanted to stare at her extraordinary body, at the necklace of white beads around her waist, but turned back as Vauban said: 'How bad?'

'Vomiting. Diarrhoea. Food poisoning.'

'She take her meds?'

It was the question of an old Africa hand.

'Yeah, we're both on malapram. She thinks she ate some bad nuts.'

'Bad nuts,' the Frenchman repeated, nodding to himself. There were indistinct tattoos on his stomach and left bicep. The floral insignia on his forearm was barely visible in the moonlight.

'Were you in the Foreign Legion?' Kite asked.

Vauban puffed out a cloud of astonished smoke and said: '*How do you know this?*'

'Your tattoo.'

Vauban followed Kite's gaze down to his arm. 'Most people think it is just some ink I like. I tell them it was done in Marseille a long time ago.'

'So you served?'

'For less than one year. I was very young. I had a lot of madness in me, you know? A lot of violence. It was a way of channelling that. Then I found my correct path with journalism.'

'Marseille? That's where you're from originally?'

'Close by. Rousset. You wouldn't know it.'

Kite noted the slight change in atmosphere between them; it was partly the late hour and the cool ocean breeze, but mostly the knowledge that they would now

72

be working together. Vauban was being less confrontational, less obnoxious. Perhaps Kite had Fatou to thank for working her magic.

'How long have you been with us?' he asked, stealing another glance inside the room. He saw a copy of the *New Yorker* on the floor next to a jar of moisturiser and a carton of Camel cigarettes. There was an almost empty bottle of Chivas Regal by the window and some fruit juice, both surely as hot to drink as bathwater.

'I am not *with* you,' the Frenchman replied, making inverted commas with his fingers. 'Michael is an old friend. He knew my father. He is like family to me. I know the nature of his work. I do favours for him. Occasionally he does favours for me.'

'What kind of favours?'

'This job, for example.'

Kite concealed his confusion in another question.

'Does Fatou speak English?'

'Not a word.' Vauban accompanied the remark with a sly smile. 'But she talks with her body.'

'What about the package? I assume we're still going to Dakar?'

'Of course. The clock is ticking.'

Kite nodded towards the hut. 'You seem pretty relaxed about it.'

'Maybe,' the Frenchman replied with a grin.

'So what's the situation?'

Leaning casually against the wooden hut in his tight white briefs, topless and sexually sated, Vauban looked like a rock star taking a break between groupies. He drew on the cigarette then abruptly stubbed it out on the wooden balustrade. Falling embers sparked in the darkness.

'The situation is we go to Dakar tomorrow.' He looked into the room and at last decided to close the door. 'The girl goes back to her family. I have a car. We drive into the city. There's a team waiting for us, close to Rue Kennedy.

73

They say they have located Bagaza. They need me to confirm his identity. I'm the only one who has seen him, spoken to him, dealt with him.'

'You were in Rwanda?' Kite asked, knowing the inevitable answer.

'I was there.'

'And you encountered this man? You saw what he did?'

The conceitedness went out of Vauban as he said:

'I saw it. Bagaza is the devil.'

Kite did not know how to respond. The Frenchman looked momentarily sickened.

'Mike said he escaped from Rwanda via Tanzania last year. Is he being protected by the Senegalese?'

Vauban shrugged. 'This is what the team has been looking into. So far so good. We find out tomorrow.'

Tomorrow. Kite looked across at his own hut, worrying about Martha.

'What time do you want to leave?' he asked.

'We eat breakfast, we go.'

'If my girlfriend is still sick, she'll have to come with us. I have a friend in town. She can stay with him.'

Kite was sure that if Eric Appiah was in Dakar, he would look after Martha. Vauban reacted with astonishment.

'You're *serious*?' The arrogance was back, an implication in his tone that Kite was embarrassing himself. 'You can't bring a girl on a job like this.'

'You think I'm going to leave her here on her own?' Kite knew that Vauban would likely report everything back to Strawson but he didn't care. 'We'll drive to my friend's house, drop her off, then go on to meet the rest of the team.'

Another shrug. Vauban rolled his eyes, made a slight adjustment to the elastic of his underpants and muttered: 'We should get some sleep.'

Kite still had a hundred questions. If Vauban was the only person who could identify Bagaza, why wasn't he already in Dakar? And what did Vauban mean when he said that Strawson was doing him a favour by mounting the operation? Since when was BOX 88 in the habit of doing favours for French journalists?

'Who found out Bagaza was in Dakar?' he asked.

'I did,' the Frenchman replied quickly. 'Through my contacts.'

'And we're taking him . . . where?'

'They have a boat waiting. That's how we get him out. They take Bagaza in the apartment, get him to the port, load him onto the ship.'

'Just like that.' Kite assumed that a team of Falcons, BOX 88's surveillance specialists, were keeping an eye on the target. Closers, the military arm of the agency, would be on hand to finish the job. Even so, getting Bagaza out of Senegal sounded a lot harder than Vauban was making out. For a start, he wondered who else might be looking at the Rwandan. In New York Kite had studied a BOX operation which had been torpedoed at the last moment by the sudden appearance of a German intelligence team working against the same target. He assumed that Bagaza was wanted by at least three rival entities: the Rwandan government, for a start, the French DGSE and possibly the Canadians, who were in the business of running Hutu war criminals to ground. If any of them were in Dakar, BOX needed to know about it.

'Who else might be interested in him?' he asked. A shadow passed beneath the hut. Both of them froze, but it was only one of the cats coming back from a night on the tiles. 'Any intel on that?'

Vauban produced another of his trademark shrugs, as if to suggest that such questions were beyond his remit. His response only added to Kite's gnawing anxiety that the operation was being made up on the hoof. The whole thing felt like an extended improvisation with Vauban – an untrained maverick – at its centre.

75

'I guess I'll find out tomorrow,' said Kite. 'So we're agreed?'

'Agreed about what?'

'Martha comes with us tomorrow. We go via my friend's house in Dakar.'

'If you're sure that's what you want, Locklang, that's what we do.'

9

Kite had been asleep for no more than an hour when he was woken by the sound of Martha retching into the toilet again. As he went to help she stretched out her arm in a gesture of desperation, tired and strung out by the long night she had endured.

'I'm so sorry,' she said, still apologising in that British way of hers for something which was beyond her control.

'It's fine,' Kite told her. 'Don't worry. You just need to rest.'

She already looked as though she had lost a stone in weight. Her tanned skin had turned grey under the feeble electric light. Kite wondered when to tell her about Vauban, about going into Dakar to stay with Eric. How the hell was he going to explain that he was going to have to leave her?

As soon as there were signs of life in the guest house he left the room to telephone Appiah, walking the short distance from the hut to the reception area. Mamadou was at the desk, dealing with a young Ivorian woman with whom Martha had played backgammon two nights earlier. They exchanged pleasantries and the woman walked out to her waiting taxi, a rusting Renault with a chipped custard-yellow paint job.

'Can I call a friend in Dakar?' Kite asked, indicating the phone on the cluttered desk. It was the only means of reaching the outside world.

'Of course!'

Mamadou asked Kite for the number and dialled it, handing him the receiver and leaving the office so that Kite might have some privacy. One of the cleaners, a voluminous woman from Toubab, waddled past the open door and greeted Kite cheerfully in Wolof.

Appiah picked up.

'Eric?'

'Is that you, Lockie?' Though it was still early in the morning he sounded lively, evidently thrilled to hear from his old friend. 'How are you, man? I hoped you would ring. You been having a good time down there? Let me guess. You're bored. You want to have some fun now, right?'

'I wish I could say that.'

'Has something happened?'

Kite explained that Martha was ill. There was no need to embellish or exaggerate the story. Then he told the first of many lies.

'I'm in an awkward situation,' he said. 'I've been offered the chance to team up with a photojournalist here and to go with him today into Dakar to interview someone for the *New York Times*. He needs someone who speaks French and English. It's a big scoop, a VIP. But I can't leave Martha alone.'

'You want to bring her here? Or I can come down to Toubab and look after her?'

'If we could come and stay with you that would be incredibly kind.'

'You know my house is your house, Lockie.'

He loved Appiah in this moment: the kindness and unthinking generosity of an old friend. Kite thought of his mother, who would have questioned every molecule of

78

his shabby cover story. What photojournalist? Since when were *you* stringing for the *New York Times*? But not Eric. If he had doubts about what Kite had told him, he wasn't about to voice them.

'If she could come for twenty-four hours, if you could keep an eye on her until she's feeling better, that would be fantastic.'

'You're not staying too?'

'Well, it sort of depends what time this guy shows up. He's due at the airport at three but could be delayed . . .'

Again, Appiah did not interrogate the details of Kite's story. He said it would be fine for Martha to stay, that there was a guest room they both could use for as long as they needed it. Kite wrote down the address of the house and what sounded like straightforward instructions for getting there. When he was done, he thanked Appiah, hung up and walked back to the hut to tell Martha what he had planned.

She was getting out of the shower, holding on to the wall for balance. Kite had grabbed two fresh towels from the reception area and handed her one.

'Feeling any better?'

'A bit.'

'This is where it gets complicated.'

She sat on the edge of the bed and looked up at him, tired and confused.

'What do you mean?'

'Philippe is my contact.'

'Who's Philippe?'

'The French guy we were talking to last night.'

Martha looked amazed. '*Him?* Really?'

'He was sounding me out. We have to go to Dakar this morning, start the operation.'

'You can't leave me here like this,' she said, astonished that Kite was even considering such a thing. 'Please don't leave me. I really feel awful.'

79

It was unlike her to stand in the way of his work, even less characteristic that she should plead so desperately. Kite suddenly saw that Martha was much sicker than she had been letting on.

'I know you do,' he said. 'Please don't worry. I'm not going to leave you here. I just rang Eric Appiah. We're going to check out, drive to his house in Dakar, he's going to put us up in his spare room. It'll be a beautiful, comfortable house. Air conditioning, people to look after you, everything you'll need. I'll go off during the afternoon to do whatever I have to do, you'll rest and get better.'

'What if it's something more serious?'

Kite looked at Martha's skin, pale as newspaper, her eyes bloodshot and sallow. He assumed she was talking about malaria.

'I'm sure you've got nothing worse than a really nasty bout of food poisoning.' He put a hand on her knee. She was shaking slightly, like the beginnings of a fever. 'And if you don't feel better this time tomorrow, there are clinics and hospitals in Dakar. Much easier to get you treated in the city. Round here there's probably nothing but voodoo witch doctors who'll make you eat chopped up goat's hair washed down with yak's milk.'

'They don't have yaks in Senegal,' she said, managing a weak smile.

It was a brief moment of cheerfulness in an otherwise gloomy morning. Kite heard Vauban walking out of his hut speaking to Fatou in French. They were checking out. Encouraging Martha to get dressed, he packed their rucksacks and retrieved the money from the rafters. He showered, ate a quick breakfast of bread and jam and processed cheese, then settled the bill. All the time Martha waited in the hut, lying on the bed, trying to rest, an electric fan doing its best to combat the relentless heat. Kite dreaded the journey that lay ahead for her and prayed that Vauban had at least rented a car with air conditioning and a comfortable back seat.

No such luck. As he carried their luggage out to the dusty area in front of the guest house, he was confronted by the sight of a dented Toyota Corolla which looked as if it had several times driven the length of Africa. One of the tyres was almost bald, the rear windscreen cracked and there was a piece of rubber sealant hanging down from the chassis.

'What a piece of shit,' he said. 'Why didn't you rent a Landcruiser?'

'They were out,' the Frenchman replied. He flung a pair of shoes and a canvas overnight bag into the boot. The Toyota tilted slightly to one side. 'I can change it with Hertz in Dakar.'

Kite had walked Martha from their room, holding an umbrella over her head to protect her from the sun. No fewer than five members of staff had gathered to see them off – Mamadou and Oumy, two chefs and a chambermaid. They all seemed concerned by Martha's condition. Kite remembered something his mother always said about flying through turbulence: 'If the stewardesses look frightened, you know you're in trouble.' Did they think that Martha was suffering from something more serious than food poisoning?

He laid a beach towel on the broiling back seat, encouraging her to lie down. She was dosed up on Imodium and said that she was fine to sit and just wanted to get to Appiah's house as quickly as possible. Martha sipped occasionally from a bottle of water but had eaten nothing for more than twelve hours. Kite put a plastic bag at her feet in case she was sick on the journey. Not for the first time, he privately wondered why the hell Strawson had encouraged them to come out to Senegal as a couple. He resolved to get her to Eric's house and then to see how she was feeling. They had a return flight booked in forty-eight hours. Kite was determined that Martha would be on it. The sooner she was back home, safe in the arms of her parents in Swiss Cottage, the better.

'Who's your friend in Dakar?' Vauban asked as he started the engine. He had not yet addressed a word to Martha.

'Local. Senegalese,' Kite replied. 'I was at school with him in England.'

'And you trust him?'

Kite was about to say: 'A lot more than I trust you' but thought better of it. Instead he went with: 'Of course' and reached for his seat belt. There wasn't one.

'You have directions?' Vauban was adjusting the mirrors. 'Getting around Dakar is a pain in the ass.'

'We'll be fine.' Kite pulled out the street map Strawson had given him as well as the directions he had written down in the office. 'Eric told me the way.'

They were soon heading into Toubab, dust and insects coming in through the open windows, the Toyota groaning in low gear as it strained uphill. The same strong, upright women in brightly coloured dresses were carrying plastic buckets and heavy sacks of grain at the sides of the main tarmacked road. They passed a man sitting in a worn armchair in the shade of a wildly overgrown tree, a group of women holding up chilled bottles of water like volunteers at a marathon. Vauban smoked, steering nonchalantly with one hand. He did not ask Martha how she was feeling; he was not concerned about her comfort. They passed the same shacks and abandoned concrete structures at the edge of town, the same boys kicking the same football near the bushes that were surely full of snakes. This time the boys waved delightedly at the car and even ran beside Kite's window for a time before Vauban accelerated away. The dry potholed tracks leading off the main road were bordered by stones and lean-to shacks of corrugated iron. Kite saw an old man in rags slumped in the shade of a blood-orange bougainvillea, a rat as big as a domestic cat feasting on roadkill a few hundred metres further on. The carcass of the animal had been stripped clean. Its bones glowed white in the sun.

For the first twenty minutes or so, Martha seemed fine. Then suddenly she asked Vauban to pull over. He acted as though he hadn't heard until Kite barked 'Stop!' and the Frenchman gracelessly slowed down, parking close to a roadside stall selling biscuits and Nescafé. While Martha leaned against the burning metal bonnet and retched, Vauban walked over to the stall and bought a glass of instant coffee. Martha was gasping as Kite tended to her. Flies buzzed around them.

'Do you want to go back?' he asked, one of those questions to which the answer can only be 'Of course not'. Even if Martha had implored him to return to the guest house, Kite would have tried to talk her out of it.

'Just need to catch my breath,' she replied.

It occurred to him that he could take her straight to the airport and ask Appiah to escort her home, but that was way beyond what he felt he could expect of his friend. Besides, she surely wasn't well enough to fly. Kite had visions of his girlfriend being taken off a plane in Paris and rushed to hospital while he was stuck in Dakar watching Bagaza.

He looked up. Vauban was staring at them as he sipped his coffee, the central casting war reporter in desert boots, ripped jeans and a powder blue T-shirt. Even at the edge of a busy African highway in ninety-degree heat, he looked ready to seduce any woman who strayed into his path. A bird cried out over the sound of the passing traffic. In a kind of breathless daze Martha said: 'Was that a parrot?'

'I think so, yes.'

'Dakar isn't safe for you,' she added suddenly, struggling for breath. 'Remember what the guidebook said. You could get mugged, have something stolen . . .'

She ran out of energy on the final word. Kite said: 'Please don't worry. I know how to look after myself. I'll be fine.'

'Ready?' Vauban called out.

His patience tested, Kite shouted back: 'Buy me a coffee, will you? Black. Two sugars.'

The Frenchman obliged, handing the vendor a few coins and bringing a small plastic cup back to the car. As he handed it to Kite, a truck sped past, kicking up a stone which hit the side of the Corolla with a crack like a racquetball.

'So we can go?'

Kite came up behind Vauban as he opened the driver's door.

'Ever been sick, Philippe?' he snapped. He had to raise his voice in order to be heard over the buzz of a passing motorbike. 'Ever had food poisoning? Ever had to go to hospital?'

'Sure.'

'So maybe show some compassion. She's doing the best she can.'

Yet there was something inescapably humiliating about his situation. When he should have been giving his full concentration to the operation, Kite was instead nursing his sick girlfriend. In doing so he was demonstrating a sensitivity, a softness, which was anathema to the machismo of their trade. It was like the heat; Kite knew that Vauban would never complain about it, just as Kite would never let anyone know how flattened he felt by the relentless, enervating humidity. Male pride and bravura were the orders of the day. By caring for Martha, he was diminishing his status as a man.

They drove without incident for about half an hour. Martha again apologised for 'causing so much fuss' and set her face to look stoic, even though Kite could tell that she was crippled by cramps and often close to being sick. On two occasions her stubbornness clearly prevented her from asking Vauban to stop; she would rather suffer in silence than have him think of her as a weak, helpless woman. The hot wind blew through the car. She lay across the back seat with her eyes closed, unable to suppress the occasional groan whenever the Toyota hit a pothole or tested its suspension on an uneven section of road. Kite occasionally reached back and stroked her hair. He was worried about her, but at the same time constantly calculating how soon he would be able to get away from Appiah's house to join the team in Dakar.

They were back in the open landscape of baobab trees and pylons when the Toyota suddenly lurched to one side of the road and skidded on the dirt-track hard shoulder. Kite knew instantly it was a puncture.

'Fuck,' he said as Vauban matched him with a French equivalent: '*Putain!*' The car slowed to a halt as a truck sped past, sounding its horn in sadistic triumph.

'Got a spare?' Kite asked when they had established that the front left tyre had blown. Inevitably, when Vauban looked in the boot, having lifted out all their luggage and put it on the side of the road, he found only a pool of dried oil and a couple of prehistoric cigarette butts.

'You didn't check when you rented the car?' Kite asked.

'This is Africa, Locklang. Things don't work like that.'

There was no point in arguing further. The bad luck had revisited them. Martha was inside the car, too weak to get up. She would cook in the back seat if they didn't fix the tyre. Kite made a decision.

'We're leaving,' he said. 'We'll hitch into town.'

'Abandon the car?' Vauban replied.

'London will cover the expense. The rental company doesn't give you a spare, they can't expect you to find a garage in the middle of Senegal when one of their tyres explodes.'

Vauban seemed to think this was a good idea. A rural bus slowed beside them, expressionless passengers rubbernecking the two stranded white men and their stricken Japanese car. As the driver moved away the noise of the bus's accelerating engine was like an old tractor struggling through mud. Suitcases and boxes and huge cotton sacks were secured to the roof by frayed ropes and lengths of twine. It looked as though something would fall off at any moment.

'We hitch?' said Vauban, saying 'hitch' like 'each'.

'Or if a taxi comes past,' Kite suggested, more in hope than expectation. He ducked into the Toyota to check on Martha. She had put a thin scarf over her head to protect her face from the punishing sun. He explained his plan and she sat up slowly, asking if it was OK simply to abandon the rental car in the middle of nowhere.

'That's Philippe's problem. I want to get you to Eric's house. You'll be much more comfortable there. We stay out here it could be six hours before someone finds us a new tyre. Can't exactly call the AA.'

So they waited by the side of the road, mad dogs in the morning sun, watching car after car, truck after truck, speed past them without stopping. Eventually a middle-aged man driving a Renault pulled over to offer them a lift. Just in time: Vauban had been trying to persuade Martha to get out of the car and stand on her own with her thumb out while he and Kite hid in the Toyota.

'Then they'll stop,' he had said. 'For a beautiful European woman travelling alone, they think they hit jackpot. You can do it, can't you? Just for a few minutes.'

Their saviour turned out to be a plumber from Kaolack named Maguette who said that he was heading in the general direction of Appiah's house. With boxes and tools occupying the front seat, there wasn't room in the Renault for all three of them, so Vauban stayed behind, telling Kite he would meet him at the Imperial café on Place de l'Independence at 4 p.m.

'Don't be late, Locklang,' he said. 'All the team will be there.'

10

Driving away from the stricken Toyota, Martha's head resting on his lap, Kite became convinced that their situation would now improve: Martha would be looked after, he would join the operation and help BOX to snatch Bagaza. There was a kind of soldier inside him, a fascination for conflict; he wanted to be tested in this place, to prove himself both to Vauban and to Strawson. He just needed to get Martha to safety and all would be well.

But Maguette was a frustrating mixture of good intentions and geographical ineptitude. It transpired that he had been to Dakar only twice before, spoke very little French, even less English, and could not read a map. Eric's directions referenced various landmarks – Place de l'Independence, as well as government buildings and the Presidential palace – but Maguette seemed not to be familiar with any of them. Kite pictured Dakar as a fat peninsular, shaped like a fish hook jutting out into the Atlantic, with the airport and the beaches at Ngor and Yoff to the north and the majority of commercial and ministerial buildings clustered in the south in an area known as Plateau. Maguette was familiar only with Sicap, a large neighbourhood halfway between the two. The Appiah house was in Fann, the city's most exclusive and salubrious quarter, though not one which was marked on Strawson's street map. Kite knew that it was close to the Corniche, the coast road on the western edge of the city, but could not get Maguette to head towards the ocean. Time and again he kept taking the wrong turn, heading back in the direction of the airport or south towards Plateau. Kite eventually lost patience, giving him a hundred francs as a gift and leading Martha into a hotel where she sat in the air-conditioned lobby sipping water while Kite used a payphone to call Eric. Within fifteen minutes Appiah had turned up in a spotlessly clean Landcruiser and was driving them to his house.

'You don't look too bad,' he said to Martha, eyeing her in the rear-view mirror. He was wearing a Chicago Bulls T-shirt and what looked like a brand-new pair of Air Jordans. 'Lockie made it sound like you were dying or something.'

'I'll live,' she said. 'It's so kind of you to have us to stay.'

In front of them was one of those Senegal sights which would have been unthinkable in the ordered, sensible West: two barefoot boys in shorts and ragged T-shirts, no older than ten or eleven, catching a free ride on the back of a bus. Their feet were balanced on a wooden running board, their fingers clinging to the frame of the rear doors.

'Since when did you start working as a journalist?' Appiah asked as he made a slow right-hand turn into a quieter neighbourhood of palm trees and expensive German cars. 'You didn't say anything about it the other night.'

'Came out of nowhere,' Kite replied. 'This French guy just needs a helping hand, so I said I'd go along. He's paying me a hundred dollars. That'll keep me and Martha on the road for a few more days.'

It was another lie of the sort with which Kite was so strangely at ease. Appiah would never meet Vauban and have the opportunity to test the story; Martha would certainly never tell Kite's friend the truth about his activities.

They pulled up in front of a large whitewashed villa surrounded on all sides by a high concrete wall. Kite could see barbed wire across the top. A couple of fixed closed-circuit cameras covered the grounds. A security guard at the gate gave Appiah a respectful wave and stepped back to allow the Landcruiser to pass beneath a raised wooden barrier. They parked directly in front of a three-storey building in the colonial style with a heavy front door opened on cue by a uniformed butler.

Kite stepped out of the car. They were a world away from the mess and chaos of downtown Dakar. Birds chirped politely in the trees. A trio of gardeners were working separately in the grounds, watering, weeding and sweeping. A Wimbledon-green lawn was somehow flourishing under the ceaseless glare of the African sun. Kite could see the blue sparkle of a swimming pool in the distance and a corner of fencing around a basketball court. Taking their rucksacks from the back of the Landcruiser, he felt a droplet of water fall on his nose. Looking up at the bright clear sky, baffled by the possibility of rain, he realised that a nearby sprinkler had honoured him with a stray spray.

'What a place,' he said as the butler took Martha's rucksack and led them inside.

'Yeah, not bad I guess,' Appiah replied, and there was a moment between them where Kite acknowledged how little he had known about Appiah's life in Senegal. At Alford they had bonded because they were both outsiders: Kite the boy from a modest background born in a distant corner of Scotland; Appiah the wealthy son of a rich Senegalese businessman. Both of them had been sent to an elite boarding school at thirteen with some vague parental idea that the experience would improve both their characters and life prospects. Yet Kite now understood that they had also been opposites: Appiah's privilege was comparable to that of his closest friend, Xavier Bonnard, whose family owned homes in London and Paris, in Verbier and Gloucestershire. To walk into Eric's lavish Dakar home was to walk into the equivalent of an ambassador's residence or five-star hotel.

'Let's get you to your room,' Appiah suggested.

Martha had shut herself away in the bathroom while Kite handed their dirty clothes to a shy, veiled maid who whisked them off to be washed and ironed. Leaving Martha to rest, Kite and Eric ate a lunch of gazpacho, cold chicken and Parma ham as swallows made quicksilver shadows on the surface of the swimming pool. The meal was served and cleared away by yet more staff. Appiah explained that he had booked a private doctor to come to the house at four o'clock. Kite thanked him effusively, offering to pay, but Appiah wouldn't hear of it. Feeling the lie as something miserable inside him, Kite said that he would be back to check up on Martha in the early evening. In truth he did not know if he would ever return to the house. More likely BOX would billet him in a flea-bitten hotel with Vauban while the team tried to work out where and when to seize Bagaza. Kite was effectively passing Martha into the care of his friend. If anything happened to her in the next twenty-four hours, she would be Eric's responsibility.

Shortly afterwards, his face and arms covered in suntan lotion, a Brown University baseball cap on his head, Kite left the villa. He was carrying a soft pack of cigarettes and a small rucksack in which he had packed a fresh set of clothes and 40,000 French francs. He had no other shoes but the worn pair of Dunlop Green Flash in which he was standing. Hailing a cab two blocks from the villa he gave directions for Place de l'Independence, arriving more than half an hour early for the planned meeting. He was hopeful that he would finally discover what role, if any, he was to play in Bagaza's arrest; at the very least he expected to be told exactly what was going on.

The Imperial was an old French colonial watering hole, straight out of Graham Greene, with a collapsed atmosphere of furtive afternoon drinking, of secret assignations between white men and much younger black women. Kite thought that he saw his old geography teacher from Alford sitting at the bar beside a local girl in a bright yellow tank top, but he was mistaken; it was just a silver-haired, sunburnt Dutchman trying his luck with one of the locals. Card games were being played in a rear saloon; a sign advertising Baileys Irish Cream hung over the door like a crucifix. Kite went outside and sat at a table for four beside the noisy square. He did not want to be spotted indoors, hiding from the heat and bustle of Dakar in air-conditioned comfort. Better to be watching the clockwise traffic on Place de L'Independence: the angry, impatient cars belching clouds of black exhaust; ambulance sirens and police klaxons widely ignored by the locals; street vendors with counterfeit watches and shoddy jewels pinned to the lining of their jackets. A small speaker competed with the outdoor clamour, piping 'Sympathy for the Devil' from a hi-fi onto the terrace.

Kite was on his second cup of coffee when he saw a taxi pull up on the opposite side of the street. A man of about fifty wearing Aviators, a crushed linen suit and Panama hat got out, looking for all the world like Hannibal Lecter in the final scene of *The Silence of the Lambs*. The man paid the driver and turned to face the Imperial. It was only as he was removing his sunglasses that Kite got a proper look at him.

It was Strawson.

11

'How are you doing, kid?' he said, casually greeting Kite as if he had last seen him at breakfast. Strawson had shaved off his straggly beard. The tip of his nose and his pale cheeks were slightly sunburned; he had an uncharacteristic air of being pressed for time. 'Why the hell you out here in this heat? Let's go inside.'

Kite picked up his cigarettes and followed him into the bar, where they sat at a table under a speaker blasting out 'Gimme Shelter'.

'How long have you been in Senegal?' Kite asked.

Strawson took off his jacket and set the Panama hat on a chair beside him. He was wearing a blue cotton shirt, the armpits grey discs of sweat.

'Six days. Where the hell is Philippe?'

'Coming at four.' Kite indicated a small clock on the wall framed by a moulded plastic Michelin Man.

'Should have been here yesterday.' Angrily Strawson demanded: 'What the hell were you guys *doing* at the beach?'

'He only showed up last night.' Kite noted the look of surprise on Strawson's face. 'Nobody called me at the guest house to explain what was happening. The three of us drove up this morning. Martha is ill.'

It appeared to take a moment for the American to understand to whom Kite was referring.

'She is? What's she got?'

'Food poisoning. Worst-case scenario, malaria. She'll be fine. Hopefully. She's staying with my friend Eric at his parents' house in Fann.'

'Fann?'

'It's an expensive neighbourhood in Dakar.' Kite pointed in the general direction of the Corniche, pleased to be able to teach the boss something he didn't know. 'There's a doctor coming to look at her this afternoon.'

'And yet you're not there. What does Eric think you're doing?'

'I told him I was working on a story with Philippe. He needed a simultaneous translator, someone who speaks French and English.'

'Philippe speaks fluent English.'

'Eric doesn't know that.'

Strawson nodded slowly. He had taken on the slightly haunted look of the unrested long-distance traveller.

'So she's out for cover. You'll have to work alone. Too bad. Wanted you guys up close with Bagaza.'

'Maybe she'll feel better in the next twenty-four hours.' Kite wanted to appear untroubled by Martha's condition, upbeat and optimistic. 'Just a stomach bug, you know.'

But the American had stopped listening. Summoning a waitress, he asked for a large bottle of still water, a black coffee and a toasted cheese sandwich. Kite decided to take advantage of Strawson's deracinated state by asking some basic questions.

'To be honest, I don't really know what I'm doing out here,' he began. 'You told me next to nothing in London. Philippe says we're on the point of grabbing this guy, you have a boat waiting . . .'

It was sensitive information, easily smothered by the Rolling Stones and the noise of the heavy afternoon traffic shunting past on Allées Delmas.

'We need Philippe formally to confirm Bagaza's identity.

I have a group of eight here including two Closers. I'll explain the rest when the others show up.'

'Closers', the military arm of BOX 88, were usually ex-Special Forces employed for black ops. They would be the ones tasked with grabbing Bagaza. It had occurred to Kite that he had not been in a working environment with Strawson since the first days at the villa in France. Indeed, this was the first time in his career that he was to be part of a team; up to this point, Strawson had always sent him out into the field alone.

'Who are the others?' he asked.

'A fixer. A good man.' Strawson scratched an insect bite on his wrist. 'Omar Gueye, local Senegalese, did some work for the DGSE but we don't hold that against him. Knows the city like the back of his hand. Unlike most of the goddam cab drivers who don't even speak French. Works closely with his brother, Naby, who right now is watching Bagaza's place.'

'And the rest?'

'Coming now, you mean?' Strawson licked his thumb and rubbed saliva onto the bite. 'Ricky Ackerman. Maybe you met him in the Tower.'

'The Tower' was agency language for BOX 88 headquarters in lower Manhattan. Kite didn't remember anybody called Ricky and said so.

'Usually based out of Nairobi, came in with his wife to oversee the Bagaza grab. Nancy, Kenyan. Kind of a pain in the ass but they work well together. Again, you likely won't meet her today. She's resting. Was up all night watching the monitors. Take this.'

From the inside pocket of his jacket Strawson extracted an envelope which he passed to Kite.

'Escape passport. Peter Galvin alias. You remember him, right?'

Galvin was the legend Kite had used in Voronezh two years earlier.

94

'I remember him,' he replied, forcing a smile.

'Any problems, you make your way down to the Gambia, we can get you out from Banjul. I assume you still have the money I gave you?'

'All of it,' Kite replied, wondering why Strawson had told him that somebody would come to Toubab and take it off him. Vauban had never mentioned it.

'Good. Goes a long way here. See that waitress?' Strawson indicated the young woman who had taken his order for the toasted cheese sandwich. 'She's lucky if she makes thirty bucks a week. You put four hundred francs in her hand you just doubled her salary.'

Kite could feel the rucksack resting against his leg. He asked about the monitors.

'Stakeout position. We have a place across the street from 35 Rue Kennedy. Camera on the front door, another round the back just in case the Hutu fuck gets any funny ideas and tries to run. Here's Ricky now.'

The traffic-roar of the door opening. A thirty-something African-American with neat, close-cropped hair wearing chinos and a tight-fitting Lacoste polo shirt was heading towards them.

'How are you doing?' Strawson rose to shake Ackerman's hand. He was a slim, inexpressive man, not a drop of sweat on him. 'This is Lachlan.' Strawson ordered three beers from the passing waitress. 'Just arrived from Toubab.'

'Finally,' Ackerman replied. His eyes were dead with concentration, the handshake limp and dry. Kite was about to defend himself against the accusation of being late when Strawson spotted Omar.

'Make it four Flags, please,' he called out to the waitress in French.

Ackerman was of a similar vintage to Omar but the contrast between them could not have been starker. Where the former was wiry and buttoned-up, Omar was large and loose-limbed, exuding the relaxed self-confidence of a man who knew that he was key to the operation: without his knowledge of Wolof and Dakar, of the local intelligence picture and the power structures down at the port, BOX would likely not be able to function. Strawson did the introductions. Ackerman and Omar were already acquainted, Kite the new kid on the block.

'I have heard a lot about you,' Omar began. He spoke English with a strong French accent. His broad smile and quick, expressive eyes were like a promise of a lasting friendship. 'How are you finding Senegal? You like my country?'

'Very much,' Kite replied.

'The kid is here to learn and to help,' Strawson added, somewhat to Kite's chagrin. 'Like I told you guys, this is his first time with a standard targeting operation of this kind. We may play him into the template, we may leave him out. Martha is sick so Lockie is solo.'

Kite felt like a passenger sitting in Economy watching the curtain being closed on Business Class. He wondered how much longer Strawson would go on talking about him as though he wasn't there.

'Play me into the template?' he asked, baffled by the expression.

'It means we might have some use for you, we might not.' Ackerman's interjection was as bloodless as it was condescending. He reminded Kite of certain teachers at Alford who insisted on the exact application of arcane rules, relishing the opportunity to punish those who failed to obey them. 'But I'm sure you'll be an asset,' he added without conviction.

'Let's begin.' Strawson had chosen to ignore Ackerman's remark. Kite noted that the meeting was starting without Vauban, who was now more than twenty minutes late. 'Ricky, bring the kid up to speed, will you? Tell him what he needs to know.'

Ackerman was about to take up the invitation when Strawson interrupted him.

'Tell you what, why don't I do that?' The question was plainly rhetorical. 'About six weeks ago, Philippe got a tip-off that Augustin Bagaza was hiding out here in Dakar. Knew him from Rwanda as one of the principal architects of the genocide. Didn't trust the Senegalese to hand him over. Suspected that he was being protected either by someone in the government or by the DGSE.' Kite wanted to ask why French intelligence officers would be looking out for a war criminal, but it wasn't the moment to interrupt. 'So Philippe came to me. Suggested I might do something about it before Bagaza got himself a diplomatic passport and disappeared on the ratline. He's a piece of shit, should stand trial for his crimes and go to prison for the rest of his life. America stood aside while the Hutus murdered hundreds of thousands of people. This is a small opportunity for my government to start to put that right.' Strawson waved a fly out of his face as he addressed Kite directly. 'Omar here has done some good work for us in the past, so I had him investigate. For one thing, we needed confirmation that Bagaza was really here.'

'And is he?' Kite asked.

'Sure,' Omar replied jovially. 'To a 90 per cent certainty.'

'That's what we need Philippe to confirm.' Strawson was still being bothered by the fly. 'That last 10 per cent. He's been up close and personal with Bagaza. If we're going to grab this guy, I don't want to get to the ship, find out we've arrested the wrong person.'

'So you've been out here for a week keeping an eye on him?' Kite asked, ignoring a feeling in his gut that Strawson had a sentimental attachment to Vauban which had clouded his judgement.

'Ricky's been here six days,' Strawson corrected.

'That gave us time to acquire vehicles, motorcycles, set up camera positions at the Kennedy residence, start to get some sense of Bagaza's pattern of life.' 'Pattern of life' meant Bagaza's routine: where he ate, where he exercised,

97

where he bought food. Ackerman made a slight adjustment to the short sleeve of his polo shirt. 'To a very high degree we were confident that the individual residing at Rue Kennedy was Augustin Bagaza.'

'*Were* certain?' Kite asked, noting the change of tense. 'What happened?'

'Well you see that's just it, kid,' said Strawson, apparently amused by what had transpired. 'Ricky hasn't seen him for a while.'

12

'What do you mean you haven't seen him?'

'You know,' Ackerman replied. 'When you have eyes on someone, you follow him around, go to the restaurants he goes to, the grocery stores and coffee shops. Then you don't see him.'

The tone was unmistakably facetious. Kite cut Strawson a look as if to say: 'Am I going to have to put up with this prick all week?' Ackerman was plainly a humourless, single-minded bureaucrat with a passive-aggressive style. Kite decided to confront him nice and early.

'Thanks for the explanation, pal.' Omar suppressed a grin. 'So it was you who lost him? Did the French get him out while your back was turned? I've come all this way to be told there's no operation?'

Strawson spoke across them.

'It's not as bad as that. Last seen entering the building at Rue Kennedy three days ago accompanied by Lady Macbeth of Kinshasa.'

'Lady Macbeth?'

'Bagaza's girlfriend from Rwandan days. Congolese Hutu mistress soon to be upgraded to wife in the absence of competing candidates. Real charmer, developed a taste for murder, encouraged Bagaza personally to cut people up in

Kigali last summer. She's been seen coming in and out of the building over the past seventy-two hours. Now either our man got away without anybody noticing or he's sick. The drapes have been closed, lights going on and off. The smart money's on sick.'

'Or maybe he just wants to stay home?' Omar suggested. 'Out of the spotlight.'

'Presumably his phone is tapped?' Kite asked. He was privately astonished that all three men seemed so blasé about the possibility that Bagaza had absconded; surely Ackerman had deployed a team to investigate that possibility?

'Not tapped,' Omar replied, picking at the peeling label on his Flag. His fingernails were bitten to the quick. 'To bug you would need the ministry, the phone company. And there are too many leaks in those places.'

'Tentacles then?' Kite asked, using BOX language for listening devices. 'You said there are cameras on the entrances. Presumably we've got a microphone in a lampshade, a bug in a Gameboy?'

He looked at Strawson, who acknowledged the reference to Kite's first mission with a subtle smile.

'Nothing on the inside,' he said, applying more saliva to the insect bite. He was making it worse. The skin was now raw with scratch marks, as though a child had drawn with red crayon on his wrist. 'The French are likely watching. We go into the apartment, they know we're here. And that's the last thing we want.'

'What about a maid or a cook?' Kite asked. 'Somebody who might tell us what Bagaza is up to?'

'Doesn't exist,' Ackerman replied dismissively.

'All I've got is you guys, the Falcons, two Closers and a ship in harbour,' Strawson explained. 'I wanted twelve here but, frankly, there are not enough black faces on the books at BOX to seamlessly blend into a city like Dakar. Hence you and Martha playing the backpacking travellers.

You could be folded into the surveillance effort with plausible cover.'

'It's not quite true that we have nobody on the inside,' Ackerman interrupted. 'What about the driver?'

Omar produced a quick, dismissive yelp of amusement. Kite saw that there was some kind of private joke between them.

'You mean the guy you recruited the day before Bagaza disappeared?'

The pin of a grenade had been taken out at the table.

'You're saying the driver tipped him off?' Ackerman was plainly outraged at the suggestion that an agent he had recruited had turned out to be unreliable. 'You're saying Bagaza's left the building, and I blew it?'

Strawson was going to call for calm, but Omar did the job for him.

'Relax, Max,' he said, laying a hand on Ackerman's shoulder. 'I'm just joking with you, brother. Didn't mean anything by it. But it's been three days since we heard from your chauffeur. His car is there, but there's no sign of him. The phone number he gave you, he doesn't answer. You were right to make the approach. In your situation we all would have done the same thing.'

Kite suspected from a barely discernible flicker in Strawson's face that this was not the case; he was irritated Ackerman had acted without authorisation.

'You forget that the driver thinks I am interested in Grace Mavinga.' Ackerman passed a hand over his close-cropped hair; the fragility of his ego was plain to see. 'I told him *she* was the one we wanted information about, not Bagaza.'

Kite assumed Grace Mavinga was Lady Macbeth.

'Sure, sure,' said Strawson, playing the peacemaker. 'Jealous husband in Kinshasa paying you to track her down. Private detective finding out why she ran off with another man. It was a good story, Ricky. You did the right thing.'

'Let's assume Bagaza is sick and resting in bed,' Kite suggested. He was keen to move on. 'Let's assume he gave the driver a few days off because he didn't need him. Sooner or later the target is going to resurface. At that point we just need Vauban to identify him.'

'Exactly.' Strawson stared towards the entrance of the bar. 'Speaking of Philippe, where the hell is he?'

'Too many women, too little time?' Omar joked.

'He'll be here soon enough,' Kite pictured Vauban standing on the road beside the punctured Corolla, still waiting for a ride. 'What happens after we get a positive ID?'

Ackerman wanted to answer but Strawson again cut him off.

'Like I said, we have people at the back door, on street corners, eyes on the building from the command truck. The Closers will go into Bagaza's apartment, wrap him in a carpet, carry it out to the van. Noise cover and the chaos of the city working for us.' Strawson finally gave up on the insect bite, rolling his sleeve down to cover it. 'But a dollar for a pinch of shit it isn't going to be easy. Never is. All the time the team has been watching him, he was never alone. Lady Macbeth goes everywhere with him, like the fucking Rain Man, and she's not exactly a shrinking violet who'll go quietly. There could be government eyes on them, Bagaza is likely talking to the French. So maybe we have to go to Plan B.'

'Which is?' Kite asked.

'Which is that you bump him. Get in his face, spook him into leaving town. We lump his car, Closers take him on the open road.'

To 'lump' a car meant to attach a tracker; it was always a short-term option because of battery life.

'How do you want me to do that?' Kite asked, delighted that he had been suddenly upgraded from backpacker to active player.

'Up to you,' Strawson replied.

102

Kite looked at the others; they seemed to agree that Kite was free to bump Bagaza in any way he chose.

'Journalist?' he suggested. 'I recognised Bagaza in the street, followed him home. Don't want to cause trouble. Don't want to get him deported. Just want to hear his story so that I can write my bestselling book about the Rwandan genocide.'

'It is dangerous for you,' said Omar. His voice was quiet but authoritative. 'Bagaza is a man who kills. He has developed a taste for it. No question he carries a gun. If he feels in danger, he will put you down.'

'He's not going to shoot a journalist,' Kite replied evenly. Strawson looked at him with an almost paternal sense of pride. 'He's going to tell me it's a case of mistaken identity and that if I bother him again, he'll call the police. Then of course he panics. *If a journalist knows I'm in Dakar, that means the Americans know, the British, the Canadians.* So Augustin packs his bags and leaves town, with or without Lady Macbeth. Your plan is to grab him on the road, right, if the apartment is too risky? Get him out of the city, somewhere quiet, then the Closers hustle him into the van before the nearest giraffe has even noticed.'

Omar boomed a delighted laugh which made one of the waitresses look over and smile.

'You say this even after what I just told you, Lachlan? You have balls.' He lit a cigarette and blew the smoke towards a ceiling fan, adding: 'We don't have giraffes in Senegal.'

'I like it too,' said Ackerman quietly. It was the first compliment he had paid Kite since his arrival. Then he spoiled it by saying: 'But what about your girlfriend?'

'What about her?'

'Isn't she sick? Don't you need to go look after her?'

'She's fine, thank you.' A fly settled on Kite's hand and he flicked it away. 'The doctor visited this afternoon. A friend of mine is taking care of her.'

103

'Your Senegalese friend? Eric Appiah?'

'That's right.'

Ackerman made a point of looking at Strawson.

'Isn't he a security risk?'

'There's no risk,' Strawson told him. If he was weary of Ackerman's attitude, he did not show it. 'Martha doesn't know anything about the operation, only that she's here to give Lockie cover as his girlfriend. Even if Appiah works out that his old friend here is not who he thinks he is, there's still no connection to Bagaza.'

Kite was grateful to Strawson for defending him and shot Ackerman a look.

'Speaking of Martha,' he said. 'What's the plan tonight?' A telephone started ringing at the bar. 'Do you need me or can I go and check up on her?'

'Go check on her,' Strawson replied. 'Would be great to get her back in circulation. Omar is working the monitor until midnight, then Nancy, yes?' Ackerman nodded. 'We meet at the safe house in the morning – 7 a.m.'

A waitress had answered the telephone. She called out in Wolof to the clientele in the bar. Omar stood up.

'For me,' he said.

It had to be BOX. Who else would know that Omar was in the Imperial? Two minutes later he was back at the table with a grin on his face.

'Your driver came through in the end, Ricky,' he said, slapping Ackerman so hard on the back that he looked winded. 'Grace just called him in Saly. Our war criminal is feeling better after three days of toothache. Wants to go out tonight and celebrate his newfound liberation.'

'Hallelujah,' said Strawson. 'We are back in business.'

13

Moments later Philippe Vauban walked into the Imperial. For once he didn't look as though he had emerged from a sound stage or photoshoot for *Vanity Fair*: he was plainly shattered by the long day on the baking road. His eyes were bloodshot, his skin burnt by the sun. To Kite's surprise, Strawson didn't lambast him for being late; instead he spoke to Vauban in an oddly affectionate manner, as he might have done to an errant son or favourite nephew. Vauban was also uncharacteristically courteous in the way he interacted with the American.

'I'm sorry, Mike. Did Locklang tell you we got a puncture? His girl was sick so they went ahead. A man stopped to help replace the tyre. Turns out he doesn't know how to find a new tyre, just wants my company so he can later try to make money out of me. So I wait at the side of the road, trying to hitch. Somebody came along but he only took me as far as the edge of the city. I'm sorry, guys.' Vauban looked around, charming Omar and Ackerman with his movie star smile. 'Took me a long time to find another taxi, long time to get here.'

'You look tired,' Strawson observed.

The Frenchman pushed a hand through his unkempt hair and summoned a waitress.

'Yeah, I am a little tired,' he admitted. 'Long day. And I get these headaches from my malaria medication. I'm trying a new one. Lariam. Anybody using that?'

Kite looked over at Strawson, who swore under his breath.

'Stay away from that shit, Philippe. Makes your mind go psychedelic. You read the small print? Anxiety, depression, psychosis. Get off it, you hear me? Better to contract malaria. I knew a guy in Thailand went crazy on Lariam, panic attacks, mood swings. Ended up beating his wife half to death. Lockie, didn't I tell you and Martha to avoid it?'

'You did,' Kite replied.

There was certainly something different about Vauban; the arrogance had gone. It was as though he had lost some of his invincible self-confidence out on the road. Kite put it down to the fact that he had barely slept.

'So let's work out next steps,' Strawson suggested.

According to the chauffeur, Grace Mavinga had booked a table at Lagon, a famous Dakar fish restaurant on the waterfront not far from Imperial. It was decided that Ackerman and his wife would go to the restaurant ahead of Bagaza. Kite and Vauban were to stick together, operating out of a taxi driven by Omar which would park on the access road to the restaurant. Once Vauban had corroborated Bagaza's identity, Strawson would decide when and where to grab him.

'Maybe we even take him outside Lagon,' he suggested. 'Philippe confirms we have the right target and we do it straight away. The access road leads directly to the port, Tom and Danny get him onto the ship, they're in Gibraltar by Tuesday.'

'You want to move that soon?' Ackerman asked.

'Not such a good idea outside Lagon, boss.' This from Omar. 'The petit Corniche is the only road in and out. Something or someone blocks the Closers' exit, it's . . .'

He was searching for a term in English. Kite helped him out.

'A choke point.'

'Exactly. The Closers have nowhere to go. Besides, there are too many people around there. Guards, cops, joggers.'

'Time is not on our side,' Strawson replied. 'I want this thing done as soon as possible. Soon as Bagaza gets his hands on a passport, he's gone. We never see him again.'

'What makes you think he'll get the passport in the next few days?' Kite asked.

'Instinct. There are too many variables. We don't have control of the locals, of the French. We've been lucky so far. Bagaza getting sick bought us time. If we can't take him outside the restaurant, I want to house him tonight and move him in the next twelve hours.' Omar nodded his consent. Ackerman looked anxious. 'What are we waiting for?' Strawson asked. 'I've got two Closers at the Savanna costing me a thousand bucks a day. You think little Augustin wants to stay in Senegal for the rest of his days? His Hutu friends are already in Texas and Marseille. There's a ratline out of Dakar and he intends to get on it.'

The logic of Strawson's argument was clear; they were up against the clock. Vauban, looking strung out by all the talk, drained his coffee and ordered another.

'How do we communicate with one another?' Kite asked.

'I have pagers in the taxi, also radios,' Omar told him. 'Everything on channel 35.'

'Got it,' Kite replied. 'And weapons?'

The question was met with a disapproving stare.

'Not for you, kid.' Strawson reached for Kite's wrist and squeezed. 'You're a backpacker, remember?'

'I thought I was a journalist.'

'Don't get smart. You're whatever the operation needs you to be. Now, any further questions?'

Plenty, thought Kite.

14

Night had fallen.

Kite left the Imperial and went out into the dark, hot city, flanked by Omar and Vauban. The BOX 88 taxi was parked two blocks away on an unlit street where cats and hookers prowled in the shadows. Omar had the radios and suggested they test them, so they sat in the baked interior of the old Peugeot 205 making sure that the equipment was working and teaching Vauban how to communicate through clicks without having to speak openly on channel 35. Ordinarily Kite would have hidden the radio in his clothing with a lapel microphone, a covert earpiece and a wire running down the sleeve to a handheld PTT; that was how he had been taught in the depths of the Manhattan winter. But it was too hot for clothing of that type; besides, sweat would soak the earpiece and might cause a short circuit in the wiring. In Dakar it would be more practical to carry the radios in their pockets as walkie-talkies, to speak discreetly and to dump them at the first sign of trouble. There were also pagers, one each for Kite and Vauban, with a warning from Omar that the technology in Senegal was unreliable. Nor would it be easy to find a working phone box.

'A lot of the public phones were smashed in protests against the government,' he explained. 'If you need to make a call, try a hotel or a restaurant.' He handed each of them a pile of coins, like a father dishing out pocket money before a visit to the sweet shop. 'If you see the sign "Telecenter" on the street, it's a place where you can phone. You pay for the duration of your call. Very few people here speak English but of course you must be careful with what you say.'

There was almost an hour to kill until Bagaza was due at Lagon, so Kite went into a Lebanese-owned hotel on a nearby corner and rang the villa.

'Eric, it's Lockie. Just checking in. How was the doctor? How's Martha?'

A deep intake of breath.

'He hasn't shown up yet. Had an emergency. Coming in about an hour. Martha is resting. I gotta say, she doesn't look good, man. Got a kind of rash now on her chest and arms. Says it's very itchy, like she wants to scratch it all the time.'

'Have you seen something like this before?'

'Me? Here? No. But I'm not a doctor.' Much of the characteristic bonhomie was missing from his voice. 'You should come and look after her if you can. She needs you, Lockie. I feel kind of awkward always asking through the door how she's doing.'

Kite reached for a cigarette but realised he had left his packet on the back seat of the Peugeot. Surely the doctor would give Martha a course of antibiotics for the rash and she would recover within two or three days? He knew that he believed this because he *wanted* to believe it; he could not stomach the thought of missing out on the Bagaza capture. It was the nature of his ambition, of his selfishness. Martha was tough. Martha was uncomplaining. Kite told himself that she had known the risks coming out to Senegal and wouldn't blame him for doing his job.

'I can't come and see her now,' he said. 'The politician is about to get here. Philippe needs me.'

'Jesus. Can't this guy find someone else in the whole of Dakar who can translate? How hard can it be? There's probably somebody in his VIP entourage studied at the Sorbonne, did an MBA at INSEAD. I could even do it, for fuck's sake.'

'He doesn't trust anyone else.' The second-rate lie enveloped Kite like the cloying air in the hotel lobby. 'Hates it when politicians have their own people translating. Wants it to be someone he knows.'

There was a disgruntled noise at the end of the line. Nevertheless Appiah seemed to accept what Kite had told him. He asked when he expected to be back.

'Hopefully soon,' Kite replied, though he had no idea how long he was going to be with the team. 'Sounds as though I might even be home at the same time as your doctor. I'm so grateful to you for taking care of Martha . . .'

'Yeah, yeah. No problem, man. I can tell you're busy. I'll go up to her room now and tell her you called.'

'Thanks, Eric. I owe you.'

'Forget about it.'

Kite hung up and looked around. A young boy had come in off the street. He was dressed in rags, pitifully thin and dirty. He held out his hand muttering *'Donne-moi des francs, donne-moi des francs'*. Kite was about to give him the change from his phone call when the receptionist came out from behind the desk and shooed him off with a loud curse. Kite followed the boy outside, gave him a handful of coins and returned to the taxi. Omar was sitting at the wheel, Vauban beside him.

'We go?' Kite asked.

Omar suggested that Kite and Vauban walk the short distance to Lagon to familiarise themselves with the neighbourhood. He would go ahead in the cab and park with line of sight to the entrance. There would be other members of the team in the area: someone on a motorcycle as well

110

as two Falcons in a Renault 5. Kite had memorised the street map in Imperial and knew how to get to the restaurant: they should go back to Place de l'Independence, walk through Kermel market and head towards the Corniche.

'Be careful around there,' Omar warned. 'Rich people go to Lagon, all the French. Sometimes there is trouble.'

They set off. Kite was carrying the small rucksack containing his clothes, the radio and pager, the money and the escape passport. Vauban had clipped his pager to the waistband of his trousers: he looked like a roadie backstage at a rock concert.

'Everything always looks the same to me in Dakar,' he said as they passed a bank. 'Shithole city with shithole streets.'

A feeble ocean breeze stirred the tops of the palm trees. At the northern end of the square, small boys were excitedly kicking a punctured leather football, squealing as an old man, hobbling with the aid of a walking stick, made his way gingerly between them. Young women with the look of office workers and secretaries were loitering at the edge of the road, presumably waiting to be picked up by boyfriends or members of their family. A Senegalese flag had collapsed in the tired, hot wind. People were sitting on benches so as not to exert themselves in the heat.

'This way,' said Kite, smoking a cigarette as he led Vauban down a broad, unlit street. Three men on prayer mats were facing a concrete wall, silently performing the evening *salah*. There was a rancid smell of rotting fish as they passed the blue-black dome of Kermel market. Here the men were more tightly bunched together on a long, rattan carpet, each of them bowing in slow deference towards Mecca.

'Fools,' Vauban muttered in English. It was all Kite could do not to seize his arm and tell him to show more respect. But there was more to come: 'They think Allah is going to save them from this? They think there is a god helping them?'

Vauban gestured towards the piles of rubbish and discarded plastic bottles lining the road. Ahead of them, a vast modernist tower, like the headquarters of some intergalactic potentate in science fiction, soared into the night sky.

'That's where all the money goes,' Vauban continued. 'Central Bank of West Africa. Audis and mistresses, langoustines and blow jobs for the government. For the rest of them?' He turned and pointed back at the men. 'Scraps of food – and prayer.'

They arrived at the ocean road to a chorus of birdsong and distant barking dogs. A container ship blinked on the horizon. As Kite and Vauban emerged from a narrow alley, a mangy dog darted between them. Ahead, through a screen of trees, Kite could see the tip of the Lagon jetty, a necklace of lights stretching out into the bay.

'There's the restaurant,' he said.

'They do not know who they are feeding,' Vauban muttered. 'A pig is coming.'

Kite assumed that Ricky and Nancy Ackerman were already in place, nibbling Senegalese peanuts and making marital small talk as they waited for Bagaza. Two men jogged past on the road breathing heavily in the intense evening heat. Kite's shirt and trousers were soaked, his face pouring with sweat. Vauban looked as though he had been standing in the rain for five minutes without bothering to find shelter.

'Fucking hot,' Kite said, allowing himself a rare complaint about the weather. 'Let's go to the beach.'

They found a set of wooden steps leading down to the sand. Sitting at the bottom they could observe the comings and goings in Lagon while remaining screened by over-hanging foliage; the restaurant was close enough for Kite to pick up a smell of charcoal and grilled prawns. The little beach made him think of a sandpit his father had built for him at Killantringan, four square metres of plastic

112

toys and seashells, the sand as dry as Bondi one day, as wet and muddy as Murrayfield the next.

'Tell me about Bagaza,' he said.

15

Vauban produced a bottle of Evian from his bag and shared it with Kite while mosquitoes swirled around them, fighting the offshore breeze. The water was lukewarm and tasted of chlorine.

'He should have been stopped but nobody cared.' Vauban picked up a small stone and threw it onto the sand. 'Nobody noticed. Rwanda was a sideshow, a thing that was happening on another planet. What did you know about it? I imagine almost nothing.' Kite set the bottle on the step but was not given time to respond. 'It was April of last year.' Vauban's short-temperedness had dissipated; his voice was low and matter-of-fact. 'Nelson Mandela was about to be elected. That's what the world cared about. Not ethnic cleansing in Yugoslavia. Certainly not Tutsis dying in Kigali. Who could even point to Rwanda on a map?'

'I don't think I could have done.'

'Of course you could not.' Across the narrow stretch of water, Nancy Ackerman sneezed and dabbed her nose with a napkin. If she had looked up she might have been able to make out Vauban's pale, dirty chinos at the bottom of the steps. 'Rwanda didn't export anything – only small amounts of tea and coffee – and nobody went there as a

114

tourist unless you wanted to pretend to be David Attenborough and sit in the jungle embracing gorillas. It is actually a very beautiful country. The morning mist in the hills around Kigali, the children singing, there are volcanoes, all the colours and sounds of East Africa. Or at least there used to be.'

A tiny bird swooped in front of their makeshift hideout, touching the water before skimming away. Vauban took out a cigarette. He was about to light it when Kite stopped him.

'Not here,' he said. 'The flare of your lighter will draw attention. The glow of the cigarette.'

With a grunt of acknowledgement, Vauban tucked the packet back into his shirt.

'You know the genocide got less than thirty seconds most nights on CNN?' He was opening and closing the lid of his Zippo. 'A friend from London told me the BBC dedicated more time to football results than the massacre of half a million Africans. As for God, what happened to *Him*? Is he the same God those men were praying to?'

'I don't know,' Kite replied, thinking of the line of tightly packed men on the rattan mat bowing obediently in the heat.

'It was God's priests who aided the murderers. It was God's churches which became the places of killing. Tutsis flocked to those churches, risking their lives through the night, through the roadblocks, escaping the death squads so that they could seek sanctuary in a holy place. When they sealed the doors to prevent the Hutus coming in, you know what those bastards did? They threw grenades into the churches. I heard all this with my own ears, saw it with my own eyes. The churches were Rwanda's gas chambers.'

'Jesus,' Kite whispered, horrified. He remembered something he had heard during a lecture at university and repeated it: 'When it comes to murder, human beings are very inventive.'

'*Oui.*' Trapping a mosquito on the back of his hand, the Frenchman wiped the bloodied remains on his trousers. Kite saw that the lower part of Vauban's right leg was covered in tiny bite marks, like a measles rash. One of the bites, close to his ankle, had become infected; it was capped by an amber scab which had leaked pus onto the skin. 'Did you know the rate of killing in Rwanda was actually faster than Auschwitz, nearly three times the speed?' Vauban's voice was louder now and he was talking faster. 'So many people had not been killed on our planet so quickly since the atomic bomb on Nagasaki.'

Movement in the restaurant. A young couple, both white, were being shown to a table on the far side of the jetty. They looked European, pale and out of place. When they sat down neither of them spoke to the other. The man immediately looked at his menu while the woman checked her lipstick in a compact mirror.

'And Bagaza?' Kite asked.

The waves rolling onto the beach grew louder, the wake from a passing ship.

'He was the orchestrator of it all,' Vauban replied. 'It was his voice on the Radio Mille Collines telling the people that the president had been killed by Tutsi rebels and that as a consequence the government had declared a curfew. I heard that sick, sarcastic psycho at all hours of the day and night, time and time again. "All the loyal population of the republic must take up arms to confront the cock-roaches." It was Augustin Bagaza who told the people of Rwanda that their Tutsi neighbours were murderers. It was Augustin Bagaza who told the Hutus to be rigorous, vigilant, to go out and to commit murder. "Our work has only just begun. This time we must finish the job. We've let them off the hook too many times before. We have the power and the right to possess this country. The Tutsis have killed our president. They are getting ready to kill you. To attack is a legitimate self-defence. You must eradicate the Tutsi enemy before they eradicate you." In French we call it *"la banalité du mal"*.'

'The banality of evil.'

'*Exact.*' Vauban again reached for his cigarettes, removing the packet from his shirt before realising the mistake. 'Bagaza was the voice of the killing, the one who denounced anybody opposed to Hutu power. It was Bagaza who ensured that they were butchered. It was Bagaza who encouraged the Tutsis to seek shelter in churches, knowing that Hutu soldiers, Hutu police, villagers, would descend on those churches and prosecute the killing. I wrote about him, but nobody cared.'

'I heard that a few hundred UN soldiers could have stopped the genocide but did nothing.'

'Of course they did nothing!' Kite indicated that Vauban should keep his voice down. 'The UN could have closed the radio station to stop the spread of lies and propaganda, but they did not do this. Even when their own soldiers were killed – ten Belgian blue berets captured and beaten and murdered – they did nothing. And the French? My own people? They armed the Hutus! They evacuated their own staff from the embassy in Kigali, they abandoned their Tutsi employees, and as soon as the French diplomatic families were safely at the airport, the massacres began.' Vauban picked up another stone and tossed it onto the beach. 'I can still hear the screams. I can still hear the sound of people pleading for their lives.'

'I'm so sorry,' was all that Kite could think to say because it was obvious that Vauban, for all his self-regard and preening vanity, was utterly traumatised. 'You have seen some terrible things.'

'Don't feel sorry for me,' he said, tapping the Zippo against the step. 'Feel sorry for the beautiful young woman I found on the road with her skirt hitched up and her underwear around her knees. She had been raped. Her throat had been opened up with a machete. Feel sorry for her.'

Vauban's voice caught on the memory. Kite sensed that he was concealing something.

'You knew her, didn't you?'

The Frenchman looked at him, eyes shot with grief, astonished that Kite had intuited the truth.

'Yes, I did.'

Kite reached out and put his hand on Vauban's back. For some time neither man spoke.

'Everybody has a sad story from Rwanda,' Vauban said eventually, ending the silence. 'That is mine.' He sounded utterly broken. 'I knew it was only a matter of time before they killed her. She would not leave the country. I found a way out for her, but she refused to go.'

'What was her name?'

'Her name was Sylvie.'

The slow tapping of the lighter began again, joining a sudden chorus of birdsong as a car moved past on the road above them.

'Such sadism, such inventiveness, such cruelty. I often reflect on what human beings are capable of.' Vauban's words were difficult to hear above the noise of the parking car. 'The Hutus killed men outright but sometimes left the wives and daughters to bleed to death as a punishment for bringing Tutsis into the world. Where did they get ideas like that if not from Radio Mille Collines and Augustin Bagaza?' Vauban looked at Kite, as if imploring him to answer. 'Who encouraged them to believe that rape and torture and mutilation were acceptable acts of self-defence? He did. The snake coming here to dinner. The monster in Dakar who lives as a free man, eating *daurade* and drinking Canard-Duchêne, while my Sylvie rots in the ground.'

Movement to the left. Vauban's demeanour suddenly changed. Kite followed his eyes across the narrow stretch of water. A man and a woman were strolling along the nearside of the jetty, a waiter showing them to a table. The man was a prosperous-looking African of about forty-five wearing a pale grey suit and white shirt. The woman was at least twenty years younger, elegant in a floral print dress with high heels and large hooped earrings.

One glance at Vauban told Kite who they were. He looked haunted, sweat pouring down his face.

'That's him.'

16

As the butcher of Kigali and his Lady Macbeth sat down, Kite sent four clicks on the radio to confirm that the target's identity had been established. Augustin Bagaza ostentatiously flapped a napkin into his lap. He was neither as tall nor as thickset as he had appeared in the photographs Kite had been shown in London: those had made him look like a huge, abrasive thug. Grace Mavinga adjusted the strap of her dress. It seemed every man in the restaurant was staring at her.

Vauban spat on the sand and cursed in French.

'Let's just fucking kill him now,' he said. 'Mike is too slow, too careful. Ackerman is a fucking bureaucrat. I want Bagaza dead. I will kill him myself.'

It sounded like the sort of thing men say when they have no intention of doing anything other than acting tough. Kite remembered the first time he had set eyes on Vauban at the guest house: the cool, beachside *poseur* sipping a Flag and hitting on Martha. He seemed now to be an entirely different person. Confronted by the sight of Bagaza, he looked haunted, a man whose composure had been stripped away as if by some merciless and incurable disease.

'That's not what we're here for,' he told him quietly.

'You think I can live, I can work, I can *feel* anything while this monster is free?'

The lapping surf dragged Vauban's words out to sea. There were two clicks on the radio; they were being summoned back to the taxi.

'Come on, he's settled in, let's go,' Kite was worried that Vauban was at risk of blowing the operation. 'We've got to check in with Omar.'

Reluctantly the Frenchman followed him back up the steps. Omar had parked some distance from the entrance around a narrow bend in the road. Kite opened the passenger door of the Peugeot. Vauban sat in the back without saying a word. The smell of sweat and old cigarettes was the smell of Dakar at night.

'Chauffeur is parked over there,' Omar told them, indicating a dark blue Citroën. 'So it was definitely Bagaza?'

Vauban was smoking a cigarette and breathing loudly. Kite answered for him.

'It's Bagaza.'

Omar whispered a Wolof phrase in apparent relief. A taxi passed and stopped in front of the entrance. As two men got out, one of them paying the driver, Omar hunched forward.

'Wait a minute.' He took hold of the wheel. 'These guys . . .'

'You know them?' Kite asked.

The men were both white with the look of well-financed European ex-pats. No wives or girlfriends in tow, a business-like sense of purpose in the way they moved and spoke to one another.

'The shorter one is from the French embassy. Yves Duval. Clever, devious, likes the local girls a little too much. Everyone assumes he's DGSE although he has business interests in Dakar, Abidjan. I never saw the other guy before.'

The second man was not as tanned as his colleague and looked beaten by the heat. Kite assumed he had recently flown in from France.

'Coincidence?' he asked.

'Who knows?' Omar waved a fly out of the car. 'Lagon is a famous place. Everybody comes here to eat. The French do a lot of business here, spend a lot of money. Could be related to Bagaza, could be something else.'

Kite could feel the voodoo bad luck moving beneath his skin again. He sent a series of clicks on the radio for Ackerman to make contact. Three minutes later he heard the American's voice on the open channel.

'I'm out of earshot. Go ahead.'

'Two white males just arrived. The taller one, blue shirt, is Yves Duval. French liaison.'

'Copy. I passed them just now. Seated inside, not with Bagaza. I know the other guy. Met him in Paris at an event in the Louvre. Maurice Lagarde.'

Ackerman coughed loudly, indicating that Kite should stay off the radio. Someone had moved within earshot of the American's position. When the threat had passed, he returned to the conversation.

'The situation has developed here. Our friends have yet to order. Asked for a table for three. They're waiting for someone.'

More coughing. Ackerman sent a click signal to indicate that he was heading back to the jetty. Kite put the radio down and pointed to the glove compartment.

'Can I borrow your binoculars?'

Omar took out a pair of Celestrons, wiping the lenses before handing them over. No longer smoking, Vauban had closed his eyes and was leaning against the headrest, humming a tune. Omar looked at Kite as if to say: 'He's crazy, let him sleep.'

'Is it normal for Bagaza to meet people?' Kite asked. 'You ever seen him with anyone other than Mavinga?'

'Only ever with his woman. Likes to keep a low profile, stay out of sight. But remember, he's been gone for three days.'

'So why Lagon? Makes no sense to show his face. It's like having dinner at the Ivy. Who's joining him?'

'I guess we wait and see.'

Vauban sniffed noisily, as if the two men were disturbing his rest, then suddenly lurched forward, possessed by a violent anger.

'Could you stop fucking shouting?' he said, though neither man had raised their voices.

'Calm down,' Kite told him. 'Nobody was shouting. It's your Lariam.'

The Frenchman appeared to accept this explanation and leaned his head back again, muttering about the heat. Kite hoped Strawson would send him back to the hotel. Now that he had positively identified Bagaza, his usefulness had passed.

'I'm going back to the beach, see what I can see.' As he opened the door of the cab, Kite caught Omar's eye. 'Come and find me if you need me.'

'Will do,' Omar replied. 'I have a feeling this is going to be a long night.'

17

Kite walked back along the road, passing the entrance to Lagon. He saw a young Senegalese man sitting on the ground beside a Honda motorcycle. He might have been a paid guard keeping an eye on the bike, but equally could be part of Strawson's team. Kite did not acknowledge him.

He found a narrow path down to the beach. It was dark but there were still groups of young Senegalese men gathered on a stretch of sand south of Lagon, some swimming in the ocean, others standing around talking and showing off to girls. Kite found a secluded spot about a hundred metres from the restaurant. He brought the binoculars up to the jetty. Panning right to left he could see Ricky and Nancy Ackerman on the city side, two tables away from Bagaza. Beyond them, the young white couple who had ignored one another when they arrived were now talking animatedly, laughing over glasses of wine. He could not yet tell if they were a surveillance couple putting on an act or just civilian tourists who needed alcohol to loosen up. There was no sign of Duval or Lagarde.

Kite put the Celestrons down and waited. Seconds later Bagaza was on his feet, greeting a man in a well-cut Italian suit. Kite focussed the binoculars on the new arrival. He was African, younger by about five years,

124

with the slick, easy nonchalance of a well-travelled executive. Kite noted the patent leather shoes and expensive wristwatch; emerald-green cufflinks glinted in the light. The man wanted to demonstrate that he had money; a government minister would have concealed his wealth under a mattress and dressed for dinner in an off-the-peg jacket. So was this guy local or from out of town? Handsome with a conman's smile, Bagaza's guest was the sort of person Kite's mother would have described as a 'Flash Harry'.

Kite studied the body language between the three featured players. They had evidently met before. Mavinga seemed comfortable in the man's company and there was laughter as he sat down; this wasn't a dinner to which she had been dragged reluctantly. Kite radioed Omar who told him that he had seen the man getting out of a taxi outside the restaurant; he was not known to anyone on the surveillance team.

'So he's not government?' Kite asked.

'Unlikely.' Kite thought he could hear Vauban snoring in the back seat. 'Lagon is too exposed, too public. Maybe he's just a friend.'

Kite continued to watch the group for some time. Plainly in an ebullient mood, Bagaza ostentatiously ordered the more expensive dishes on the menu, pointing at a platter of iced shellfish on a neighbouring table while his friend refilled their glasses.

'What do you think?'

Kite almost dropped the binoculars. Strawson had crept up behind him, the sound of his approach concealed by the rolling waves and the traffic on the petit Corniche.

'Jesus. Gave me a fright.'

'No shit.' Strawson looked up at the jetty. 'Didn't I teach you to keep eyes in the back of your head?' When Kite didn't answer he added: 'Nice little place you found. What's going on?'

'There's something about this guy. The one with the suit and the chunky watch. He doesn't look local.'

'We've never seen him before. Could be anybody. Right now we have a bigger problem.'

Kite felt the needle of a mosquito on his arm and flicked it away. It left a small droplet of blood on the skin which he wiped on his trousers.

'What sort of problem?'

'Lady Macbeth left the lights on, drapes open. Guess what Naby sees through the window?'

'Idi Amin playing backgammon?'

'Very funny.' Strawson wiped sweat from his face with a sodden handkerchief. He was still wearing the white suit, the hems of the trousers stained and frayed. 'Suitcases. Lots of them. Shrink-wrapped and ready to fly. They've spent the last three days packing. They're clearing out of Dakar.'

'So this is the last supper?'

Kite raised the binoculars. Bagaza was laughing again. It took half a second for the sound to echo across the water; by the time Kite heard it the Rwandan was reaching for a basket of bread.

'And they choose to spend it with this guy. They're celebrating. Oysters and langoustines. Why?'

It did not take long for Kite's question to be answered. No sooner had he finished polishing off his first glass of champagne than Bagaza's guest reached into his jacket and pulled out an envelope. Without ceremony, he quietly slid the package across the table. Bagaza pushed the bread basket out of the way, picked up the envelope and placed it in his lap. Mavinga watched all this intently. And now all three were smiling, refilling their glasses and raising a toast.

'There are your ratline passports,' said Kite.

'That what it looks like?' Strawson did not have a pair of binoculars of his own and was relying on Kite to describe what he was seeing.

'Makes sense. Their bags are packed, the apartment has been cleaned out. Could be money he owes him, a contract, a deed. Maybe he already has the passports. Doesn't really matter though, does it? Evidently Bagaza is leaving Senegal.'

'Then we have to take him tonight.'

'And the French?'

'What about them?' Strawson sounded like he didn't care. 'It can't be coincidence they're in the same place at the same time on his last night in the city. Maybe they have a meeting planned for later. Maybe Lagarde being here is an all-clear signal for Bagaza to make his move. None of that changes the fact that if this operation is going to succeed, it has to succeed tonight.'

'Do you still want to take him in the apartment?'

'Where else do you suggest?' There was suddenly an edge of impatience in the American's voice. 'Flights start leaving around 5 a.m. We can't stop him getting on a plane. I've got two guys outside Rue Kennedy. Most likely Bagaza enjoys a long, leisurely dinner, settles his check, accompanies Lady Macbeth back home and the Closers wrap him up.'

'And if they don't go home?'

Strawson had been sitting just behind Kite on a small wooden crate. Climbing to his feet with the groan of a middle-aged man whose joints had seized up, he said: 'That's when we improvise. That's maybe when we need you to play the eager cub reporter.'

Kite looked back at the jetty. 'You see the couple on the far side of the deck?' Strawson took the Celestrons and pointed them at the restaurant. 'Blonde woman with her back to us, man in a polo shirt across the table?'

'Sure.' The American moved the binoculars fractionally to his right. 'What about them?'

'Are they ours?'

'Negative.'

127

'An hour ago they were barely speaking. Now it's all laughter and conversation and taking their time over the food.'

'You think maybe DGSE?'

'If we're doing it, what's to stop them doing it?'

'Nothing,' the American replied. 'Maybe they want Bagaza for themselves. Maybe they want to escort him all the way to the airport. One way or another, we're about to find out.'

18

It was reported on Kite's radio that Bagaza's party had yet to order their main course. Strawson reckoned it would be at least another hour before the meal finished and gave him permission to quickly telephone Martha. Strawson's radio had stopped working. He borrowed Kite's, telling him to keep his pager switched on in case the team needed to make contact.

'Don't hang around and don't go far,' he said, handing him a sheet of paper on which he had written down the number of a satellite phone. 'Grab something to eat then get back to Omar. Any problems, you call in. Someone will be manning the phone 24/7.'

Kite had photographic recall and committed the number to memory. He walked uphill in the direction of Place de l'Independence, late-night traffic circling in the heat. On Rue Félix Faure he found a Telecenter and quickly dialled the villa.

There was no answer. Kite tried the number again but there was still no reply. He walked outside, smoked a cigarette then returned to the booth to dial Eric's house a third time.

Still the number rang out. He could not work out why nobody was answering. Surely a maid or butler was around to take messages, even if Eric had gone out and left Martha sleeping?

It was almost half-past ten. Three doors down from the Telecenter was a restaurant serving local food. Kite was ravenous and ordered a plate of chicken yassa, sitting alone at a table by the window so that the slight breeze from the street might cool him. He took the pager out of the rucksack, set it on the table and finished an ice-cold bottle of Coke in four thirst-quenching gulps. As he set the bottle down the waitress shot him a look, asking if he wanted another. Kite shook his head, indicating that he was in a hurry. He was anxious to get back to Omar and worried about Martha. Perhaps Appiah's staff didn't live at the villa and went home at the end of each day. Maybe Eric reckoned that Martha's condition was improving and had left her to rest while he went to see friends for dinner. But what if things were more serious? What if the doctor had recommended that she go to hospital?

The chicken had still not arrived. The sugar and caffeine in the Coca-Cola had had no discernible effect and Kite was still starving. He checked his watch. He was due back in less than ten minutes; Lagon was at least a five-minute walk from the restaurant. His intention had been to eat quickly and then to try the Appiah villa one last time, but the slow service was holding him up. Signalling to the waitress, he asked what had become of his food, but she was mutely unapologetic, indicating with a shrug that it would come when the chef was good and ready. Kite went to the bathroom and washed his hands. Coming out, he caught his reflection in a mirror. A cartoon white man in the tropics stared back at him, sweat pouring down his face, Kite's T-shirt clinging to his torso as if the waitress had thrown a bucket of water over him.

Another five minutes went by. A cat appeared beneath the table and curled around Kite's feet, begging for food. He had nothing to offer, not even a salted crisp or monkey nut.

130

He smoked another cigarette and considered giving up on the chicken, but didn't want to go all the way back to Omar's taxi only to find that Bagaza was still eating. Martha's illness pricked at Kite's conscience like the needle sting of a mosquito. It was his duty to protect her and yet he had failed to provide even a basic level of care. Was this to be his future in BOX? Not a lone wolf surviving on his wits in France and Russia, but a small cog in a larger machine, waiting for orders, obliged to put his private life on the back burner?

Another five minutes had gone by when at last the food was brought to him. The sauce tasted of the sweat of the man who had prepared it, yet Kite wolfed down the chicken with the ravenous hunger of a convict, sucking on the bones as he checked his watch and anxiously eyed the pager. By ten to eleven he was done and tucked enough money to cover the bill under an ashtray. Flies were fighting against the breeze trying to get to the remains of his dinner. As he wiped his mouth on a piece of tissue the pager hummed. Kite looked at the read-out.

CLOSERS RA MS OG – KENNEDY ASAP
LK NG NA – THIOSSANE. LK CONTACT SVP. (RA)

It was a general instruction from Ackerman to the principal members of the team: Strawson, Ackerman and Omar were going to Rue Kennedy with the Closers, presumably to wait for Bagaza. Kite, Nancy and Naby were being sent to Thiossane, which Kite assumed was a street or the name of a prominent landmark in Dakar. 'Contact SVP' meant that Kite was to ring the satellite phone at the hotel as soon as possible. Picking up the rucksack, he thanked the waitress and went out onto Rue Félix Faure, heading for the Telecenter.

It was shut. He almost kicked the locked door in frustration, but his anger was tempered by the presence of a homeless woman, not much older than Martha, sleeping with two very young children on the corner of the street.

'*Argent*,' she said, holding out her hand.

Kite took some coins from his pocket and gave them to her. Beneath the folds of her dress a baby stirred. The child's lips were chapped, the mother's clothes caked in dirt. She thanked him with a weak smile. Turning away from the locked door, Kite considered running down to the petit Corniche but decided to go back to the restaurant to see if they had a working phone. The waitress was wiping down his table as he walked in. She told him that there was no landline in the building. Nor did she think Kite would be able to find a phone unless he went into a hotel. Taking out the pager, he showed her the word 'THIOSSANE'. The waitress had never seen a pager before and stared at the screen in wonder. She did not appear to understand what she was looking at. Kite tried saying the word in a variety of different ways, varying his accent and pronunciation, but there was no change in the girl's expression. Through the open kitchen door he could see the chef smoking a cigarette at the back entrance; perhaps he would know.

Then it struck him. At the beach, Eric had talked about nightclubs in Dakar. Kite was sure that he had mentioned 'Thiossane' as the name of a place in the old city run by Youssou N'Dour. That would make sense: if Bagaza was planning a celebratory send-off, quaffing champagne at Lagon before heading to a nightclub, Thiossane would be a logical destination. It was so hot that they probably planned to change their clothes at the apartment and then go on to the club.

'*Boîte de nuit?*' he said to the waitress. 'Thiossane. Youssou N'Dour.'

'*Oui*,' she said uncertainly. 'Youssou N'Dour.'

'It's a nightclub?' he asked again in French. 'You know it?'

132

'Yes. I know it.' She seemed surprised that Kite was not aware of the place. 'It's in the north.'

She did not have an address and her French was not good enough to give adequate directions. Now running very late, Kite clipped the pager to his belt and went outside in search of a taxi. As he was walking east towards Avenue George Pompidou, a short, wiry man with matted dreadlocks appeared from a side alley offering him hashish and *'jolies filles'*. Kite walked on. The man followed him for a few paces then prodded him in the back, again saying 'Hashish'. Kite turned around.

'Touch me again and I'll put you on the floor,' he said in quick, clear French. 'I don't want your drugs. I don't want your women. Walk away.'

The man backed off, stepping out onto the road. Fired with adrenaline, Kite hailed a passing taxi, an old Citroën seemingly held together with prayer and duct tape. The brakes squealed as the driver pulled over to collect him. Kite climbed into the back seat and gave the name of the club.

'Comment?'

'Thiossane,' he repeated. *'Boîte de nuit. Le chef, c'est Youssou N'Dour.'*

Without responding, the driver moved the stick into first gear and pulled away from the kerb. There was a catapult hanging from his rear-view mirror like some relic of a Biblical feud. The engine rattled and backfired before accelerating with a sudden jolt.

'You know the place?' Kite asked.

'Yes,' the man grunted in Wolof.

The back seat was a hot metal box without ventilation: Kite tried winding down the windows but both handles had snapped off. Seeing what he was trying to do, the driver leaned over and lowered the passenger window, all the time weaving in and out of traffic.

They passed the Imperial, now dark and closed, two kids on a moped riding pillion beside them. The noise of the taxi's engine was so loud that the boy on the back looked over at the Citroën and laughed. Kite's driver swerved to avoid a jaywalking pedestrian, the same old man with the walking stick who had been hobbling across the square hours earlier. Kite turned in his seat to look at him; as he did so the taxi's engine shuddered and popped, the driver cursing as he lost speed. Then just as soon they were accelerating again, moving downhill, passing an old colonial building marked 'Hôtel de Ville'; it looked like it belonged in a prosperous French country town. To the east was the port, spots of light in the darkness, and somewhere a ship waiting to take Augustin Bagaza to justice.

'How far is the club?' Kite asked in French as they swept past the railway station.

No response. Seconds later, the engine backfired again and there was the same sudden loss of power. The Citroën slowed to a shuddering crawl, vehicles passing on both sides; Kite heard the disquieting screech of skidding tyres as a truck hit the brakes behind them. Men swore through open windows as they passed the taxi. Kite's driver managed to steer to the relative sanctuary of a lay-by before the engine finally gave out.

'Fuck,' Kite exclaimed, climbing out of the back seat into the thick heat of the night. 'What happened?'

The driver did not answer. He had already opened the bonnet and was impatiently studying the engine. Kite remembered a long-ago mechanics seminar at The Cathedral, an affable Cockney teaching him about the inner workings of the Lada Niva. The driver was reaching for the fuel line; if it needed replacing then their journey was over. With no time to waste, Kite turned to face the oncoming traffic and looked around for a replacement cab.

A group of young men were loitering nearby. The oldest of them was a fit, good-looking Senegalese of about twenty with a neat beard and darting, mischievous eyes. He was sitting astride a moped in a Chicago Bulls singlet wearing a box-fresh pair of Air Jordans.

'Where you from, sir?' he asked in French.

'*Londres*,' Kite replied, not wanting to be drawn into a pointless conversation.

'And where you going?'

It occurred to him that the men might have been to the club.

'Do you know Thiossane?'

They looked at one another.

'Sure. Of course. We know it.' The kid on the moped indicated the stricken taxi. 'I give you a ride? My name is Sadio.'

Kite wondered what they were doing lurking by the edge of the road so close to the port. There were no homes nearby, not much to do or see, just stray dogs on distant train tracks and an old man selling coconuts from a wooden cart. He thought of Martha reading from the guidebook at the beach, making fun of the author in a high-pitched, matronly voice: '*There is a thick network of pickpockets. If you are followed by a street urchin turn immediately to the police.*'

'How far is it?' he asked.

None of the young men appeared to understand Kite's question. He asked it again. At that moment a cab with its light illuminated swept past, moving uphill. Kite was too late and missed it.

'Maybe ten minutes,' Sadio replied.

The taxi driver was still examining the fuel line, patiently checking it for leaks. Kite looked at the moped. It was an old Vespa with new tyres.

'How much to take me there?'

'How much you pay me, sir?'

'A thousand?'

It was a lowball offer and was greeted as such.

'Three thousand,' came the reply.

They settled on two. Kite explained to the taxi driver that he was in a hurry and gave him a 500 note for his trouble. With a nod to his friends, Sadio climbed onto the moped, inviting Kite to sit pillion.

'What's your name?' he asked, turning the key in the ignition.

'Peter,' Kite replied.

There was a metal bar behind his back which he held for balance, feeling the hot air against his skin as the Vespa lurched away from the lay-by. Kite could smell a long day of stale summer sweat on Sadio's clothes, the name PIPPEN emblazoned across the singlet. Plateau was soon far behind them, the Dakar of Lagon and air conditioning, of white men and cappuccinos. As the moped weaved through the traffic, Kite had the sense of moving from a European city into the obscurity of the African night; everything in front of him was unknown. The French had given themselves streetlights and tarmac and brasseries, the trappings of a civilised life; they had left the rest of the country in darkness.

At the top of a slow incline Sadio made a turn inland; Kite felt the back wheel slip beneath him but Sadio was skilful and adjusted his weight quickly to compensate. There were now no more cafes and well-lit hotels, no restaurants serving champagne and oysters, just market stalls shrouded with tarpaulins, women finding their way by not much more than the light of the moon, herds of goats asleep on street corners watched over by smoking men. They were suddenly on tracks of dried mud and loose sand in narrow streets without illumination. With no means of orienting himself, Kite had to surrender to Sadio's knowledge of the potholed, criss-cross city. He felt like a man who had been blindfolded and was being led, step by staggering step, through some vast, mysterious mansion. As the moped zipped past shuttered shops and shacks illuminated by bright white bulbs, he began to think that they were heading in the wrong direction. It didn't seem possible that a nightclub could exist in such a place. Yet Kite could not bring himself to believe that Sadio was deceiving him; there was something in his nature which invited trust.

'Sorry, Peter!' he called out in French as he suddenly swerved down a side street at such speed that Kite was almost thrown from the moped. 'Now we arrive!'

Seconds later they had pulled up at the edge of a wide boulevard lit solely by the lights from passing cars. There was a putrid smell of uncollected rubbish. Sadio pointed to the building directly in front of them.

'Thiossane,' he said.

19

They had arrived at the back of a single-storey warehouse bordered on each side by low-rise housing. Kite climbed off the Vespa to a background rattle of cicadas. He could hear the low thump of live music and felt a steady beat beneath his feet, underground rhythms smothered by sand and concrete. He looked around for Naby and Nancy Ackerman, but they were nowhere to be seen; each of the parked cars along the street was empty. Was he too early or had he come to the wrong place? Was everybody already inside?

'You want I wait?' Sadio asked.

Kite had not yet given him any money for the journey and said: 'Yes.'

He walked down one side of the building and came to the main entrance. Vendors hawking cigarettes and Hollywood chewing gum were gathered on the pavement. One of them had an urn of café Touba, a spiced, sweet coffee native to Senegal. Kite bought one and drank it on the street, all the time scanning for surveillance. A young woman was selling mangoes from a wooden stall set back from the dusty road. The entrance was manned by an overweight security guard in a black leather jacket who nodded Kite through on sight. The music was suddenly louder, the rhythmic fusion of drums and electric guitar, the throat-wail of a male singer's voice rolling out into the night. Through a curtain Kite could see a live band at the back of a large, crowded room: there were two men on hand drums, two more on guitars, a keyboard player and a male dancer in a woollen hat prancing around in front of the stage. Kite was shown to a table by a young woman in a stained red dress. Two electric fans, as big as the propellers on a light aircraft, were doing their best to move air around the venue. Kite looked for Grace and Bagaza but could not see them. Nor was there any sign of anyone from the team. He asked the waitress if there was another venue in Dakar with a similar name and she looked at Kite as though he was congenitally stupid.

'What you drink?' she asked in English.

'Flag,' he replied, dropping into his seat.

A song ended to cheering and rapturous applause. Members of the audience got out of their seats, walked up to the stage and handed banknotes to the lead singer, like customers in a strip club trying to ingratiate themselves with the dancers. The waitress returned with Kite's lager, popping the cap and wiping the neck of the bottle with a paper napkin. He lit a cigarette to give himself something to do with his hands, wondering how long Sadio would be prepared to wait. To his left, a large group of Senegalese were slapping their hands on the table in time to the beat of a favourite new song; to his right, an out of place white couple were staring gormlessly at the stage, as though they had been expecting to come to some local version of the Hacienda and had no interest in what was happening.

Then he saw them, appearing through the crowd like the half-remembered faces from a dream. Bagaza and Mavinga were seated towards the end of a long line of tables on the opposite side of the club, dressed in the same clothes they had been wearing at Lagon. There was a bottle in front of them, white wine by the look of it, and

139

a relaxed, drunken quality to their body language. The fixer who had given them the passports was nowhere to be seen, the seats on either side of them taken. Kite thought back to the pager message. Strawson, Omar, Ackerman and the Closers had all gone to Rue Kennedy, presumably to grab the target. For whatever reason, Bagaza had eluded them. So why hadn't the rest of the team come up to Thiossane?

It was time to go to Plan B, he told himself, remembering the conversations with Strawson. *You bump him. Get in his face, spook him into leaving town.* At Imperial the others had agreed that Kite would play a journalist looking to interview Bagaza about the genocide. There was nothing to stop him doing that now. Omar's warning, that Bagaza was a man who was most likely armed, a murderer who had killed and would kill again, made no impression on Kite. He yearned for the confrontation, for the opportunity to test himself against such a man. It was a mixture of courage and vanity: he wanted to do something which would later impress his colleagues. Besides, his reputation within BOX 88 would suffer if he did not seize this opportunity.

Picking up his Flag and the rucksack, Kite made his way across the room to a vacant stool about twenty metres from Bagaza. Just at the point when he was about to sit down, there was a power cut. The lights, the music, the fans – all of it went out to an accompanying groan of frustration. Nobody moved in the eerie green illumination provided by fire exit lights at the four corners of the warehouse; laughter and conversation continued throughout the blackout. Kite looked towards Bagaza but it was too dark to make out his face; nor could he see Mavinga. Had they sensed that they were being watched and would now take the opportunity to slip away? Stubbing out the cigarette, Kite went quickly outside to check the street.

The tradesmen were still hawking coffee and cigarettes. The only lights around the club were oil lamps and small fires. There was no sign of Bagaza or the woman. As Kite turned back to the Thiossane entrance, a taxi on the opposite corner blinked its lights. Kite could not make out the number plate and walked a few steps closer. It was Omar's Peugeot. A different man opened the driver's door, gesturing discreetly at Kite to return to the club. He assumed this was Naby, Omar's brother. Kite did as he was advised, reassured that others were now watching Thiossane from hidden vantage points.

As he made his way back to his stool, the electricity returned. Kite sat to quiet cheers of relief and a smattering of applause. Bagaza and his lover were still side by side at the table drinking the last of their white wine. When the lead singer announced the name of the band's next song, Grace let out a cry of delight and tipped her head back to absorb the first few bars. Bagaza looked on impassively.

Kite waited. He reached for his pager, hoping that more information had been circulated about the whereabouts of the team. It was no longer clipped to his belt. He felt in his pockets. It wasn't there either. He reached down and rummaged through the rucksack but knew with a sinking feeling that he had attached it to his trousers when he left the restaurant. It had likely fallen off during the journey with Sadio.

He sat up straight, telling himself that this changed nothing. He must still provoke Bagaza into leaving, either by accompanying him to the exit or by making him think that there was a risk he was about to be seized. By now the Closers would be outside or perhaps waiting for him at Rue Kennedy.

A chance soon came. As the audience applauded the end of the song, a woman in a bright orange dress stood up and vacated the seat next to Bagaza. Shouldering his rucksack, Kite weaved between the tables to a wild chorus of drums and wailed singing. Having reached the seat, he glanced at Bagaza and sat down.

At first the Rwandan did not react; Mavinga looked briefly at Kite, at once wary and oddly flirtatious. Up close he saw how striking she was: flawless skin and full lips, calculating eyes softened by low light. He looked ahead, facing the band, and caught the smell of Bagaza's after-shave; the mass murderer had recently anointed himself with a fresh application of eau de cologne.

'Great band!'

When there was no response, he said it again.

'Great band!'

'What did you say?'

Turning to face him, Bagaza had shouted his reply in English.

'I said great band. Incredible synchronicity, passion.'

Their eyes met. Kite was amazed by the gentleness of Bagaza's expression; it was a face entirely without malice. Grace ignored them, lost in the frantic chorus of the new song.

'You are English?' Bagaza asked. His voice was clear and deep, tailored for broadcast.

'Yeah! My name's Peter. Peter Galvin. I'm a journalist.'

Even this revelation did nothing to shake the target out of his benign state. He merely nodded and went back to watching the singer. Kite decided there was no point in delaying the inevitable.

'I was told I would find you here.'

It was as though Bagaza had been struck in the back of the neck by a dart. He turned.

'What was that you said to me?'

'I was told I would find you in Dakar.'

'Who said this?'

Kite was surprised that Bagaza had not immediately feigned confusion or bought time by claiming that he was a victim of mistaken identity. It was obvious from his reaction that he knew the game was up.

'I'm afraid I can't tell you that.'

142

'Peter? That is your name?'

'Peter, yes.'

'You say you are journalist?'

There was a kind of quick, street cunning in Bagaza's eyes.

'A writer, yes.' Kite's heart was drumming at a speed quicker than the frantic rhythms of the band. 'I've been looking for you all week. Missed you at Lagon tonight, but they said you were coming here.'

It was exactly the right tactic. The word 'they' had an electrifying effect.

'Who said this? The owner of the restaurant?'

'No. Other people.'

Assailed by a wild improvisation between keyboard and drums which had sent the crowd into a frenzy, Bagaza stared ahead. The long months on the run, the back-handers and secret deals, the aliases and lies – had it all been for nothing? If a journalist had managed to track him down to Lagon and Thiossane, that meant any number of Western intelligence services were more than capable of doing the same.

'Who do you think I am?' he asked.

'You are Augustin Bagaza.'

'No, no, my friend. That's not what I mean.' The Rwandan reached across Kite's back, pinching the shoulder muscle with his hand: 'What sort of *man* do you think I am?'

Kite thought of Lionel Jones-Lewis, his creepy house-master at Alford, running his hand up and down his back when he was fourteen years old. This was an entirely different kind of assault. His voice dried up as he tried to reply.

'That's what I'm here to find out.'

'Oh, you will find out.' Bagaza looked at Grace. 'Who else knows this? Who else can find me here? Your newspaper?'

'I'm a stringer,' Kite replied. 'I work alone. This would be an article for the *New Yorker* magazine. In due course I have plans to write a full-length book about the massacres.'

'You call it a massacre?'

'I don't like the term "genocide".' Kite was improvising. 'I prefer to hear both sides of the argument, Hutu and Tutsi. That's why your memories and analysis would be so invaluable to the magazine's readers. For balance.'

'Who are you?' Mavinga had suddenly leaned across Bagaza, not because she had heard what Kite had said but because his presence was ruining her enjoyment of the music. Bagaza spoke into her ear, presumably in dialect. Kite saw the shock of whatever he had told her flash across her face.

'Get away from us,' she said, spittle landing on Kite's cheeks and lips. He smelled alcohol on her, the ether of his father's breath. 'Fucking journalist. We have nothing to say to you.'

'Take it easy,' Kite replied. The intensity of her fury was disturbing: he remembered Strawson's remark about Mavinga encouraging Bagaza to 'cut up' Tutsis during the genocide. Fearing that they both might think he was alone and therefore vulnerable to attack, Kite said: 'I have a fixer here in the club keeping an eye on me. He knows who you are. He knows the risk I am taking by talking to you.'

To bolster this baseless claim, Kite looked over at the bar. For a startling moment he thought that he glimpsed Vauban, but it was just a trick of the light. The band announced that they were taking a break and a pretty waitress approached Kite asking if he wanted something to drink.

'He is not our guest,' Mavinga replied in French, standing up and heading off in the direction of the toilets. 'And he is not staying.'

Yet Bagaza remained. This was the man whose words had convinced tens of thousands of Rwandans to commit mass murder; a psychopath who had gleefully encouraged his countrymen to slaughter with gun and machete. Kite could not square Bagaza's reputation with the hunched,

144

contemplative figure beside him. He pushed his chair back, aware how easy it would be for Bagaza to sink a knife into his guts and slip away before anyone in the club had noticed.

'Look,' he said. 'You can't hide forever. People know that you're here. They know there's a black market in diplomatic passports. That's what you're after, isn't it?'

'I thought my lady told you to fuck off?' Bagaza leaned back in his chair, allowing Kite to see the barrel of a revolver in the waistband of his trousers. 'Yeah, that's right. I don't talk to scum journalists. So you get out of this place, out of my face, Mr Peter Galvin. You tell anyone you saw me here, it ends badly for you.'

Kite found that he was not afraid; Bagaza was lashing out because he was cornered. Sweat cooled on his body; for the first time in hours Kite felt comfortable in the saturating heat.

'I'm sorry you feel that way,' he replied. 'I wanted to give you an opportunity to tell the world your side of the story. A lot of people blame you for what happened last year. They speak of you in the same way people speak of Eichmann and Pol Pot. Now the name Augustin Bagaza will always be associated with mass murder.'

'Let it be associated with whatever you like. You think I care? You think I have been called by this name in over a year? You think Augustin Bagaza still exists? I am leaving Dakar. I am leaving Senegal. You cannot stop this. The people who told you about me, whoever they are, they cannot stop it either. Maybe you just got lucky and saw me in the club tonight. Maybe you are not who you say you are. Maybe you are a fucking British spy working for a government that was too weak, too racist to help the people of Rwanda in their time of need. Maybe you don't understand anything that went on in my country. Maybe you're just a fool.'

'It's been a pleasure,' said Kite, though he was now

145

unsettled, not so much by Bagaza's words but by the transformation in his attitude. He had never encountered a man with such quick and easy access to hate.

Mavinga was coming back from the bathroom, her face gleaming with sweat. When she saw that Kite was still at the table, she shot Bagaza a look of revulsion.

'I will leave you in peace,' Kite told him, hoping that somewhere in the club there was someone in the team who had witnessed their encounter. 'It was nice talking to you.'

Mavinga returned to the table. She did not look at Kite. Bagaza stood up and stepped towards him.

'Be careful, young man.' He was smiling as he spoke, raising his voice above the din of the club. 'It will be very easy to have you killed. You would be wise to leave Dakar as soon as possible.'

20

Shaken by Bagaza's words, Kite walked back towards the bar, scanning the club for members of the team. The only person looking at him was the waitress in the stained red dress; she flattered him with a provocative smile. Ignoring her, he walked out through the main doors, determined to find out who was around to help him. Passing through a thick cloud of mosquitoes, Kite made for Naby's cab.

The Senegalese had been waiting for him. As soon as he saw Kite he got out of the Peugeot and walked over.

'Do you have eyes on them?' he asked, without introducing himself.

'You're Naby?' Kite asked.

'I am,' he said. He was about five years younger than his brother, not as relaxed nor as self-confident, but with the same look of calm intelligence. 'Go back inside. Wait for me there.'

Kite did as he had been instructed, clocking Bagaza and Mavinga at their table as he walked in. They were deep in conversation. A few minutes later, seated on a tall stool at the bar with a Flag in his hand, Kite spotted Naby waiting for him in the short passage at the entrance. Grabbing his beer, he walked over to speak to him.

'What's the situation?' he asked.

147

'There was trouble at Rue Kennedy.'

'What kind of trouble?'

'The French kind. The Closers were waiting. Then suddenly the police are all over the van, asking why it's parked there, finding the weapons. Mike thinks Duval or Lagarde tipped them off.'

'They were *arrested*?'

'They won't hold them. Dakar police, you know?' Naby made a gesture which Kite could not accurately interpret; either he was suggesting that the local police were hopeless and easily overpowered or that a few hundred dollars would be enough for them to turn a blind eye.

'Are the French here? Is Duval in the club?'

'I didn't see anybody.'

'But the others are on their way? Nancy? Omar? Ackerman?'

Kite glanced at Bagaza and Mavinga. They had stopped talking and were sitting back, seemingly gathering their thoughts.

'No. We are the only ones left.'

Kite was stunned.

'What? Just you and me? No Closers? Where's Mike? Where's your brother?'

'No Closers. Ackerman got caught up in the raid. Mike and my brother are trying to work out next steps. Maybe they pull the plug. Maybe they come up here. What's your feeling about Bagaza?'

'My feeling is he's a piece of shit and we should arrest him. But how do we do that without the Closers?' Kite wanted to get on the radio to talk to Strawson but knew the protocol; in the event of an operation being exposed, personnel were instructed to dump any communications equipment. 'Why did we get the message to come up here?'

'They finished dinner early. Ricky overheard Bagaza talking about going to Thiossane to celebrate. Thought they were going to stop off at Kennedy, but they just kept driving.'

'Do we stand down?' Kite asked.

'I didn't get that order. And until we do, we stay with the target.'

'Where's Philippe?'

'Forget about him. Mike sent him back to the hotel.' A very thin teenage girl and a much larger, older African man pushed past them, heading outside. 'Omar says he should go to hospital, get himself checked out. There was a craziness inside him.'

'He's not wrong about that.' Kite remembered the revolver shoved into the waistband of Bagaza's trousers. 'Do you have a weapon?' he asked.

'Of course.' Naby seemed to find the question naive. 'Why?'

'Bagaza is armed. Itching for a fight. Got a spare?'

Naby laughed. 'You have no fear, do you? My brother told me this! You want to shoot him down in the street? In the middle of Thiossane?'

Naby reached back and withdrew a pistol from the waist-band of his trousers.

'Take this,' he said. 'I have another in the car.'

Kite took it, unzipped his rucksack and slipped the gun inside.

'Who does Bagaza think you are?' Naby asked.

'He might think I'm a journalist. He might think I'm a spy. Either way he knows that people are looking for him. He lost his cool with me. They both did. They're probably panicking and working out what the fuck to do next.'

'They will try to run,' Naby replied. 'They will go for the airport.'

'They definitely won't risk the apartment.' Kite glanced over at Bagaza's table. 'I don't want this fucker to disappear. Surely there's someone on the team who can help us?'

'How did you get here?'

Kite told Naby about the ride on Sadio's moped and was suddenly struck by an idea.

149

'Give me five minutes,' he said. 'Keep an eye on them. If they leave, try to lure them into your cab. I'll follow.'

Naby agreed and Kite walked outside. Sadio was standing nearby with a group of three young men. When he saw Kite, he raised his hand and said: 'Yo! Peter!' as if in imitation of a character in an American film. His new friends looked impressed.

'Your moped,' Kite said in his clearest French, acknowledging the others with a nod. 'How much?'

Sadio did not appear to understand the question.

'How much to buy your bike?' Kite repeated, pointing at the Vespa.

This time he understood, but in the wrong way. He began to tell Kite what he had paid for the moped, that it had been second-hand when he had purchased it from a dealer in Pikine.

'No, no. I asked how much do you want for it?'

Laughter. Gales of it. Sadio looking at Kite as though he was either crazy or patronising or both. It was time to let the money do the talking.

Kite opened his rucksack. He reached inside and felt the hot steel of Naby's gun. He pulled out the envelope of cash and extracted 10,000 French francs. One of the young men whistled. Another muttered something in Wolof. Sadio neither showed that he was offended by the proposal nor pleased at being offered such a large sum.

Just then: a staff door opened at the back of the warehouse, about fifty feet away. A hinge creaked and a young African man appeared in the alley. Kite recognised him as one of the barmen from the club.

Two people materialised beside him. The first was Bagaza. The other, holding his hand, was Grace Mavinga.

21

Kite stepped to one side, concealing himself in the shadows of an apartment building. He took another 10,000 francs from the envelope. He was now offering Sadio the equivalent of £2,000 for a third-hand moped with a top speed of 40 mph.

'I want to buy it,' he said quietly. '*Maintenant.*'

The French word for 'Now' had a clarifying impact. Sadio's eyes widened at the prospect of getting his hands on enough money to feed his family – and most of his friends – for the best part of a year.

'OK,' he said coolly and went to snatch the money. Kite knew that he was taking a risk. Any one of the men could make an opportunistic grab for the rucksack, assault Kite and take off with the spoils. There was no need to sell the moped to this strung-out British tourist with sweat pouring down his face. They could mug him for the cash; nobody would be any the wiser.

'Keys first,' said Kite.

Sadio handed them over, his new friends watching the exchange, transfixed. Meanwhile Bagaza and Mavinga were walking into the darkness of the back streets. As they vanished from view Kite straddled the moped, started the engine, handed the money to Sadio and secured the rucksack on his shoulders.

'Helmet,' he said in English, suddenly aware that his face would be too easily seen in the headlights of oncoming cars.

'What did you say?' Sadio replied. Kite had forgotten the French word for 'helmet' and mimed putting a hat on his head. He needed Sadio to hurry; the target was getting away. Then, suddenly realising a solution, he stepped off the bike, lifted the seat, found a helmet and put it on.

'Ah!' Sadio exclaimed. *'Mon casque!'*

'Merci,' said Kite, adjusting the strap, lifting his feet from the dusty pavement and almost going over the handlebars as the moped lurched forward. He heard laughter behind him as he moved off. Mavinga and Bagaza had been out of sight for almost a minute. A taxi appeared at the bottom of the alley on the opposite side of the club. Kite saw Naby at the wheel; he must have seen the target leaving the club and rushed to his car. If Naby could somehow loop around the block and approach from the south, Bagaza surely wouldn't suspect that he was surveillance. But if Bagaza's driver was waiting on a parallel street, or another taxi crossed their path in the meantime, Kite would likely be the only one capable of giving chase.

He drove past the cab, sounded the moped's horn and turned so that Naby would see his face. He then looped back towards the narrow street where he had last seen Bagaza and Mavinga. They were about a hundred metres away on the corner of a busy road with traffic passing in both directions. Kite braked quickly and switched off the engine. There were clothes hanging from a line just above his head. He reached up and unclipped a small T-shirt, took off the helmet and tied the T-shirt around his face to disguise his features. With the helmet back on, it felt as though he had encased himself in a hot towel.

Bagaza was hailing a cab. Kite prayed that Naby had made it. A taxi pulled up but there was no way of seeing the driver's face. Bagaza opened the rear door for Mavinga then went round to the opposite side and ducked into the back seat. Kite was freewheeling downhill, without headlights, and now switched on the engine as he followed the taxi onto a metalled road. As soon as he had made the turn, he tucked in behind a truck belching fumes into his face; he swerved out to breathe cleaner air and to try to get a glimpse of the taxi's number plate.

To his amazement he saw that Naby had managed to pick them up. Kite had no idea where Bagaza intended to go. A small aircraft flew over the road, descending towards Yoff. That meant they were going north – in the direction of the airport.

After about half a mile the truck Kite had been following abruptly turned off, leaving the Vespa too close to the cab. Kite throttled back, allowing the taxi to get about seventy metres ahead of him. Another bike buzzed past, then a brace of taxis; Kite tucked in behind the second, all the time keeping an eye on Naby's distant bumper. Flies and mosquitoes and the dust of the city struck his face continuously; even with the T-shirt covering his mouth and nose Kite managed to swallow an insect, spitting it out into the fabric as best he could. His eyes were watering constantly. He wiped them with the back of his hand and almost lost balance when the moped hit a chunk of loose concrete; he swerved to correct himself and was reprimanded by the driver of a passing car, cursing him as he overtook. Many of the vehicles coming towards him were without headlights; from a distance it looked as though Kite would hit them, only for the vehicles to slide past at the last second.

Naby's taxi was moving west, presumably heading for the Corniche and the fastest route to Yoff. Kite made a tight left turn to follow. He was hunched over the handlebars, driving in conditions which were completely alien to him: he could hear nothing but the lawnmower rattle of the moped's engine, his body so encased in sweat that it felt as though he was riding in a wetsuit.

Ahead, out of the blue, police cars. Yellow lights strobing against whitewashed walls. A roadblock for Bagaza, preventing him from entering the airport, or just a coincidence? Naby immediately turned off, presumably under instruction, heading back towards the old city. Kite followed into a dimly lit residential area where parked cars were coated in a film of red desert sand. He had been driving without headlights so that he would be less visible to Bagaza or Mavinga if either one of them turned around; as a consequence it was difficult to see the contours of the road. Accelerating to catch up with the taxi as it crossed an intersection, Kite's front wheel hit a patch of oil and the moped skidded at an angle which almost forced him off the bike.

Then, suddenly, Naby stopped. He had come to a halt in a small square surrounded on three sides by shuttered shops and closed market stalls. Kite pulled over and cut the engine. He was within touching distance of a herd of sleeping goats. A young man peered out at him from beneath a torn blanket, then closed his eyes and went back to sleep. The taxi was about a hundred metres away, the engine still running. In a patch of light halfway along the street, a dog scuttled out of a building and vanished into the gloom. It was extraordinarily quiet. Just the hum of crickets and the low rumble of distant traffic. Kite thought he recognised the street from earlier in the day; had he driven along it with Martha while searching for Appiah's villa? On one side of the road was a low wall, on the other a high wooden fence wrapped in tangles of wire and cable. Were they back in Fann? Perhaps Bagaza had a safe house here, somewhere to lie low while he worked out his next move.

The driver's door opened on the left-hand side. Kite saw immediately that something was wrong. Naby emerged from the car, knees bent, then slowly stood up with his hands on his head. Kite could sense his fear and swore under his breath. Naby now turned so that he was facing away from the taxi at a ninety-degree angle to Kite's position. He took a single step forward, hands interlinked behind his neck.

The engine growl of another plane coming in low from the south. Kite looked up at the night sky then back at Naby as he heard the sudden metallic crack of two gunshots fired less than a second apart. Naby's head erupted in blood and tissue. His body was thrown forward onto the ground. Bagaza got out of the taxi on the far side, moved quickly into the driver's seat, closed the door and drove away.

Kite was so stunned that he almost came off the stationary Vespa. His hands shaking, he tried the key in the ignition. The engine turned over without catching. *Jesus*, he whispered. *Jesus*. He tried the ignition a second time. The engine fired. The man beneath the blanket, woken by the sound of the gunshots, stared at Kite.

It was obvious that Naby could not be saved. When he pulled up alongside the body, Kite saw that the left side of his brain had disintegrated. The second bullet had struck him close to the heart; streaks of blood, black as oil under the night sky, had soaked the ground behind him. Kite was certain that Mavinga had fired the gun; Bagaza had been on the other side of the taxi. One of them must have recognised Naby from the club. In his eagerness to pick them up, he had not had time to alter his clothes or appearance in any way.

Kite fought an impulse to give up; the sight of the body had revived a sudden memory of Billy Peele, his friend and mentor cut down by gunfire in France six years earlier. It would have been easy to turn the moped around and drive back to Eric's villa. Strawson would never know that Kite had followed the target out of the club and witnessed Naby's murder. Yet Kite was determined not to quit. Whispering a desperate apology to his colleague's lifeless body, he twisted the throttle and raced through

155

the neighbourhood in a state of numb determination. Two hundred metres on, he glanced to his left and saw the tell-tale dent in the taxi's bumper at the bottom of a deserted street. Bagaza was indicating onto a busy road.

Kite waited until the taxi had disappeared then sped to the corner. He realised that he was back on the Corniche, the hot salt smell of the ocean rushing past him. His mind moving like a pinball, he pulled down the T-shirt from his face and sucked in great gulps of sea air. He kept thinking about Naby, about Strawson's likely reaction to the tragedy. Did Omar's brother have a wife and children? Kite knew so little about the private lives of the men and women he encountered in the secret world. He thought of his own father, dead before the age of fifty, his body helicoptered off a Scottish beach on a grey April morning. In shock at what he had witnessed, Kite swore, with defiant certainty, that he would avenge Naby Gueye and bring both Bagaza and Mavinga to justice.

He could still see the taxi up ahead. In the slipstream of an empty bus he was buffeted by a sideways Atlantic gust which pushed him perilously close to the edge of the Corniche. The moped jumped on the uneven road as, up ahead, the lights on Bagaza's taxi flared red, braking in a queue of traffic. Kite was grateful for the chance to stop and wiped his eyes as the hot Vespa engine rattled beneath him.

Petrol. He had not even thought about it, but now looked down and saw that the dial was close to empty. To slowly putter to a stop while Naby's killers vanished into the night would be the cruellest injustice. The traffic moved on again, Bagaza shunting forward. Kite's helmet was a vice pressing against his skull, the T-shirt no longer giving any protection from the sand and grit blowing into his face. The taxi turned off the Corniche, heading south-east towards Plateau. Kite misjudged his speed, driving too quickly down a quiet residential street. If they turned they would see his face, white arms braced across the handlebars, the moped buzzing like some giant insect. Kite braked and pulled in behind a parked minibus, the Vespa skidding to a halt on shingle. The taxi moved further and further into the distance. Kite knew that he would have to risk going back onto the street or lose Bagaza entirely, but the neighbourhood was deserted, offering him no guarantee against being spotted or heard. He pulled out and tailed at a slow crawl, passing a stray dog in the gloom who looked poised to run out in front of the bike. The taxi's brake lights flared red again and Kite accelerated in case Bagaza made a sudden turn.

Then he saw that the cab had stopped. A light came on in the interior as Bagaza switched off the engine and opened the driver's door. Kite veered onto a hard shoulder of rubble, squinting in the gloom. He saw Grace get out of the taxi and follow Bagaza into a building on the eastern side of the street. Kite waited until they were out of sight, then rode very slowly to within about fifty metres of their position. There were well-tended houses and a couple of restaurants nearby, but not a soul in sight. A little further on was what appeared to be a brand-new, three-storey hotel.

Kite removed the helmet and the T-shirt, lifted the seat and put both inside the Vespa. His hair was wet through, his clothes soaked in sweat. He felt mummified by the heat. He crossed the road, passing an old woman who had suddenly appeared and was walking in the opposite direction.

'Telephone?' he asked in French, desperate to call Strawson, but she merely shrugged and moved on.

The front door of the hotel had a glass panel with a window to one side through which Kite could make out a reception area. Mavinga was a silhouette opposite a figure behind a check-in desk.

Five minutes went by. A cat slipped out of the darkness, brushed against his legs, then slunk off into the night. Kite was extraordinarily thirsty, the adrenaline of the night coming off him as he watched the hotel. He was fighting to stay alert. If the hotel was full, Bagaza and Mavinga would come out and continue their journey south. Kite would be forced to follow them a second time; he reckoned he had enough petrol for another couple of miles, but no more.

Yet the longer he waited, the more certain he became that they had been given a room. Grace's silhouette had vanished. A light came on in a second-floor bedroom. The cat came back and miaowed at Kite as he watched from the shadows, waving mosquitoes out of his face.

Then, confirmation. Bagaza at the window, closing the curtains. He had left the taxi parked outside, a careless mistake if a witness had taken down the number plate. Would he realise and come back out? Kite gambled that they would both stay put until morning and walked up to the entrance.

22

The night manager was seated behind the reception desk reading a French academic textbook about biochemistry. He was a young, bespectacled Senegalese with an attentive air who did not seem at all startled when the bedraggled Kite walked in off the street asking if he could use the phone.

'*Êtes-vous un client de l'hôtel?*'

'No,' Kite replied in English. 'I don't have a booking. I was going to call you from the airport, but I didn't have time.'

With an apologetic smile, the night manager explained that he did not speak English and had failed to understand what monsieur was trying to tell him.

Reverting to French, Kite explained that he had come straight from the airport where his luggage had failed to turn up. His father was still at the terminal attempting to retrieve it. They wanted two rooms for three nights, bed and breakfast. And could he possibly use the telephone so that he could call his father at the Lost Property office and direct him to the hotel?

'Of course, sir.'

Kite registered with the Galvin passport, paying cash for the rooms. He was then pointed to a Bakelite phone on the opposite side of the reception area. The night manager explained that the cost of the call would be charged to his room. Then he went back to his textbook.

Kite dialled the satellite number from memory. He listened to it ring out with the same mounting frustration he had felt six hours earlier in the restaurant. At long last someone picked up.

'*Oui?*'

It was Vauban.

'Philippe?'

'*C'est moi.*'

He was the last person Kite had expected.

'Where's the boss?'

'Mike? Right now, I don't know. What's up, Locklang?'

There was a strange lack of urgency in his voice, no trace of stress. He might have been lying in bed with a girl, nonchalantly lighting a post-coital cigarette, or smoking a joint on the beach.

'I need to speak to him.'

'Like I said, he is not here. He ask me to answer the phone. So that is what I am doing. I am answering the phone. I feel good. I feel powerful.'

'You feel *what*?'

'Where are you, Locklang? Let's talk about Bagaza. It's time.'

'Are you OK, Philippe? You sound stoned.'

'*Moi?* Stoned?' The Frenchman laughed. 'No. I don't smoke tonight. But I feel great. I feel like I understand what we all have to do, yeah? I have understood this for a long time. I just didn't . . .' His voice drifted off, then returned to complete the thought: 'I just didn't understand. I feel like I finally know God. I can make miracles happen.'

'Look,' said Kite, alarmed. 'I need you to concentrate. It sounds like the Lariam you've been taking is still messing with your head.'

'Don't fucking patronise me, OK?' Vauban's sudden anger was as disconcerting as his mood of mellow tranquillity.

160

'I can concentrate. I see things much clearer than you, in fact.'

'I am not patronising you, Philippe. We have a very serious situation. I need you to call the boss.'

'Mike? Sure. I can reach him. What has happened? What is your situation, friend?'

'Just listen to me carefully. I need you to write this down.' Kite doubted that Vauban had the wherewithal to grab a pen and a piece of paper but went ahead anyway. 'The man we are all looking for. I know where he is. Tell the boss to get a team to the Hotel Té Dungal as soon as possible. I will meet them on the corner of Rue A and Rue 4. Did you get that?'

'Rue A and Rue 4. *Oui.*' Vauban's tone was suddenly sharper, as if he was finally aware that there was something serious at stake. 'Hotel Té Dungal.'

'I will find out what room they are in. Tell the boss that our Senegalese brother from the taxi is down.'

'What does it mean "down"?'

'It means the taxi driver's brother is out of the game. Not coming back. The woman got rid of him.' Kite had no patience for the absurdity of the *en clair* language. He wanted to spell it out. *Naby is dead. Grace Mavinga shot him in cold blood.* But protocol was protocol.

'I told you he was dangerous, Locklang.' The remark was amused and carefree. Vauban did not seem to have understood that it was Mavinga who had pulled the trigger. 'This is why he has to be stopped. I saw this a long time ago. This is who we are dealing with. Bagaza is the devil.'

'Yes, you already said that.' Kite looked at his watch. 'You need to reach the boss. Tell him I will see him as soon as possible. Try to bring the Closers if he can. It gets light at seven and this feels like a busy neighbourhood. OK?'

'*Très bien.*' A nonchalant promise, the *boulevardier* organising to meet a girl for brunch in Place des Voges. 'They will see you.'

'Get some rest, Philippe,' Kite told him, but Vauban had already hung up.

He took a deep breath. He was concerned that Vauban was not well enough to have understood what was being asked of him. The night manager had spent the duration of the call reading his biochemistry textbook, making occasional notes on a small pad; he did not look up when the call ended. Kite ran a hand through his damp hair and dialled Eric's number. He had expected the phone to ring out for some time, but Appiah answered almost immediately.

'This can only be you, Lockie.'

'It's me.' The night manager looked over. Kite offered him a friendly wave. 'I'm really sorry to ring in the middle of the night. I wondered how Martha was doing.'

'She's not good, man. She's in hospital. I had no way of reaching you.'

'*Hospital?*'

'The doctor came. He didn't like what he saw. Thinks she may have dengue fever. It's a kind of malaria. She has a rash on her back. That can be a sign.'

Kite was blindsided. 'Is anybody with her?'

'No, Lockie.' Appiah sounded strung out. 'They made me leave. It's the middle of the night. I guess she's asleep. Don't worry. It's the Principal, best hospital in town. She has her own room, she's being well looked after, I promise. You want me to give you the address? I can meet you there.'

Kite wanted to be at Martha's side, to comfort her, yet he could not leave the hotel until Strawson arrived. He would have to stay put for at least another hour.

'I could be there by five,' he said. Appiah gave him the address. 'But you don't have to meet me there. You've done more than enough. I'll call you afterwards.'

'It's no problem. You might need someone who speaks Wolof, who can ask the doctors the right kind of questions.'

162

'What exactly is dengue fever?' Kite asked. 'What did the doctor say?'

'Maybe she doesn't have that. They took some bloods. The results will be back in the morning.' Appiah cleared his throat. There was a sound on the line as though somebody was in the room with him. 'In a few hours, I guess. What happened to you?'

'Long story.' It suddenly occurred to Kite that the landline might not be secure. Appiah's father was a prominent businessman; any number of government ministers or foreign powers might have taken an interest in him. He said: 'The interview took forever.'

'Sure, Lockie. You had to get it done.'

It seemed a strange thing to say.

'I'm really grateful, Eric. For everything.'

'Sure.'

As Kite put the phone back in its cradle the night manager looked up and nodded. If he suspected that Kite had not been speaking to his father at the airport, he did not show it; his expression was blandly accommodating. Kite spotted a bottle of water in a small breakfast room off the lobby. He asked if he could take it and the night manager fetched it for him. They exchanged words about the heat, joking that October was the very worst time for tourists to visit Senegal. Kite said that he had spoken to his father but sadly there was still no sign of the luggage. He asked to be shown to their rooms and was taken to a small, simply furnished bedroom on the first floor next to a slightly larger room with a stained yellow bedspread and a view of the taxi. The doors and the walls were flimsily constructed and offered scant privacy; Kite could hear a female voice on the floor above. The night manager said that there were only three other guests staying in the hotel. Monsieur Galvin was welcome to move to another room if he wished. Kite told him that he was perfectly happy. Then, after the night manager had gone, he left the light on in the room and went out onto the street. He wanted to check the room's position relative to the target. He was directly below Bagaza. The voice he had heard was Mavinga's. Their bedroom light had now been switched off.

Kite longed to sleep, just to lie down for a couple of hours, to shut out the heat and the bad news, but he was badly shaken up by what had happened. Besides, there was still work to do. The Closers would need to know everything about the hotel; floor plans, exits, blind spots. To research this he went up to the second floor and located a fire escape at the back of the building; when he pushed the door open Kite saw that he was standing at the top of a steel staircase leading down to a quiet back street where a man – presumably a guard – was asleep in a chair against the wall of a private house.

He went back to his room and took a shower. The water running off his body was the colour of mud. He could hear a woman moaning in pleasure and wondered if the sound was coming from the room above; Bagaza, the tender monster, making love to Mavinga. Less than an hour had passed since she had shot Naby. It made Kite's blood run cold.

Just before five o'clock in the morning he changed into the fresh clothes from the rucksack and lay down on the bed. The mattress was as hard as a pavement, the heat broiling. A ceiling fan turned uselessly above his head, barely disturbing the air. While Kite waited for Strawson, he tried to work out if he was vulnerable to arrest. Had the man tending the animals at the top of the street seen his face? Kite was sure that by then he had been wearing the T-shirt across his nose and mouth, making it impossible to identify him. But that same man would have been able to provide the police with a description of the Vespa, perhaps even a number plate. To ease his nerves, Kite went back to the lobby, walked down the street and wheeled the Vespa along a narrow alley about two hundred metres from the corner of Rue A. There was a plastic storage tank on one side of the alley which stank of chemical waste. He rested the moped against it, wiped down the handlebars and returned to the street.

It was still very quiet in the neighbourhood, just the occasional bark of a dog and the hum of cars moving past on a parallel road. Kite kept trying to understand things from the police's point of view: would they announce that they were looking for a young white European male in connection with Naby's murder? After all, Kite had been seen talking to him in Thiossane. Yet it was surely too early for that connection to have been made. More likely they would be searching for the taxi. If a passing police patrol spotted the Peugeot parked outside the hotel, Bagaza was finished.

Just then, headlights on Rue 4, coming from the south. Kite lit a cigarette and waited beside an empty skip which stank of manure. A mosquito bit him and he cursed. The vehicle slowed as it approached. The passenger door opened. Vauban stepped out. He was wearing a filthy linen jacket, an overnight bag slung over his shoulder.

'*Salut,*' he said, waving with fake enthusiasm.

The car did a U-turn and returned in the direction from which it had come. Kite knew just by looking at Vauban that there was no chance of Strawson and the team showing up at the hotel. He had come alone without passing on Kite's message.

'What the fuck are you doing here?' he said. 'Whose car was that?'

'Some guy borrowed it for me,' Vauban replied, an explanation which made no sense. He walked up to Kite, swaggering with manic energy. The Lariam had sunk deeper into his brain. 'I wanted to get here right away. No taxis in Plateau this time of night.' His eyes were wide open, unblinking. 'How are you doing, Locklang?'

165

'You shouldn't have come.' The Frenchman did not appear to have heard him. It was as if another person had taken possession of his body.

'This is the place?' he asked, looking up at the hotel. 'Té Dungal?'

'Did you hear what I said?' Kite held him back because Vauban had started walking towards the entrance. 'You shouldn't have come here. Where are you going? Where's Mike?'

Still he did not respond. Kite said: 'Where are the others?' and at last received an answer.

'The others? Oh man, they're coming soon.' Vauban looked down at his boots and scuffed the sandy surface of the road. Kite knew that he was lying. 'There was trouble with the police. Did you hear about it? Did Naby tell you? Mike is trying to regroup the team. Ricky's wife went up to Thiossane to look for you.'

'Naby is dead.'

'What?' Vauban's face was a rictus of confusion and then suddenly completely without expression. He stared off into the distance and grinned. It was like dealing with an addict. Kite thought of his friend, Xavier, high on coke and mushrooms at a hundred parties. Vauban was similarly lost in a world of strange visions and looping ideas; it was impossible to get through to him.

'What the fuck?' he said suddenly in French, with the same dangerous shift in mood Kite recalled from the phone call. 'What do you mean I shouldn't have come? I am chosen. I can work miracles. Who the fuck are you to say this to me, Philippe Vauban, just a kid from Scotland?' He prodded Kite in the chest, goading him on the deserted street. Kite was so disturbed by his deranged, aggressive behaviour, and so anxious that Vauban might scupper what remained of the operation, that he gave serious consideration to knocking him out. Then he saw that one side of his jacket was weighed down by something heavy. Christ, was he carrying a gun?

Kite tried to reason with him.

'Listen.' He pointed up at Bagaza's room. 'We have to keep quiet.' The Frenchman clocked the window, rolled his eyes and pressed a finger to his lips, miming a sinister 'Shhhhh!' Kite played along with the game, saying: 'Let's get you into a taxi. You should go home.'

'I had to come up here,' Vauban replied, with a playfulness which turned instantly into a barely concealed rage. The swings in his temperament were frightening. 'I have to see Bagaza. I have to make justice.'

With that he put his overnight bag on the ground and unzipped a side pocket.

'Philippe, wait . . .'

Vauban rummaged around inside the bag. When he stood up, Kite saw to his horror that he had taken out a machete. Removing the gun from the inside pocket of his jacket, Vauban then walked towards the hotel carrying both weapons. Kite tried to reason with him, putting a hand on Vauban's shoulder to pull him back, saying 'Philippe, no, give them to me!' but the Frenchman simply shrugged him off, turned and pointed the gun at him.

'Fuck off!' he said in English.

Kite was sure that he was going to fire, but instead Vauban walked into the hotel. As the door swung shut behind him, he heard him aggressively asking the night manager what room Bagaza and Mavinga were staying in. It was not possible to hear the reply. Kite approached the entrance, scanning the street for signs that passers-by might have witnessed what was happening, but there was nobody around.

'The Rwandan scum,' Vauban was shouting in French. 'Where is he?'

Kite came into the lobby, saying Vauban's name. The Frenchman spun around, saw Kite, raised the gun and fired.

The shot missed him by no more than six inches, hitting a strip of timber on the wall. Kite ducked back into the street, horrified. The night manager scrambled into the office. Through the window Kite could see Vauban grab the registration book, the gun on the counter. His own weapon was upstairs in his rucksack. Without it there was nothing he could do to prevent what was about to happen.

'Philippe, please!' he shouted. He looked up and saw that Bagaza had switched on the light in his room. 'This is not who you are. This is not the way. Your medication has made you crazy.'

He was of course ignored. The situation was hopeless. Vauban made his way towards the staircase, the machete hanging casually by his side. Kite inched his way back into the lobby. At the last moment Vauban paused and turned, raising a hand to his mouth; he looked like someone trying to remember if he had left the gas on. Kite quickly retreated out of sight. He heard Vauban mutter something in French and then watched him climb the stairs.

As soon as he was out of sight, Kite shouted: 'Call the police!' There was no response from the night manager. Surely someone had heard the gunshot and raised the alarm? Kite sprinted up to the first floor. Vauban was nowhere to be seen. He unlocked his room, grabbed the rucksack from the bed and took out Naby's gun.

Afterwards he would struggle to remember what came first: the sound of the flimsy door on the floor above being kicked in or the first of two gunshots fired in quick succession.

Kite went back out into the corridor. He had a notion in his mind that he could still somehow stop Vauban. He pictured Mavinga waking up to the sight of a deranged intruder armed with a gun and a machete intent on killing her lover; it would later astonish him that he had possessed some atavistic desire to protect her.

Kite climbed the stairs to the second floor. Halfway up a middle-aged African man, naked but for a pair of thin white shorts, ran past him, hurrying to safety. Kite could hear Bagaza begging for his life. What he saw from the landing shocked him profoundly. The Rwandan's naked, bloodied body lying on the floor in the open doorway, a hand raised feebly above his head. Vauban was standing over him and now repeatedly brought the machete down on his arms and shoulders.

'Please,' Bagaza pleaded in French. Vauban cracked open his skull, the awful impact of steel hacking at bone and flesh again and again as he taunted him.

'This is what you did!' he shouted. His disembodied voice was terrifying, possessed. Vauban had taken off his shirt and jacket as if taking part in a ritual killing. His torso was covered in sweat and blood. 'How does it feel? This is what they did to my girl!'

Bagaza's motionless body took the blows. Kite saw Grace at the back of the room. She was standing by the window in a red slip. She bent down, apparently looking for something on the ground. Kite called out, 'Philippe, for Christ's sake!' but Vauban was very far away, lost in a stupor of frenzied violence, each swing of the machete weaker than the last until finally he stopped and seemed to realise, with an awful clarity which briefly swept away his psychosis, what exactly he had done.

At that moment Grace found the gun with which she had shot Naby and pointed it at Vauban. Rather than fire immediately, she instead ordered him to drop the machete and to stand facing the wall.

'Let's talk, this is a mess,' Vauban replied in a pitiful voice, but Mavinga stepped around Bagaza's motionless body in an attitude of determined, organised counter-attack.

'Don't turn around!' she ordered.

Kite was less than ten feet away, transfixed. He could not fire his own gun unless fired upon; it was an iron law of his training. She had picked up her handbag and some clothes. It was obvious that she intended to run. As she stepped out of the room, Vauban lunged at her from behind the door and she fired, twice. Kite heard Vauban's body hit the ground. In the same moment Mavinga ran to the landing, passing Kite on the stairs without even seeming to realise that he was there.

Kite rushed into the room, almost slipping on the blood in the doorway. Vauban was dead; the injuries to his brain were worse even than Naby's head wounds. Kite could hear voices outside the room and looked out of the window to see Mavinga getting into the taxi and driving off.

The sight of her escape cleared Kite's mind. He realised that he was in great trouble. Vauban and Bagaza were dead and Mavinga gone. Strawson would not vouch for him if he was arrested. Kite would be disavowed by BOX 88. Those were the rules.

So he moved fast, back into the deserted corridor where rivulets of Bagaza's blood were now flowing towards the stairs. He ran to his room, wiped down the sink and the shower head and the toilet cistern, grabbed his rucksack and sprinted to the first-floor fire escape.

The door would not open. Kite was sealed inside the hotel. He could hear voices gathering in the lobby below, people too fearful to come upstairs in case the gunman was still active. He rushed back to the landing, climbing the stairs two at a time to the second floor. The fire exit he had used before opened easily. He looked down. The guard who had been asleep outside the house had gone; perhaps he had heard the shots and run. Kite sprinted down the metal staircase, blood on the soles of his trainers causing him to lose his footing on the bottom step and twist his knee. When he had regained balance, he looked around. He had to get away from the hotel without being seen.

Between two of the houses in the quiet back street there was a narrow passage. Kite could not see if it was blocked off at the far end. With no alternative he started down it in complete darkness, walking straight into a thick spider's web which coated his face. He cleared the gluey strands from his eyes and mouth. His thin shoes crunched on broken glass as he moved forward in the gloom; there was foliage on both sides of the passage and planks hanging loose from fences. Kite stepped over them and at last saw the lights of a car about twenty metres ahead. Ducking under a cable he made it to the end of the passage and looked quickly in both directions to make sure that he would not be seen. He was certain that he had come out on Rue 2; if that was the case, his moped was about fifty metres away to the east. Kite calculated that it wasn't worth the risk of trying to reach it. The Vespa was almost out of fuel and the noise of trying to start it would alert passers-by. Better to walk calmly in the direction of the old city and hope for a cab.

He got lucky. Though Kite could hear sirens in the distance approaching the hotel, no police vehicles passed him. At a busy junction a taxi flashed its headlights and, when Kite raised his hand to flag it, careered to the side of the road to collect him. He gave directions to the Principal then sat back on the worn leather seat, wondering why the hell the operation had been allowed to fail so catastrophically.

23

'So what was the reason?' Isobel asked.

They were still in the living room in Stockholm, Ingrid fast asleep upstairs, the house as quiet as a ticking clock. Kite pressed the screen on his phone and saw that it was almost two in the morning. He had a final inch of Ben Scotia in front of him. Isobel had been drinking green tea since midnight.

'A perfect storm of bad luck, bad planning and bad comms. It turned out Michael's wife was very sick, she died just a few weeks later. Michael had known that he couldn't give the operation his full attention, so for the first few days Ackerman was making a lot of the smaller decisions on the ground. Recruiting Bagaza's driver turned out to have been a very stupid move. The driver alerted Duval to an American presence in Dakar and consequently the DGSE were watching out for us at Lagon. Ackerman had met Lagarde in Paris and was easily spotted. He was eventually fired, became a schoolteacher in Detroit.'

'What about Eric? How did you spin it?'

'I told him the truth. I told him what happened.'

'How was that possible? Were you allowed to do that?'

'Martha was delirious. When Eric was with her, she had let slip why we were in Senegal. She told him I was working

172

for the Foreign Office, that I was a spy. I was in danger, she was very worried about me. Babbled something about Eric needing to save me, something along those lines. He put two and two together, understood immediately how important it was that his family and the other members of staff in the villa didn't find out.'

Isobel had been in a mood of sustained consternation for the previous hour, listening to Kite's story with mounting horror. He knew what she must surely be thinking: that he had been heartless to leave Naby's body in the street, not to mention ruthlessly self-interested in abandoning Martha to her fate.

'Were the police looking for you?'

'They were looking for a young male British citizen named Peter Galvin, but they didn't have much to go on. The Galvin passport was fake, they had no photograph to circulate, no way of connecting me to the moped. As far as I know they never found Sadio. The night manager had seen my face, he knew I was British, that I was acquainted with Philippe and had tried to stop him. He was able to describe me to the police, but the photofit they put together, the facial composite, was hopeless. Made me look like Gene Hackman. I just laid low at Eric's house until Martha got better.'

'You make it sound easy.'

'It wasn't easy, believe me.' Kite slugged the last of the single malt. 'The problem was the phone call I'd made to Eric's house from the hotel. If the police looked at the records then they'd come to the villa and we'd have a major diplomatic incident on our hands. So Mike went into overdrive, got the Turings to erase all phone records from the hotel between midnight and 6 a.m., also any evidence of me calling the Appiah villa from Toubab. God knows how they did it as quickly as they did, but they got it done.'

'So you made contact with Strawson again? He hadn't left the country?'

'That was the frustrating thing. He'd been in the hotel all along. When I rang he had momentarily left the room, leaving Vauban in charge of the satellite phone. Philippe realised that I had Bagaza cornered and got it into his mind that this was the opportunity to kill him. By the time Mike got back, Philippe was on his way.'

'How did Strawson react?'

'Given that I was alone, he said I did everything right, including getting out of Senegal. Augustin Bagaza dead was better than Augustin Bagaza living under a new identity in Buenos Aires or Mississippi. Of course Mike felt responsible for what happened to Naby and Vauban, even though he had long believed that Philippe had a death wish. Foreign Legion, war junkie, sex addict.'

'And Bagaza? Naby? How were all the murders explained?'

'Naby was said to be working for a foreign intelligence agency surveilling a known Hutu *genocidaire* who killed him. Vauban was a French war reporter with PTSD and a hideous paradoxical reaction to Lariam. He hacked Bagaza to death. Grace Mavinga acted in self-defence, then fled the scene of the crime never to be seen again.'

'Never?'

'We think she got out of the country on the new diplomatic passport. When BOX ran Bagaza's Lagon contact to ground, more than three weeks had gone by. He gave us the name on the passport as well as the identity of the Senegalese official who had supplied it. But by then Grace Mavinga – or whoever she was pretending to be – was long gone. Strawson's best guess was that she did what Martha and I were supposed to do and crossed the border into the Gambia at Banjul.'

'How did you get out?'

Kite remembered the ensuing days as if they had happened only weeks earlier: Martha's strength gradually returning, her revulsion at Vauban's actions, her disbelief at the nature of his death. She had insisted that Kite had been right to leave her at the villa with Appiah. Was there a flicker of envy in Isobel's eyes as he told her all this, the long-suppressed realisation that Kite's relationship with Martha – the passion and turbulence of fifteen long years together – somehow trumped their marriage? Or was she just tired after a day of childcare and a long night of secrets?

'As soon as Martha was better, Eric drove us up to St Louis. We stayed at the Saint-Exupéry place, the Hôtel de la Poste, then walked over as backpackers into Mauritania. There was a crossing point at Rosso near the mouth of the Senegal River, boats going over all the time. We paid a truck driver to take us up to Nouakchott then caught a flight to Casablanca.'

'And Eric has worked for MI6 ever since? How is that possible? He's Senegalese, lives in Dakar.'

Isobel still believed that Kite was a senior MI6 officer; she knew nothing about the existence of BOX 88.

'He's not on salary. He's not trained. He acts as what we call a support agent.' This much was true, although Appiah had a freelance relationship with other services. 'If we need help in West Africa, MI6 sometimes turns to Eric. He can house people, act as a middleman, move money around, that sort of thing. He has a vast network of contacts across the region, fingers in a thousand pies. If he encounters somebody or something of interest, he'll get in touch, see if we want to take it any further.'

Isobel picked up her empty mug. It looked as though she needed a long time to process all that Kite had told her.

'And he's encountered somebody or something of interest recently, hence his call tonight?'

'Yes.'

'Do you think it's about Grace Mavinga?'

'What makes you say that?' Kite asked, in the way that you might ask a fortune teller to explain a prediction.

'Nothing.' Isobel carried the mug into the kitchen. 'I just wondered what had happened to her. She was

175

sleeping with a mass murderer. She killed Vauban. Seems strange that she was able to get away with it, to vanish for so long.'

Kite was silent. He had the sense that his wife wanted to hear nothing more of the whole sorry saga. He put his glass down next to the small silver box his father had given him as a christening present. He picked up the box and opened it. The inscription inside the lid read: *To Lachlan. From Da.*

'We should get some sleep,' he said, anxious to speak to Appiah as soon as possible.

'So you'll call him in the morning?'

'First thing,' he replied.

24

After fleeing the Té Dungal hotel, Grace Mavinga had driven for almost two hours, abandoning the taxi when it ran out of fuel, then riding a bus into Touba, a city about 180 kilometres east of Dakar. She had the equivalent of a hundred US dollars in her handbag as well as the new passport; everything else had been left behind at Rue Kennedy. In Touba she walked half a mile to a guest house and slept until dusk, fearful that the police would come for her and that she would be arrested the moment she stepped outside. There was a market nearby where she bought some clothes, toiletries and a new wig, shorter and less elaborate than the extensions she had worn for Augustin, as well as a *hijab* and some black plimsolls.

She spoke only rudimentary Wolof; the women who served her knew that she was an outsider. Grace took on the withdrawn, conservative characteristics of a devout Muslim woman. Where once she had worn Italian dresses and expensive French underwear, she now needed to look impoverished and forsaken. The second night she slept on a crowded, sweltering bus going south-west towards Kaffrine, mosquitoes picking at her skin, passengers moaning as they slept. She knew it was vital to keep moving. The bus stopped every half-hour, Mavinga ticking off the tiny towns – Colobane, Panal, Diarhao – wondering whether to risk the diplomatic passport at the frontier or to stay in Kaffrine for as long as it took the police to stop looking for her.

She grieved for Bagaza, but only in the way that she might have grieved for a neighbour's dog that had been run over by a passing car; that is to say, her feelings were short-lived and sentimental. She had hoped that he would take her to a new life in the United States where, once they were settled and she had earned a green card, their relationship would fizzle out. She was intensely angry about what had happened in Dakar, her rage directed principally at the English spy who had evidently followed them from Thiossane and watched as his crazed friend killed Augustin. Mavinga felt no guilt or regret at shooting this man; she only wished that she had also killed the spy.

Looking back, she had run from that room as she might have run from a burning building. Her actions had forced her into a life of poverty; she had relied on Bagaza for food and clothing, for a roof over her head. She had given up her studies in Kinshasa to be with him and was now effectively stateless: she could not go back to Zaire, not with the country overrun by Hutu refugees; nor would it be safe to stay in Senegal. It shamed her that she was obliged to survive on peasant food – buying *pain akara* and *ndambé* on the street for a few francs – and yearned for all the treats she had taken for granted in Dakar, the wines from Burgundy and Bordeaux, *soupe de poisson* at L'Oasis, *thieboudienne* at Chez Loutcha. Yet Grace was also possessed of immense energy and natural cunning. At all times she was thinking of ways to conceal herself, to evade capture, to change her appearance and alter her behaviour so that she left no trace of herself in the memory of others. Augustin had once been a stage actor of some renown in Kigali; he would have been impressed by her talent for shape-shifting and disguise. Mavinga saw her face printed in a Dakar newspaper, but it was an old photograph, taken when she was nineteen, smartly dressed and strikingly beautiful. After only two days it was already as though a different woman was staring back at her, not at all like the thin, devout Muslim in a *hijab* that Grace had become. As the hours and days went by, she had felt reassured that nobody would recognise her. She was defiant; pride would not allow her to fail nor to be captured. She knew that her strength of character was far greater than the British spy who was anyway most likely back in England by now, complaining and crying about the terrible things he had witnessed. Europeans were soft. It comforted Mavinga to picture Peter Galvin as a man who would be visited by nightmares for all eternity.

On the fourth day, she stole a handbag belonging to a young professional woman staying in the room adjacent to hers at a small hotel in Kaffrine. As soon as she had the bag in her possession, Mavinga left town in a taxi which she paid for with money from the woman's purse. It was the third time she had stolen another person's belongings, on each occasion targeting a woman of roughly her age and appearance in the hope of finding documents which would allow her to cross the border; she did not trust the Lagon passport and had sewn it into the lining of a small suitcase she had bought in Touba. With this woman she got lucky. She was carrying a Malian passport as well as what Grace assumed was a lucky ten-dollar bill; she exchanged this for francs in Tambacounda, paid a man to take her photograph then glued her veiled face into the Malian document, easily removing the existing picture with a nail file and some white spirit.

Her new name was Aminata Diallo. She took a night bus to the border at Kidira. There were hundreds of people queuing at the frontier – fruit growers and peanut farmers, men in worn suits, women of all ages, many with small children strapped to their chests.

179

Mavinga scanned the notice boards for her photograph, wondering if her nineteen-year-old face was tacked to the walls of the guard huts on both sides of the Falémé River: WANTED. FOR MURDER. But she was allowed to pass without difficulty, taking out Diallo's passport and briefly removing her veil so that the guard could see her face. She was not required to pay a bribe. She did not even have to smile. She was just one of a hundred women shuffling into Mali that morning, a woman looking for a bus to take her to the capital.

It was in Bamako, a city at the edge of the desert, dustier and even hotter than Dakar, that Grace Mavinga provided the first clue to her whereabouts. Yves Duval, the DGSE officer who had been tracking Bagaza in Dakar, would later describe it as her only mistake. Grace Mavinga would come to see it as the moment which marked the beginning of the rest of her life.

25

Using a secure phone, Kite called the Moran Hotel in Chiswick just after eight o'clock local time and asked to be put through to Mr Graham Campbell.

'One moment, sir.'

Appiah picked up after a short delay, took down Kite's number and called him back from what he described as 'the burner phone I'm using for this situation'.

'And what is that situation, Eric?'

'Do you listen to podcasts?' Appiah seemed to be starting the conversation with some friendly chit-chat. 'In the car? The shower? I just got back from the gym, like to listen to them while I'm working out. Is it the kind of thing you're into, Lockie?'

Kite was sitting in a busy breakfast café in Djursholm. He had a bowl of fruit in front of him and a cup of black coffee. He had ordered scrambled eggs fifteen minutes earlier, but they had never shown up.

'Occasionally,' he replied. 'If Isobel recommends something then I might listen to it. She's a fan of Rory Stewart and Alastair Campbell. *The Rest is Politics*. Says it helps her to understand how the British think. Why?'

'Have you heard of one called Woodstein?'

'As in Woodward and Bernstein? Watergate?'

'Exactly. It's listened to all over the world, gets a lot of attention. Investigative journalist called Lucian Michael Cablean, used to be with the *New York Times*, left when the social justice warriors took over. Made a name for himself digging up big political and espionage stories from the past. Had a bestseller a few years ago about the Red Brigades, wrote another book on Shining Path which was nominated for a Pulitzer.'

With a feeling of quiet dread, Kite knew where Appiah was heading.

'And he's stumbled on something?'

'Not exactly stumbled.' Appiah's connection momentarily cut out then returned at a slightly lower volume. 'It concerns your friends in Dakar in '95.'

'I had a feeling it might.'

'Do you remember that two men went into Lagon restaurant just after Bagaza and Lady Macbeth the night you were watching the restaurant with Philippe Vauban? One of them was local DGSE, the other had just flown in from Paris.'

His memory fresh from relating the story to Isobel, Kite recalled their names instantly.

'Yves Duval and Maurice Lagarde.'

Appiah sounded an appreciative whistle.

'Your memory, Lockie. As good as ever, my friend. So both of them, in very different ways, have been causing a lot of problems lately. Lagarde left the Service maybe twenty years ago, tried to make his fortune in Iraq, it didn't work out. He takes a big financial and reputational hit, his wife leaves him, his friends from the Service stop talking to him because he's such a pain in the ass. He gets married a second time, loses contact with his kids, that relationship doesn't work out either. So now he's sixty-three, sixty-four, living off a small state pension in a rented apartment in some shithole suburb outside of Bordeaux.' Kite assumed that Appiah was getting his information from the DGSE

182

but didn't interrupt to check. 'Here's the problem. Lagarde is angry. Humiliated. He writes a memoir about his two decades as a spy, tries to publish it in France, gets told he'll go to prison if it ever sees the light of day.'

'And someone outside DGSE has now seen the manuscript?'

'As usual you have gone directly to the point. Somebody leaked the Dakar section to Lucian Cablean.'

Kite tapped his teaspoon on the bowl of fruit in percussive frustration.

'Now why would they do a thing like that?'

'Only Doctor Hans Zarkov, formerly of NASA, has provided any explanation.'

It was an old joke from their school days, 'Flash' on *Queen's Greatest Hits*, but Kite wasn't in the mood for joking around.

'Seriously, Eric. Who leaked it?'

'The working assumption is somebody who wanted to demonstrate that Duval, and indeed dozens of people in the French political and intelligence apparatus, knew that Augustin Bagaza was running around Dakar and didn't take appropriate steps to arrest him. Or somebody inside DGSE who just wants to fuck the British and the Americans, take the heat off Paris. Macron recently sealed government documents relating to France's complicity in the genocide for another twenty-five years, so people have been asking questions. Bottom line, a Pulitzer-nominated American writer with over a quarter of a million followers on social media, not to mention a spotless reputation for crusading journalism, is now sitting on a serious scoop, the unsanctioned assassination of a suspected *genocidaire* by MI6 and CIA in the autumn of 1995.'

'Hang on a minute.' Kite laid down the spoon, stood up and walked outside so that he could speak more freely. 'Bagaza wasn't a suspect, he had the blood of thousands on his hands. He was murdered – not assassinated – by a

French journalist and former soldier with acute PTSD whose mind had been addled by Lariam.'

'I know that, Lockie. *You* know that. Michael Strawson, rest in peace, knew that. But that's not the version of history in the memoir.'

'Lagarde wanted to make things look as bad as possible for us and for the French?'

'*Exactement.*' Appiah's connection again briefly cut out. It was several seconds before the encryption software on Kite's phone restored the line. 'But it gets worse.'

Kite was pacing outside the café. The plate of scrambled eggs had at last been brought to his table. The waitress gestured at him through the window and he indicated that he would come back inside.

'How much worse?'

'Cablean works at Columbia University. He has a law degree from Yale, an M.Phil. from Cambridge, an M.Sc. from the London School of Economics. In other words, the guy is not stupid.' The warm interior of the café enveloped Kite as he returned to his table. 'He looked up Vauban's family. Eventually found his mother, spoke to her at length. Now Madame Vauban has several screws loose. She told Cablean that her husband, Vauban's father, had worked for a man named Michael Strawson. Saved his life on one occasion. Told him they both worked in a secret Anglo-American intelligence agency known only to select officers in CIA and SIS.'

'Christ. She knew the name?'

'She did not know the name.' It was like a superstition: neither Appiah nor Kite would say 'BOX 88', even on a supposedly secure line. 'Her name is Brigitte, as in Bardot. Thanks to her, Cablean thinks her son was a paid assassin, recruited by Strawson to kill Bagaza in cold blood. The stories about Lariam, about PTSD, were put out after the incident to the press by the CIA. Brigitte told Cablean those were government lies.'

'And has anybody tried to correct these lies, to speak to Cablean?'

'That's where you come in. The source I've been talking to is London DGSE, a good guy called Jean-François Fournier. Kind of a crusader. We've been working on something together, something separate that's related to Duval and Grace Mavinga. That's how I was made aware of the Lagarde problem. Right now, Paris is listening to Cablean's phones, looking at his laptop, following him around New York, waiting to see how far this thing goes. Maybe they try to stop him, maybe they let the broadcast go ahead. Cablean has interviewed two Senegalese who were on Mike's team in '95, both of them happy to take $200 from a famous journalist to spill the beans on what they knew and what they saw. They confirm the presence of an Anglo-American intelligence unit in Dakar watching Bagaza and Mavinga in October of '95, also the sudden appearance of a rival DGSE team at Rue Kennedy headed by Yves Duval which led to you guys standing down. In other words Cablean has all the little details he needs to put his story together, to broadcast and start a firestorm.'

Kite calculated the likely outcome of the podcast's release. Public knowledge of an unnamed, off-the-books Anglo-American intelligence unit known only to select members of CIA and SIS might sound like a useful rumour without basis in fact, but broadsheets in Europe and the United States would quickly pick up on the story and put pressure on their respective governments to comment. No formal reaction would be forthcoming and the story might eventually serve only as fodder for conspiracy theorists. However if the name 'BOX 88' ever became public knowledge, and proof emerged of the Service's existence, there would be a political earthquake. Kite consoled himself that any journalist who tried to get to the bottom of Cablean's accusations would know that Michael Strawson, Philippe Vauban and Augustin Bagaza were already dead and therefore unavailable for comment. Furthermore, nobody had seen Grace Mavinga for more than twenty-five years.

'Who from our side is talking to Cablean?' he asked, staring down at his rapidly cooling eggs. 'Richard Ackerman?'

'Don't think so. I'd have to check.'

'He was sacked shortly afterwards. Might relish the opportunity to tell his side of the story, grind an axe. Any mention of Sadio, the kid who sold me the moped?'

'None.'

'Omar? If he looked into Naby's family, I assume Cablean found him.'

'Omar has always been loyal to you, Lockie. Still mourns Naby. Wants nothing to do with the investigation unless we nail Mavinga. When that happens, he wants a piece of her.'

Kite didn't at first acknowledge the significance of the word 'nail'; he was trying to think of others who might remember his face.

'What about the night manager? What was his name? Demba something?'

'Diatta. Cablean found him too. The guy is good, no wonder he likens himself tb Woodward and Bernstein. Diatta is now running one of the big tourist hotels in Casamance. He remembers that the phone records from the hotel were destroyed. Cablean knows who had the power to do that. The Americans. The French. We've got to assume Diatta told Cablean everything he could remember about Peter Galvin. Then of course there are the statements he made to the police, eyewitnesses who saw you in Thiossane talking to the principals, plus a passing security guard who clocked you taking a cab three blocks from the hotel five minutes after Grace shot Vauban.'

'The prize for Cablean has to be Lady Macbeth,' Kite remarked quietly. 'If he finds her and she talks, he has the whole story. What's this about investigating her and Duval?'

'They became involved after '95. They're protecting each other. It's a long and dirty story. I'll explain when I see you. Don't worry about that for now. Worry about Cablean.'

His ignored eggs now congealed, Kite skewered a slice of browned banana and swallowed it with a lukewarm slug of coffee. He could not work out the link between Duval, last known to him as a serving DGSE officer in Senegal with alleged business operations in Dakar and Abidjan, and Grace Mavinga, the Congolese girlfriend of a Hutu war criminal. He asked again how the two of them were connected, but Appiah would not enlighten him.

'So what would you suggest I do?' Kite asked. 'We can't exactly put a block on a podcast. There's no international jurisdiction. Even if Paris threaten a lawsuit and it doesn't go out in France, what's to stop somebody listening to it in Germany or Brazil or Timbuktu. Come to that they can just use a VPN.'

'There are elements in *la boîte* who *want* this story to come out,' Appiah replied. '*La boîte*' was an industry nickname for the DGSE. 'It'll embarrass the president, make life difficult for London and Washington. Heads will inevitably roll. But I don't advise that you do *nothing*, Lockie. Besides, there's something else you should know.'

'Tell me.'

'Cablean went to Toubab, spoke to Mamadou. He's now the boss at the guest house, runs the place. Been there thirty years. Told Cablean about the visitors' book.'

The waitress approached Kite's table. She looked tired and impatient for Kite to settle his bill. Kite indicated that she should come back when he had finished his conversation.

'I wouldn't have signed the visitors' book in Toubab.'

'You didn't. But Martha did, using the surname Raine and leaving an address in Swiss Cottage. After what happened somebody from the team came to the guest house and ripped it out. But Mamadou remembered you, remembered Martha. Told Cablean you left the next day, even though Martha was sick. That's the only explanation I can think of.'

'The only explanation for what?'

'For the fact that Lucian Cablean has the names 'Lockie' and 'Martha Raine' in a file on his laptop and a note beside each one saying "FIND THEM".'

26

With the money he had earned from two bestselling books, one of them translated into fifteen languages, the other nominated for a Pulitzer Prize, Lucian Michael Cablean had bought a two-bedroom apartment in a high-rise on the Upper East Side of New York City boasting spectacular views over Roosevelt Island and the East River. Cablean wasn't a Big Ego, Master of the Universe type, but at night, looking down at the glittering lights on FDR Drive, it was hard to suppress a feeling of immense personal triumph at the way his life had worked out. He was happily married, professionally lauded and blessed with good health. He earned $275,000 a year for what he considered to be very little work indeed as Visiting Professor of Journalism at Columbia University and commanded high six-figure advances on both sides of the Atlantic. As his friends liked to point out, through sheer hard work and dogged determination Cablean had achieved all this before the age of forty-five. His detractors – mostly mid-level academics and non-fiction writers with a fraction of his sales – claimed that he had been criminally lucky in his choice of subjects and wildly over-praised both as a writer and public intellectual.

Cablean rose at dawn most mornings and used a gym three blocks away, running for twenty minutes followed typically by fifty lengths of the swimming pool. He would then return to his apartment, have coffee with his husband before the latter went off to work, then respond to any emails which had come in overnight. From the moment he woke up to the moment he fell asleep, Cablean's mind was full of whatever story he happened to be working on. The Lagarde memoir, specifically the assassination of Augustin Bagaza and its associated cover-up, had occupied his thoughts for almost three months. Cablean was constantly wondering how to shape the material. He had everything he needed on Bagaza himself and had spoken at length to Lagarde on a visit to Bordeaux. But he still needed someone from MI6 or CIA to corroborate – or at the very least comment upon – the charges levelled in the memoir. That meant tracking down the elusive Martha Raine in the hope that she would lead him to her former boyfriend, 'Lockie'.

It was an hour-long, fifty-block walk from Cablean's front door to Columbia. He kept a bicycle on the ground floor of the building and frequently cycled to work via Central Park, occasionally stopping for something to eat at Effy's or Piksers Deli. This particular Manhattan morning was threatening rain, so he decided to take the subway. Putting on a pair of headphones and finding Peter Gabriel's 'So' on Spotify, Cablean walked out onto East 63rd Street, passing a neighbour from the 27th floor coming back from a run with whom he exchanged a brisk nod.

Across the street, waiting for his target in an Oldsmobile parked on the corner of York Avenue, Mohammed Suidani extinguished a cigarette, stepped out of the car and proceeded to follow Cablean at a distance of about thirty metres.

Three hours earlier, thousands of miles away on the other side of the Atlantic Ocean, Eric Appiah had been coming to the end of a cappuccino at an Italian delicatessen on Chiswick High Road. He had called Kite in Stockholm and was looking forward to seeing him later in the day to discuss the Cablean podcast and to apprise him of the DGSE's enquiry into the activities of Yves Duval and Grace Mavinga. He had noticed that the deli sold cannolis and ordered two to take away before finishing his coffee and heading out onto the street.

It was a crisp spring day in west London, a cold sufferer ducking into a chemist for medication, a barber shop across the road doing a brisk trade in beard trims and wet shaves. As Appiah looked around for a taxi, his phone rang. The number came up as 'JFF', his contact listing for Jean-François Fournier, the DGSE officer leading the investigation into Duval and Mavinga.

'You don't usually call me on this phone,' said Appiah.

'I tried the other one. There was no answer.'

'I left it at the gym. Used it to speak to Peter Galvin this morning.'

'You reached him finally?' There was relief in Fournier's voice.

'Flying into London today.'

'And he wants to meet?'

Appiah hesitated. During the conversation with Kite, he had deliberately avoided going into detail about the Duval enquiry, reckoning that the Cablean podcast was the more pressing issue for his old friend.

'I'm seeing him later on,' he said. 'I'll feel him out, see what he thinks. Now what can I do for you?'

A black cab was approaching from the west. Appiah stuck out an arm but was beaten to it by an elderly lady brandishing a furled umbrella.

'I wanted to wish you luck this morning,' Fournier told him. Appiah was running late for a meeting with a lawyer whom both men hoped would enhance their understanding of Mavinga's complex financial arrangements in the Cayman Islands. 'If you need me there, I can be in Paddington, no problem.'

'Not necessary.' Appiah reached into the pocket of his coat and touched the bag of cannolis. 'It's just a preliminary discussion. If she gives me what I think she can give me, maybe you can join us for the second round.'

Fournier agreed with this strategy and reiterated his hope that the meeting would go well.

'And we're still on for dinner tonight at Kitty Fisher's?' he asked. 'Perhaps Galvin could join us?'

'One of my favourite restaurants in London.' Appiah wondered why Fournier was pushing so hard to meet Kite. Professional curiosity – or something else? 'Peter would love it. And a lot less expensive than Brick Street! I'll book for three of us at eight. Now it's time for me to find a cab and meet our "Deep Throat".'

'Deep *what*?' Fournier asked. They had been speaking in English and he had not understood the reference.

'The lawyer,' Appiah explained. 'Lindsey Berida. I thought *All the President's Men* was supposed to be one of your favourite films?'

'It is. Of course. But in French we use a different term for this.'

'We do,' Appiah replied, laughing heartily. 'So let's see if she's the real deal or wasting our time.'

'I very much hope the latter, my friend.'

Mohammed Suidani followed Cablean to the subway station on Lexington Avenue, tucked in behind him at a ticket turnstile, tapped Apple Pay on the read-out and proceeded onto the platform.

Three days earlier, driving away from JFK, he had put on a turban and face mask so that CCTV would not be able to match him to the moment of Cablean's execution. He was now familiar with the target's routine: the early-morning visits to the gym; the meals with his husband at a French restaurant close to their apartment building; Cablean's route across Central Park by bicycle. The clients had given him six days to make the kill; it was just a question of waiting for the right moment. As soon as it was done, Suidani was to make his way to Baltimore by train and catch a flight back to London.

He looked along the platform. Cablean appeared oblivious to his surroundings, a pair of Bose headphones clamped to his ears. There were cameras in the station, certainly, but in a more crowded environment it would be all too easy to move in behind the target and to push him in front of an oncoming train; in the subsequent mêlée, Suidani would be out of the station in under a minute. He had a loaded gun with which to fend off anybody who tried to detain him. He knew that Cablean was a famous journalist, that his murder would likely make headlines and that the police would be under pressure to find whoever had killed him. The client had told him that if he was arrested, he was to say that he was a lone wolf, an Islamist fanatic. *You had no idea you were killing a well-known writer. You did it for the glory of Allah.* But Suidani had no intention of being arrested. By the time images of a mysterious man in a face mask and turban began circulating to US law enforcement, he would be back in London enjoying the second tranche of his £300,000 fee.

Eric Appiah arrived at Paddington station two minutes before the appointed start of his meeting with Lindsey Berida. Texting her from the back of the cab, he apologised for running late but was told not to worry. She had just got off a call; there was absolutely no rush. Just make your way to North Wharf Road, find the entrance to Lovage House, press the buzzer for apartment 1228 and go up to the 12th floor.

Appiah knew little about Berida except that she had worked for a bank in the Caymans for nine years and was ready to talk about Kisenso Holdings, an entity controlled by Grace Mavinga which Fournier believed to be at the centre of a vast money laundering operation orchestrated by Yves Duval. Berida had reached out to a colleague of Fournier's at the DGSE and the meeting had been set up within a few days. Appiah had been given the task of breaking the ice: his charms, particularly where women were concerned, outstripped even Fournier's and it was hoped that he might soften Berida into indiscretions. If the meeting was a success, there would be a second, more formal interview at which Berida would be invited to go on the record.

Appiah had only passed the new development at Paddington Basin by car on the Westway; this was the first time that he had visited the area on foot. Tipping the taxi driver five pounds he made his way from Praed Street past St Mary's Hospital – where his younger sister had been born in 1978 – heading towards a canal bordered by houseboats. Office workers were queuing at a stainless-steel food truck which glinted in the late morning sun. Using his phone, Appiah located North Wharf Road then checked his appearance in the lobby window of a high-rise. A section of his shirt had come loose and he tucked it back in as he continued towards Lovage House.

Twelve floors up, tracking his approach through a pair of binoculars, Riyad Gyan announced that their visitor would likely be at the apartment within two minutes.

'He looks bigger than I thought,' he muttered in Arabic.

'Then you'd better be ready,' his companion replied.

Marianne Hette's job was to report on the activities of Lucian Michael Cablean. Senior DGSE figures in Paris wanted to know who he met, what leads he was following and when the Woodstein podcast might see the light of day. Hette's secondary responsibility was to ensure that no harm came to him. The American was threatening to expose not only DGSE secrets of the past, which a cabal of retired and still-serving officers were anxious to conceal,

194

but also the activities of Augustin Bagaza's erstwhile mistress, Grace Mavinga, who was under investigation as part of a wider enquiry into the malign activities of Yves Duval. In other words, there were plenty of people who might wish Lucian Michael Cablean dead. The last thing the DGSE wanted was blame for the murder of a leading American journalist, even if such an attack was carried out by a third party. The Service would survive the fallout from the podcast; it likely would not survive an incensed American political and media class accusing the French government of mounting state-sponsored assassinations on the streets of New York.

So when Marianne Hette spotted the young Sikh in the turban and face mask for the third time in two days, standing just six feet from Cablean on the platform at Lexington and 63rd, she knew she had a problem.

Boarding the Q train in a carriage adjacent to the oblivious Cablean, Hette had ridden three stops to Times Square while pretending to read Nabokov's *Pale Fire*. Cablean's pursuer appeared to be alone and was not, as far as she could discern, trained in anti-surveillance; for the duration of the short journey, he looked over at Cablean at least a dozen times in an anxious, furtive manner.

Times Square was packed. This appeared to suit the Sikh's purpose. As soon as both men were out of the train, he quickly moved towards Cablean, following him through crowds of late-morning commuters to a platform serving the 1 Uptown to Columbia. People were three-deep waiting for the train, Cablean trying to push through to find more space. Hette could see the Sikh slipstreaming him, touch-close.

Hette instinctively felt that an attack was imminent. Fournier had given her clearance to neutralise any threat, but she was too far back from the principals. She heard the rumble of an approaching train, saw commuters surge forward. There was no clear path to the Sikh. People were passing her on both sides. If she didn't go now, she would never reach them.

'*Putain*,' she muttered, reaching for the zipped inside pocket of her jacket.

The train was less than ten seconds from the platform.

Lindsey Berida had answered the intercom at Lovage House in a genial, sing-song voice, immediately buzzing Appiah inside. He passed a security guard seated behind a wide, uncluttered desk who was too busy watching TikTok videos to look up and acknowledge his arrival. Appiah rode the lift to the twelfth floor in an upbeat mood, optimistic that Berida would unlock the secrets of Kisenso Holdings and bring the investigation several steps closer to Mavinga's eventual arrest. There was a mirror in the lift. He again checked his appearance, noticing that the hem of his trousers had caught in the top of one of his boots.

Appiah took out his phone. The married doctor with whom he had been spending time in London had sent a text message saying that she was free to meet later in the afternoon. He replied wondering if she could join him for lunch at his hotel.

The lift doors opened. Lovage House was a new building, decoration on the top floor as yet unfinished. There were dust sheets draped over items of furniture and plastic matting on the floor. Appiah followed signs to Apartment 1228 and knocked gently.

'Just a minute!' Berida called out.

Seconds later the door was opened by an attractive North African woman in a dark business suit, her hair tied up in a bun, bright red lipstick adding lustre to a wide smile.

'You found me.'

Her accent was hard to place. As Appiah stepped inside, he noticed the smile disappear and the woman's eyes dart quickly to one side. His arms were suddenly wrenched behind his back and his wrists secured.

196

Appiah tried to turn but was pushed forward, momentarily losing balance. The door slammed shut. Looking up, he was confronted by the sight of two masked men. Berida had stepped away from the door and was holding something in her right hand. As Appiah cried out a gag was jammed into his mouth and his eyes blindfolded. Suddenly there was classical music in the room, Mozart, and the quick exerted breathing of men. Appiah was lifted off his feet. When he tried to kick out, he heard the whistle of a tie ziplocking his legs, the plastic cutting through the fabric of his trousers and pinching the skin. He screamed in pain.

'What do you know about Kisenso Holdings?'

This from Berida. Her question was strangely polite, quiet and respectful. Appiah tried to answer but there was no way of speaking through the gag.

'Where is Peter Galvin?'

He heard the glide and slam of a French window. The noise of the city was suddenly audible over the Mozart. In French one of the men said: 'Forget questions. Get his phone.'

They reached into Appiah's jacket. He tried to resist, flicking his body this way and that and kicking out with his knees. He felt weightless; the men carrying him were extraordinarily strong.

'What do you want?' he tried to say. His chest was flooded with sweat.

'Tell me the code please.'

Appiah swore through the gag. Suddenly the blindfold was off. As he opened his eyes, Appiah saw the face of his children on the home screen, then a man's thumb swiping the image away as the phone recognised his face.

'Got it,' the man said.

'Search the contacts,' Berida demanded. When she spoke French her voice was quite different, quick and impatient. 'Look for Martha Raine.'

Martha? Appiah thought. Why Martha? He wanted the

chance to speak to them, to negotiate. His sense of powerlessness was total.

'And him?' one of the men asked.

'Outside.'

Cablean was listening to the end of 'In Your Eyes' when
the Uptown 1 flashed in from the south, the weight of
commuters pressing around him, crowding up the platform.
He steadied himself, putting one foot in front of the other.
At the same time Cablean pushed out with his right elbow,
letting whoever was at the other end of the bony arm in
his ribs know that he wasn't going to be pushed out of the
way. Fucking Times Square. He should have taken a cab.

The noise of the train drowned out the song. Cablean
couldn't hear a note. He pulled the headphones down onto
his shoulders and found himself saying: 'Take it easy!' as
the crowd surged around him.

'We're all gonna get where we're gonna get!' someone
shouted.

The train came to a halt. Cablean was directly opposite
a set of doors. As they hissed open there was a surge
behind him. He heard a kind of dismayed gasp of surprise,
an unusual sound that he had not expected, but paid no
attention to it. He was more interested in getting onboard.
There was suddenly less pressure behind him. Cablean
pulled the headphones back onto his head, heard the first
notes of 'Red Rain' and stepped up onto the train.

Nobody followed. He realised that something had
happened behind him on the platform. As the doors slid
shut, Cablean saw that a young man wearing a turban and
face mask had collapsed. An elderly lady with wispy white
hair was crouched beside him.

The doors closed, the train moved away and Lucian
Michael Cablean, lost in music, continued his journey.

27

Returning home from the café in Djursholm, Kite had picked up the grab bag from his office, kissed Ingrid goodbye and assured Isobel he would be back in Sweden before the end of the week.

'Don't make promises you can't keep,' she said. 'Do what you have to do in London. Come back to us when you can.'

He had updated headquarters in Canary Wharf on the Cablean problem and informed his number two, Azhar Masood, that he was due to land just after midday. No arrangement had been made for Kite to be met at Heathrow airport, yet Cara Jannaway, whom Kite had recruited from MI5 three years earlier, was waiting for him in arrivals. She was casually dressed in jeans and trainers, her hair tied back. He reacted to her presence with a mixture of surprise and anxiety, asking why she had made the long journey from east London.

'You have a habit of tracking me down,' he said. Cara assumed this was a reference to their meeting on Kew Green prior to the Dubai operation. 'Parks, restaurants, now airports.'

'And I always seem to come with bad news.'

Kite placed his bag on the ground.

'What's happened?'

'You haven't heard? You didn't see the news?'

'Nothing.' Kite took out his phone as if it was somehow complicit in his ignorance. 'I've been talking to my wife since I got off the plane.'

Cara had never had to tell anyone that a person had died, far less a close friend of her boss who had been thrown off a building in broad daylight.

'Eric Appiah is dead.'

She saw the shock pulse through Kite. He said 'What?' very quietly, almost to himself, then looked around as if somebody standing nearby might reassure him that what he had been told was untrue.

'I'm so sorry,' was all that Cara could think to say.

'What happened?' he asked.

'He fell from a block of flats in Paddington. It's been on social media, BBC. People saying it was suicide. The police seem to be going with that. Obviously we think it's more sinister.'

Kite knew that Eric would not have taken his own life; either he had got on the wrong side of a business deal or, more likely, his death was connected to the work he was doing with the DGSE.

'Do you know if he was involved in Ukraine in any way?' Cara asked. 'Opposition groups, financing, weapons procurement?'

'I really don't know.' Kite had a sudden, vivid mental image of Eric showing up at the guest house in Senegal, all smiles and charm. 'Martha,' he said suddenly. 'Where is Martha Raine?'

'I . . . I don't know,' Cara replied. 'Why?'

'Find out for me, please. She may need protection. I don't want to call her. Not about this.'

'Of course.' Cara could not work out what link Martha might have with what had happened in Paddington. 'Do you have her number?'

'Not like that.' There was an edge of impatience to the reply. 'The Turings can place her. We have a fix on her phone. Just locate her. If she's in New York, ask The Stadium to send a team to Bank Street.' The Stadium was the nickname for BOX 88's new headquarters in Manhattan; Bank Street was Martha's home address. 'Look at her comms, see if anyone's taking an interest in her. Her married surname is Radinsky. Someone should watch their apartment. Discreetly.'

That last word was crucial. Cara knew that Martha was unaware of the steps Kite had taken to ensure her safety in the aftermath of the Dubai operation. He had been concerned that the FSB might look for her in New York and use her as bait.

'I'm on it,' she said.

'I'll get a warning to Lucian Cablean. His life could be in danger.'

Cara screwed up her face, wondering how the author of *Years of Lead* could be implicated in what had happened to Appiah. 'The Red Brigades writer?'

'He works at Columbia. I'll have somebody call him.'

'What's this all about?'

'Wait.' Kite wasn't finished. 'Eric had taken a room at a hotel in Chiswick. The Moran. He may have items there relating to an investigation he was working on with the DGSE. We need to get to them before the police do.' It was pure Kite, the man Cara knew and had worked alongside for three years. He had returned from a long sabbatical to be confronted by the worst possible news, yet rather than wallow in anger or self-pity, his instinct was to fight back. 'Find out the room number. He usually booked under the name Graham Campbell. Get me a pass key and a clean phone. I'll get whatever details I can from Scotland Yard. Presumably the Met have Eric's phone and wallet. There was probably a Moran room key in there so we'll need to move quickly.'

Cara had been awake until three with her new boyfriend and was worried that she would forget all that was being asked of her. She made a mental checklist – Martha. Room. Keycard. Phone – and created a simple mnemonic, MRKP, to jog her memory.

'There's more.' Kite had picked up his bag and was making his way through the terminal. 'Call our mutual friend at Five and ask him if he's ever taken an interest in an individual named Grace Mavinga.' He took a pen from his jacket and wrote the name on his boarding pass. 'She's in the Dakar files. See if they've anything recorded against.'

Their 'mutual friend' was Cara's former boss at the Security Service, Robert Vosse, whom Kite had recruited into BOX 88.

'I'll look into Yves Duval. He was a DGSE officer in the mid-90s based in Dakar. Now involved with Mavinga. According to Eric they are protecting each other. I have no idea why or how. SIS will likely have a file on Duval. I'll ask Vauxhall for whatever they have.' Kite gave her the boarding pass. 'How did you get here?'

'I drove.'

'Leave me the keys. Have The Cathedral bring everything to Chiswick as soon as they can. The pass key for Eric's room and a clean phone.' Kite looked at his watch. It was still on Stockholm time. He took it off, wound it back an hour. 'We can meet near the Moran. I'll be on my personal number.'

'Got it,' Cara replied, handing him the keys.

'You've forgotten one important thing.'

'What?' she asked, unnerved by Kite's quick, ordered efficiency.

'Where did you park?'

28

Cara met Kite three hours later in a deserted pub on a street running parallel to the Moran. In the intervening period he had acquired a Brentford FC baseball cap, a packet of Boots face masks and a pair of latex gloves. There was a cup of tea on the table in front of him, an old man doing a Sudoku puzzle at the bar.

'What did you find out?' he asked.

Cara went through her acronym aide-memoire.

'There was no fix on Martha Raine. The number we have for her is no longer in use. The Turings are looking at her financial transactions, social media, her husband's details, trying to get a new number and location.'

Kite felt a thump of unease. 'What's wrong with the address in Bank Street?'

'The Stadium is sending a team over to see if anyone is at home. Maybe she changed her mobile phone provider, maybe she's on holiday. Who knows?'

Kite dropped a sugar cube into the tea. 'Cablean turned up for work at Columbia this morning as usual. Maybe Martha is fine too and there's no connection. Did you get the information about Eric?'

'He was in room 306 at the Moran, booked under "Graham Campbell" just like you said. The Turings told me this would work against every door in the hotel.' Cara handed over an iPhone. 'They put some software into it, you just hold it against the door. The phone is otherwise clean, usual apps, numbers for personnel. Bob is seeing what he can find out about Grace Mavinga and the pseudonym. Maz said you called him about Yves Duval, he's talking to Vauxhall. Should be an update on all of this by five.'

'Thank you, Cara. How are you?'

'Don't worry about me,' she said. 'More importantly, how are you?'

Ordinarily Kite might have taken time to speak about Appiah, to tell her what sort of man he had been, but he was in a depleted mood, stalled by shock and grief.

'Thanks for asking,' he said. 'Maybe later, another time. I need to get to his room as soon as possible.'

It was stuffy in the pub. Cara removed her jacket, saying: 'Want me to wait here for you? Or I can bring the car to the Moran, be outside when you come out.'

'Do that. My bag is in the boot. I won't be long.'

The Moran was two minutes away on foot. Kite fitted a face mask and the baseball cap, entered via the automatic doors and walked directly towards a bank of lifts in the centre of the hotel. An elderly Indian woman in a sari joined him to the third floor, bidding him good afternoon in a sing-song voice as she stepped out of the lift. Kite waited until he had heard the click and clunk of her door closing, then made his way to Room 306.

The software worked without any problems; Kite held the phone to the handle and the lock clicked open. In years gone by, he would have had to hack the hotel security, bribe a chambermaid or even trust his facility for picking locks. He walked into the room, closed the door and put the gloves on.

The smell was instantly a memory of the cricket pavilion at Alford: Appiah's Kouros aftershave sprayed liberally after

204

every game, his fellow players mock-choking as though on poisoned gas. Kite was surprised by how few personal items he could see. Expecting shirts and suits on hangers, books by the bedside, photographs on the desk, he found only an unopened bottle of Co-Op Malbec, a copy of the *Financial Times*, a toothbrush and disposable razor. It didn't look as though Appiah had slept in the room; why then the strong smell of aftershave? Ordinarily on London visits he gave 'Claridge's' as the code for his whereabouts whenever he was using the Moran. But there was often a woman involved; his bed might change from night to night, depending on the identity and location of the latest Appiah mistress. Kite set himself the added challenge of finding her before the police did.

He opened a cupboard to reveal a well-stocked minibar. The safe-deposit box was open with nothing inside it, the drawers below it also empty. Dirty gym clothes were piled up at the bottom of the cupboard beside a pair of worn trainers. Kite picked up a running shirt, feeling the sweat of a morning workout on the fabric. In the back pocket of a crumpled pair of shorts he detected the hard outline and weight of a key. In another pocket, a pass to a Virgin Active gym. Opening his phone, Kite looked for the nearest branch and located one only a few hundred metres to the east in a business park north of Chiswick High Road.

He knew how Appiah's mind worked. Though untrained, he had designed a unique personal tradecraft – some of it suggested by Kite, much of it his own work – which meant that he never left too many clues about his whereabouts and behaviour in the same place. Contacting Kite via the art gallery had been pure Appiah: eccentric and unnecessarily complicated. It was possible he had rented a locker at the gym so that he would have a safe place in which to store information about Duval and Mavinga. The card and key were perhaps a breakthrough.

Kite lifted the mattress, looked in the toilet cistern,

opened the back of the remote control. Nothing. With the key and the membership card in his pocket, he put the baseball cap and the face mask back on, removed the gloves and returned to the ground floor. Emerging into the lobby he passed a young, attractive woman wearing a dark business suit, her hair tied in a bun. She caught Kite's eye momentarily as she entered the lift.

Cara was waiting outside.

'We've got work to do,' he told her, climbing into the passenger seat. 'I need somewhere to change clothes.'

'Change clothes?' she repeated, confused.

'We're joining a gym.'

29

The business park was a newly minted urban development of steel-and-glass office towers which took Kite back to Dubai; the buildings had the same soulless, dystopian gleam. In the centre of the complex, an artificial freshwater lake shimmered with pale foam and pond scum. Blank-eyed office workers wandered about carrying lattes and cycling helmets; security guards in high-viz jackets looked short of things to do. There were glass pods for meetings, discreet signs guiding visitors to the London headquarters of tax-dodging multinationals, joggers passing through en route to Acton and Kew.

'It's a glimpse of the future,' Cara observed. 'Even the trees look depressed.'

There was a restaurant on the north side of the lake. Cara sat outside while Kite went to the gents and changed into his running gear. Emerging into the sunlight, he signalled to her and she walked towards the Virgin Active. Kite entered twenty seconds later in face mask and base-ball cap. A middle-aged woman in a lycra bodysuit, breathing heavily from a recent workout, held the door for him as he went inside. He could hear Cara asking how much it would cost to join the gym for six months. Kite made a small performance of searching his wallet and clothes for Appiah's membership card. Having found it, he slid the card through a security reader, hoping that it would activate the doors. The card did not work. Distracted by Cara's questions, and aware of Kite's frustration, the receptionist looked up and, without asking for identification, hit a button which allowed him to enter the gym.

'Thank you so much,' he said, his voice muffled by the mask. 'Appreciate it.'

There was a dome lens CCTV camera directly ahead of him. Kite lowered his eyes, the Brentford baseball cap further concealing his appearance. Cara was now talking to the receptionist about the possibility of attending yoga classes at seven o'clock in the morning. It relieved some of Kite's tension to hear her playing the role. Ahead of him, two men appeared at the top of a staircase, both sweating profusely. Kite could hear the whoops and grunts of an exercise class, upbeat house music playing on a sound system. He passed the two men and went down to a basement area where he located the entrance to the male changing rooms.

It was a vast, over-lit area divided into separate sections; there were as many as two hundred lockers built into the walls. A smell of aerosol deodorants and chlorine hung in the air. About half the lockers were padlocked. Kite walked around, ostensibly searching for somewhere to change while scanning the locks for one that might match Eric's key. To his relief he saw that the majority were combination padlocks; only about forty required a key. Several of these were bunched around the first numbered lockers on the nearest side of the changing area. Kite assumed these were the permanent lockers, rented out by the gym to members, and set his bag down in front of them. An old man was towelling himself nearby and cut Kite a suspicious look, doubtless wondering why he had chosen to change so close to him. Biding his time, Kite stared at his phone until the man had left. Then he took out the key.

The word STANLEY was etched on the metal. Kite scanned the padlocks but few of them were branded. He chose one which looked a likely match. The key did not fit. He tried a second padlock with a similar result. Footsteps behind him. Trying a third locker without success, Kite sat down as a tall black man walked past him and settled on the opposite side of the changing area. An alarm was going off inside one of the lockers. Killing more time on his phone, Kite waited for the man to leave then tried two more locks. No success. He was now past the first batch of lockers, numbered 1 through 30, and beginning to feel frustrated. Was he going to have to try every locker in the place?

Two more men came into the changing area, both bearded, both wet from a shower. Kite took off his trainers and re-laced them. He did a Wordle and checked the cricket scores until the men had gone. They left behind a pair of sodden towels and a wet, discarded Kleenex. Cara sent a message saying that she was back at the Moran having a drink in the bar. Impatient to find the padlock, Kite tried two more doors but was prevented from going for a third by the appearance of a female member of staff. She picked up the discarded towels and grunted in disgust as she bent down to pick up the Kleenex. Kite was then obliged to wait a further five minutes while a tattooed weightlifter performed a series of half-naked, post-workout stretches, anointing himself in talcum powder. When he had finished, he waddled over to the hairdryers wearing only a pair of blue underpants. Briefly alone, Kite tried the padlock on locker 74. No luck. The lock on 76 was marked STANLEY on the reverse side but again the key did not fit.

Then it struck him. Kite looked along the wall. There was a large red padlock attached to locker 88 with an acid house smiley face stickered to it. How could he have been so slow? Appiah's key slid easily inside. Someone had come into the changing area behind him. Assuming that it was the weightlifter, Kite ignored him. He was intent on extracting whatever Appiah had left in the locker.

The first thing he noticed was a small plastic wallet. He slipped it into his pocket. At the bottom was a Tesco carrier bag next to a black zip-up holdall. Kite placed the plastic bag inside the holdall and pulled both out. The locker was now empty. The man behind him had been joined by a friend. They were talking about going to a party in Southall. Having reattached the padlock and wiped it for prints, Kite walked out of the changing room. Within a few minutes he was skirting the edge of the man-made lake and calling Cara to ensure that the coast was clear.

'Don't come back to the Moran,' she said. 'Police turned up half-an-hour ago and arrested someone. I'm trying to find out what's going on.'

30

It was quickly established that the person who had been arrested in the lobby of the Moran was the same woman in the dark business suit whom Kite had passed on his way out of the hotel. Cara's description of her – 'corporate hottie, wears her hair up, looks North African' – matched his memory of the woman who had entered the lift.

'Any connection with Eric?' he asked. He was walking towards Cara's vehicle.

'I asked a member of staff. Apparently, she was trying to break into his room using Appiah's key card. Hotel had put a block on it. A chambermaid saw her, called the manager.'

'And now the police have her?'

'Took her away three minutes ago.'

'Did you get a name?'

'No, but I called Jane, added it to her workload. She's going to find out what she can.'

They were back at The Cathedral within an hour. It was Kite's first visit to headquarters in over a year; during the Covid lockdowns BOX 88 had been temporarily headquartered in Chelsea. In that most secret of places, only a handful of people knew of his association with Appiah. One of them was his second-in-command, Azhar Masood, who emerged from his office overlooking Canary Wharf both to welcome Kite back to work and to express his condolences. Though the two men were close, there was no warm embrace, no consoling hand on the back; it wasn't their style. Instead, Masood accompanied Kite and Cara to a meeting room where two analysts were waiting for them.

'I assume someone took the phone from you?' Masood enquired.

Kite had found a locked mobile in the black holdall which he had passed to a Turing on his way up to the fifteenth floor.

'They did. Seemed to think it would take no time at all to get into its guts, find out who Eric was contacting.'

There had been little else of consequence in the bags: no notebook, no photographs, no weapon or passport, only a receipt for a private members club in Mayfair – 49 Brick Street – at which Appiah had spent more than £450 on what looked like a long night of martinis, Chateaubriand and Crozes-Hermitage.

'Is he a member of the club?' Kite asked.

An analyst seated to his left had a laptop open with access to what looked like the Brick Street computer system.

'Doesn't appear so.' He was a prematurely balding twenty-nine-year-old father of two named Jerry whom Masood had poached from Google. 'I've been able to access the membership list and reservation system. There's no record of an Eric Appiah or Graham Campbell on the books. Judging by the photographs, most of the clientele appear to be white European, white American, English ex-public schoolboys, if you know what I mean.'

'I know what you mean.' Kite caught Cara's eye. 'Brick Street is the new Annabel's.'

'I thought the old one was still going.' This from Masood.

'It is. But it's wall-to-wall Chinese and African plutocrats, Gulf money and call girls. Brick Street turns its nose up, only wants posh boys, European bankers and Americans whose families went over on the *Mayflower*.'

'So what was Eric Appiah doing there?' Cara asked, adding sugar to a mug of tea. 'Or does he get past the selection committee on account of being an Old Alfordian?'

'Must have been somebody's guest,' Kite replied, noting that Cara seemed relaxed and ebullient in Masood's company. They had been working side by side for the better part of three months. 'Can we access their CCTV recordings from the night of the receipt? See who signed him in?'

'I'll get on it,' Jerry promised.

There was a knock at the door. Freddie Lane, a veteran of both the Torabi and Dubai operations, had managed to break the security on the holdall mobile and was bringing Kite a report on its contents.

'There were only two numbers stored in the phone,' he said, settling into the seat next to Cara. 'All messages erased, no social media or WhatsApp. Just Signal and Telegram. He was being careful.'

'So do we know who he was talking to?'

Lane, never a person to shout his successes from the rooftops, said: 'Of course' in a tone of voice which suggested that Kite had underestimated his abilities. 'The first number belongs to Dr Audrey Salinger, a married GP who lives here in London.'

'Why do you say "married"?' Cara asked.

Lane hesitated, as though he was in polite company.

'Because metadata puts her phone at the Moran hotel three nights ago from about 10 p.m. until seven the following morning.'

'Eric's appetites unchanged to the end,' Kite observed. 'What else do we know about her?'

'Less than we know about the owner of the other phone, sir.' Lane held up a piece of paper on which he had scribbled some notes. 'Jean-François Fournier. Declared DGSE officer with the French embassy in London.'

'Well, well, well . . .' Masood was wearing a tie and loosened it, opening the top button of his shirt. 'Known to you, Lockie?'

'Yes. Eric mentioned him on the phone this morning. They were working together.'

Jerry was typing on the laptop, scrolling through documents, jumping from tab to tab. 'There's a Jean-François Fournier listed as a member at 49 Brick Street. Lives in Chelsea. Born 1985.'

'Bingo,' said Kite.

'Do they have bingo in France?' Cara understood from Masood's reaction that this was not a time for light-heartedness. 'Must be the beneficiary of your friend's generosity,' she added, recovering quickly. 'Martinis. Steaks. Red wine. All adding up to four hundred and fifty quid three nights ago.'

Kite was wondering if Appiah had misjudged Fournier; had the DGSE betrayed him?

'I assume we have photographs of this guy. How quickly can we get his comms?'

'Shouldn't be a problem,' Lane replied. 'If he's declared, Cheltenham will have them. We can scoop up whatever we need.'

'I want to know where he was today, where he went before and after his dinner with Eric, if he's had any contact with Yves Duval or Grace Mavinga in the last seventy-two hours. Is he leaving the country? Has he shown any interest in Lucian Cablean or Peter Galvin or Martha Raine? Get me everything as soon as you can.'

Jerry scribbled the names down on a notepad and said: 'Yes, sir.' It was almost eight o'clock. He had the appearance of someone who had been looking forward to going home to his wife and children after a long day at work.

'I just have one more job for you after that,' Kite told him. 'Then you can call it a night.'

31

The private members club at 49 Brick Street was a converted nineteenth-century Georgian mansion which had once housed Falaise, a fashionable French restaurant frequented by Kite's mother in the early 1990s. Kite remembered being taken there shortly before starting at Edinburgh University. Martha had come with him, fresh from a summer holiday in Turkey. He remembered wrought-iron tables with red-and-white gingham cloths, awkward conversations over avocado Marie-Rose, silver candlesticks encased in stalactites of wax. Afterwards Cheryl had taken a taxi home, whispering, 'She's such a nice girl, isn't she?' in Kite's ear as she kissed him goodbye. Buoyed by his mother's approval, Kite had bought a bottle of Chilean wine in a nearby off-licence, helped Martha to clamber over a gate into Hyde Park and made love to her beside the Serpentine before they were chased off by a security guard.

At some point in the intervening thirty years the entire building had undergone an expensive refit. Falaise was no more. In her place was an elite nightlife bolthole the size of a boutique hotel with multiple bars, a basement restaurant bedecked in crimson and scarlet wallpaper and a packed dance floor playing hits from Motown and the heyday of Margaret Thatcher. Kite had been there twice before, once for a work meeting and once for a friend's fortieth birthday party. He entered via a discreet door on Hertford Street, his six-year phantom membership having been placed on the Brick Street servers by Jerry two hours earlier. An attack on Jean-François Fournier's personal phone had revealed that the Frenchman was due to meet a friend for dinner shortly after ten o'clock. Kite intended to find him and, when the time came, to establish how much or how little he knew about Appiah's death.

On the basis that it was inevitable he would run into an old boy from Alford College with Brick Street membership, Kite was registered under his own name. Sure enough, descending an elaborately decorated staircase in the north-east corner, he spotted Christian Bathurst, a boy from his house, once a svelte box-to-box midfielder, now a portly financier with a full head of chalk-white hair. Making a sharp turn at the bottom of the stairs, Kite ducked out of sight, skirting the edge of the dance floor until he found himself in a lengthy queue for the bar. Fournier was likely on the opposite side of the basement, dining in one of the cellar booths which offered members a certain degree of privacy and quiet.

Kite took out his phone. There was a Signal message from Cara and a WhatsApp from Isobel. He had not yet told Isobel about Eric's death. When he clicked on her message, he saw that she had sent a photograph of Ingrid in the bath with a love heart emoji fixed to the image. Beneath this she had typed 'Missing Daddy'.

'Missing her too', he replied, then opened the message from Cara.

Any sign of him?

Kite's response was succinct.

None

Moments later, a black cab pulled over on Hertford Street. A handsome middle-aged Pakistani businessman emerged into the Mayfair night accompanied by a beautiful young woman – at least ten years his junior – wearing Louboutins and a figure-hugging red dress. A keen-eyed observer would have noticed three buttons on the cuffs of the businessman's Turnbull & Asser shirt as well as a gold wedding band on the ring finger of his left hand. He wore Church's brogues, a tailored suit and an Audemars Piguet watch finished in yellow gold, conservatively valued at £350,000.

The young woman, who wore no wedding ring, was not his wife. She was not even his girlfriend. Yet she held his hand as they walked the short distance to the main entrance of 49 Brick Street. Having queued behind a group of excited guests, most of them in their mid-twenties, the businessman approached the reception desk and introduced himself as Rehan Saleem, an alias he was using for the purpose of gaining entry. A hostess typed the name into the reservation system, welcomed Mr Saleem back to the club and typed in the identity of his companion – the entirely fictitious Lady Amelia Lambe – before wishing them both a lovely evening.

Azhar Masood now familiarised himself with the lobby. There was a sumptuously upholstered sofa at its centre, a trio of oil paintings depicting various outposts of the former British Empire and a broad oak staircase currently blocked by two middle-aged American women loudly debating whether to go upstairs or down. Immediately ahead of him was an outdoor smoking terrace packed with chattering guests; a distinct smell of Cuban cigars wafted into the lobby. Everywhere he looked, Masood saw prosperous-looking men in lounge suits and women of every age in designer skirts and vertiginous heels. The place reeked of money, of status, of a sealed-off world frequented by a privileged few. The atmosphere was one of restrained decadence, of good manners and uncertain breeding on the brink of alcohol-fuelled debauchery.

'Drink?' he asked his companion.

'Too right, Jeeves,' replied Cara Jannaway. 'Let's find the bar.'

Kite had ordered a Negroni, paying the princely sum of £32 for the privilege. Noting his surprise, a six-foot Aryan *ubermensch* in black tie made a crack about 'ze cost of living crisis' and ordered a bottle of Veuve Clicquot. Kite turned towards the dining area, pausing beside an eight-foot soft toy giraffe. His phone pulsed. Setting the Negroni on a mantelpiece crowded with African-themed ornaments, he took out the phone and read the message. It was from Mary, a Turing working the night shift in Canary Wharf.

Fournier just called his wife. Whoever he was meeting for dinner didn't show up.

Kite tapped out a quick reply.

So F left?

The answer came back seconds later.

No. Told his wife he would be home by 1.

Kite was still waiting for word from New York. He asked if BOX 88 had been able to track down Martha or heard back from Columbia University.

Nothing on either. Still trying.

He looked at his watch. It was just after midnight. Picking up the Negroni, he made his way into the dining area, passing from room to room. Each was more garishly decorated than the last: purple and crimson wallpaper and scarlet shaded lamps gave the impression of an upmarket Parisian bordello. All was laughter and candlelit conversation in half a dozen languages, balloons of cognac and half-finished plates of tiramisu. Far from hating the place, Kite relished its decadent sophistication; he had always loved the theatre of expensive restaurants, of single women in search of husbands, of husbands in search of single women. After three austere months in Sweden it felt as though he had emerged from a health clinic into the Rio carnival.

'Excuse me.' He buttonholed a passing member of staff who had the look of someone in charge. 'Is Mr Fournier dining here this evening by any chance?'

'Yes, sir.' The man had a heavy Italian accent. 'Monsieur Fournier is with us in the cellar. You would like me to direct you to his table?'

'No, thank you.' Kite smiled gratefully. 'I'd like to surprise him. We haven't seen each other in years.'

'As you wish, sir.'

Pausing by the eight-foot giraffe, Kite tapped out a WhatsApp message.

Staff confirm F here. Basement. Cellar table north side.
I'm going for a smoke.

Less than twenty feet away, settled into a quiet dining booth with a British plutocrat who had donated more than half a million pounds to the campaign to leave the European Union, Jean-François Fournier gratefully accepted the offer of a second vodka martini and wondered if his host would ever acknowledge that Brexit had been an unmitigated disaster.

'Accept it, Charles,' he said, shaking his head with world-weary amusement. 'You wanted freedom from bureaucracy, from paperwork, from foreigners like me

219

telling you what to do. Now instead you have *more* bureaucracy, *more* paperwork and foreigners who do not tell you what to do because they no longer want to do business with the United Kingdom.'

'Is that the official position of the French government?'

Charles Oliver Neustrom was a sixty-four-year-old hedge fund manager with two ex-wives, three estranged teenage children and a personal fortune estimated at somewhere between £750 and £900 million. He was a founding member of 49 Brick Street, visited the club at least twice a week, knew all the staff by name and regularly spent more than £2,000 on food and wine. Occasionally he would take home one of the Brazilian or Ukrainian call girls who slipped past reception on a nod and a wink from the management. His hair – a combined transplant and dye job – was often damp and a source of fascination to Fournier, as were Neustrom's outfits. Tonight he was sporting a bright blue designer shirt decorated with figs, avocados and pomegranates beneath a double-breasted pinstriped blazer fitted with brass buttons. Neustrom had a pot belly and smelled of coconut shower gel. Fournier had befriended him in Paris in 2011 and renewed their acquaintance after being posted to London. He hated everything about his politics, his taste and lifestyle, yet could not help admiring a man who lived his life with such brazen contempt for norms of social discourse and behaviour. Neustrom was so much more entertaining than the slicked-back City psychopaths who made up the bulk of the membership at Brick Street and Annabel's. Furthermore, as an Old Alfordian and graduate of Trinity College, Cambridge, he was a well-connected figure in London and therefore a more than useful conduit into the upper echelons of the ruling Conservative Party.

'The position of the French government is clear,' Fournier replied. 'We believe, as do the governments of Japan, Germany and the United States, that after the confinement there was a trade recovery by all the G7 nations *except* the United Kingdom. In your country everything is flat.' Here Fournier made a levelling gesture with his hand, almost knocking over a glass of champagne. 'Why is it flat? Because small businesses can no longer trade with Europe and Europe, speaking frankly, can no longer be bothered to trade with small businesses in the UK. There is too much red tape. It is expensive and time-consuming. They choose to buy their products elsewhere. Or your businesses are building hubs in Poland or the Netherlands and trading within the EU in that way. Those local jobs of course go to Poles or to the Dutch, not to workers in the UK. It is the slow economic suicide which all sensible people predicted before the 2016 referendum.'

'Total cock,' said Neustrom. Like many Old Alfordians of a certain vintage, he sounded at times like a Spitfire pilot trying to pass himself off as a cab-driving Cockney. 'What you Frenchies call *"le confinement"* is what we call the global Covid clusterfuck which messed with every economy on the planet. Throw in Vladimir's invasion and the subsequent energy crisis and you're not in any kind of position to be judging whether or not Brexit has or hasn't been a success. An S&P survey showed that private sector activity in the UK actually *outpaced* the EU for six straight months last year, so put that in your Gauloise and smoke it.'

'Excuse me?'

Both men were stopped in their tracks by the sudden appearance of a startlingly attractive woman in a figure-hugging red dress. At first, Fournier assumed she was one of Neustrom's girls, but it was to the Frenchman that she had directed her attention.

'Are you Francine's father, from the Lycée?'

Francine was the name of Fournier's oldest daughter, a ten-year-old student at the Lycée Charles de Gaulle in South Kensington.

221

'I am,' he said. 'Do you teach there?'

'Not any more,' said the woman, casting a bashful, apologetic look at Neustrom. 'I was a classroom assistant for a year. I used to babysit a friend of your daughter's. Francine was often round at the house. I recognised you.'

'You have a very good memory for faces.' Fournier wondered if this was all too good to be true. 'What's your name?'

'Amelia,' the woman replied. 'Amelia Lambe. I was just looking for a table actually. The club is so busy. I'm here with a friend.'

'Would you care to join us?' Neustrom's enthusiasm was self-evident; he was already moving cushions out of the way on the seat beside him. 'We were just about to open a bottle. As long as you promise not to talk about Brexit . . .'

'Oh no, we couldn't possibly,' Lambe replied. Backing away slightly, as though she had regretted coming over, she added: 'It's sort of a date I'm on. He wouldn't approve.'

This accompanied by a charming smile, somehow making the two men complicit in her secret doubts about whoever had been lucky enough to bring her to the club.

'Well, if you're sure and can find room elsewhere,' Neustrom replied.

A hesitation. She wanted to stay; Fournier could see it in her eyes. Amelia Lambe wanted these relative strangers to save her from the prospect of a long night listening to her date boring on about derivatives.

'Let me go and find him,' she said.

At that moment Azhar Masood was turning away from the bar holding two glasses of house white wine – astonished both by the £45 bill and by the beautiful barman who had brazenly flirted with him – when Cara materialised beside him.

'Contact made,' she said. 'Opposite side of the stairs. Drinking with a bloke who looks like Mick Hucknall – if

222

Mick Hucknall was seven stone overweight and on holiday in Bora Bora. Played the classroom assistant, they seemed to buy it. Invited us to join them. We're on a first date, I said you'd be annoyed that we're not alone.'

'Understood,' Masood replied. 'Remind me how we met.'

'Sugar Daddy dot com. But we're keeping that a secret.'

Masood smiled as Cara touched the lapel of his jacket and led him to Fournier's table. Both their phones vibrated to a group text from Mary.

Be advised. New message to wife indicates that F was meant to be having dinner with Eric Appiah. Shows no knowledge of EA murder.

'Well, well, well,' Cara muttered, aware that Kite would have received the same text on the smoking terrace. She typed out a reply:

Received. Fournier in booth behind stairs. Dining with friend. M and me joining. Suggest LK intervention within 5.

They were standing beside the eight-foot giraffe. Cara looked up at it in the way that she might have looked at a drunk in the club who was thinking of making an ill-advised pass.

'Ready?' Masood asked, ducking under the low cellar wall.

'Ready,' she replied.

Kite saw Cara's message, stubbed out his cigarette and took out the burner phone. A member of staff, passing him in the lobby, reminded sir that guests were not allowed to make telephone calls inside the club and would sir please go outside to complete his conversation.

'Of course,' Kite replied, walking out onto Hertford Street. He dialled Fournier's number.

* * *

Cara Jannaway and Azhar Masood had been the guests of Fournier and Neustrom for only a couple of minutes when the Frenchman reached into the inside pocket of his jacket to answer his ringing phone. They both studied his reaction closely. Kite was using Appiah's burner: if Fournier had been responsible for his death, receiving a call from the number would have come as a profound shock. Yet as he looked at the screen, his face widened into an amused grin and he answered in a lively, jocular tone.

'I hope you're ringing to apologise for not showing up at Kitty Fisher's,' he said in French. Cara did not speak the language, but Masood understood him word for word. 'I didn't hear back from you, so I've ended up eating in Brick Street. We're sitting here with two charming new friends. Come and join us.'

At that moment Fournier's expression changed from one of warm good humour to consternation. Both Cara and Masood noted the way his face paled, the mouth open in shock.

'I see,' he said in English. Then again, still coming to terms with what he had been told: 'I see.'

Neustrom looked up, evidently noting the change in his friend's demeanour. The opening bars of 'Tainted Love' sounded from the disco; there was a delighted whoop from the dance floor.

'Everything all right, old chap?'

Fournier was already making his way out of the booth. He balanced himself on the table as he passed the seated Cara.

'I need to take this,' he said, barely acknowledging Neustrom. Then, to the man who had called him with the news of Eric Appiah's murder: 'Who is this? Who are you?'

'Call me Peter Galvin,' said Kite. 'I was a friend of Eric's. I believe you know who I am.'

'Yes, I do,' Fournier replied. His breathing had quickened. It sounded to Kite as though he was walking away from the cellar. 'Of course I know who you are. Let me take this outside. I'm in a club. It's difficult to hear.'

There was a scratch and tap on the line as Fournier made his way to the exit. Kite pictured him walking up the same Mother of Pearl staircase he had used at the Hertford Street entrance.

'Why don't we meet?' he suggested.

'Now?' the Frenchman replied.

The door opened and Jean-François Fournier stepped outside. Kite walked up to him, lowering the phone.

'Why not?' he said. 'There's no time like the present.'

32

'You are here,' said Fournier, looking up and down the street. 'You were here all along.'

A message from Cara landed on Kite's phone.

F appeared genuinely shocked. Expected to be speaking to Appiah. Go ahead.

Fournier was in his late thirties, of below average height, with dark hair and plump cheeks. His well-cut suit skilfully concealed a slight paunch. He was the sort of man who would fit in anywhere: at a board meeting; standing over a map in the desert; eyeing up a girl in a nightclub. He had a friendly-in-all-weathers face, that particular sort of forgettable anonymity which is invaluable to a spy. There was an MI6 file on Fournier but it had not arrived in time for Kite to read it; besides, he preferred to make his own judgement about a person, face-to-face, then to check first impressions against the facts. He suspected that the Frenchman would prove to be a decent, level-headed man, perhaps somewhat conservative and dispassionate in outlook, but comfortable enough in his own skin not to make an already complicated, dangerous situation worse by playing unnecessary games.

'Why all the business with the girl?' Fournier asked. 'So complicated, no?'

'I wanted to be sure that you weren't involved in what happened to Eric.' Kite raised the phone, indicating that Fournier had been given a clean bill of health. 'My colleagues tell me you were surprised to hear what happened.'

'I spoke to him only this morning. We were supposed to have dinner tonight at Kitty Fisher's. Eric went to a meeting in Paddington. That's the last I heard from him. What the hell happened?'

'He was thrown from a twelfth-floor balcony,' Kite replied flatly. 'Who was he meeting?'

Plainly in shock, the Frenchman said quietly: 'A woman. Someone we thought would help us. Eric and I were working on a case together, an investigation.'

'An investigation into Grace Mavinga and Yves Duval.' Fournier looked up. 'He told you about this?'

'Only that they were in some kind of relationship, platonic or otherwise, and were "protecting each other", whatever that means. He said your organisation was looking into their affairs as a separate enquiry unrelated to Lucian's Cablean's Woodstein podcast. Is that correct?'

'That is correct. Cablean is one thing, Duval quite another.' For a moment Fournier was silent, evidently coming to terms with the horror of what had happened in Paddington. When he continued, his manner was distracted. 'They met in 1995 as a consequence of Duval's interest in Augustin Bagaza. He had a thing about African women. Grace caught his eye. He became obsessed with her. They formed what you might call a business partnership, though there has always been a sexual element to it.'

He broke off, shaking his head in apparent disbelief. Kite saw the extent to which Appiah's death had affected him.

'They're married?' Kite asked.

The question provoked a mocking laugh. 'Duval is married.

227

But not to Grace. This of course does not stop them from spending a great deal of time together.' He looked up at the black London sky, adding: 'It's a long story.'

'Funny. That's what Eric said to me on the phone this morning.'

'He was your friend.' Fournier extended a hand. 'I am sorry for your loss.'

'Thank you.'

He stepped into a pool of light, eyes intrigued and sharp. His nose was very slightly squashed and the tips of his ears hard and swollen, probably from youthful years at the heart of a rugby scrum. He took out a packet of cigarettes and offered one to Kite. There was a photograph on the packet of a hospital patient with late-stage throat cancer. It made Kite think of Michael Strawson.

'Eric's meeting was set up via a colleague at DGSE,' said Fournier, lighting his own cigarette before Kite's. 'Duval must have got to them.'

'What makes you say that?'

'I know him. He's sending a message. He can't kill me without provoking Paris, so he kills Eric as a way of warning others from cooperating with my investigation.'

'And Cablean? Is he next or not a big enough fish?'

'Next for Duval, you mean?'

Kite nodded, prompting Fournier to take on a slightly conspiratorial air.

'Let me tell you what happened today in New York. I have people watching Cablean, reporting on his activities, protecting him if necessary. We knew he had been targeted by Duval and Mavinga's people. We don't want the world thinking that the French government is in the business of assassinating American citizens, particularly famous ones. Besides, the Woodstein podcast is merely an irritant for the DGSE, more dangerous to you than to us, no?'

'Perhaps.'

'This morning we took down someone we believe was hired to kill Cablean.'

'What do you mean "took down"?'

'Exactly that. My agent incapacitated an individual named Mohammed Suidani on the subway at Times Square. Took his phone, which is currently being examined by our technical teams in DC.'

'Which will likely show that he was hired by Duval and Mavinga?'

'Who else would want Cablean dead?' Fournier's question was evidently rhetorical. 'Maurice Lagarde's memoir, which is the basis for the entire Woodstein story, blames Duval for not acting to arrest Bagaza when he had the chance. Cablean will doubtless say that Duval was complicit in allowing a war criminal to remain at large. Mavinga shot and killed Philippe Vauban. This will obviously become public knowledge if the podcast goes ahead. Hundreds of thousands of listeners around the world will want to know what happened to Bagaza's mistress. There will be pressure on the Senegalese police to reopen the case, on Interpol to track Mavinga down. She likes to clean up problems. She likes to get anybody out of her way who might damage her. There was a reason you nicknamed her "Lady Macbeth".'

A couple had come out of the club, arm in arm, drunkenly stumbling home. Kite encouraged Fournier to follow him down Hertford Street.

'If you can link Suidani to them, if you can prove a conspiracy, that's surely helpful to your investigation?'

'Of course.'

Kite remembered the woman in the business suit he had passed in the lobby of the Moran. He took out his phone and showed Fournier the arrest mugshot of the person who had tried to break into Appiah's room.

'Do you recognise her?'

Fournier tossed his cigarette and seized the phone from Kite's hand.

'That's Lindsey Berida,' he said. 'The woman Eric was due to meet this morning. Where did you get this?'

Kite took the phone back, saying: 'There's a lot we need to discuss.'

33

Kite and Fournier walked the short distance to the BOX 88 penthouse in Belgravia where Kite had been living prior to the Dubai operation. The apartment was much as he had left it: sterile and sparsely furnished with a smell of tobacco from the heavy smoker who lived on the floor below. A cleaner had dusted the tops of the paintings in the living room: a modernist oil of Edinburgh Castle; an etching by Lucian Freud; an Auerbach charcoal of a standing female nude.

'Are these what I think they are?' Fournier asked, taking off his jacket and looping it around the back of a chair. He had telephoned his wife to say that he was working late and would not be coming home. 'Your safe houses are better equipped than ours. We hang IKEA prints of Brooklyn Bridge and Marilyn Monroe. That's if the budget can extend to this.'

'They're mine,' Kite told him. 'I was living here for a while. Call it a storage facility.'

'You collect?'

'I have a tradition of buying a painting after a successful operation. Although that one' – he pointed to the picture of Edinburgh Castle which he had originally bought for Martha – 'was a gift to a girlfriend. She gave it back when we broke up.'

Fournier produced a worldly shrug and showed himself around; Kite assumed he wanted to be sure that they were alone. Somebody from The Cathedral had left Kite's luggage in the master bedroom. He took a bottle of Vacqueyras from the wine rack, pulled the cork and poured each of them a glass.

'Are you happy to talk in here?' he asked, following Fournier into the open-plan living room. 'You'll have to trust there are no microphones. I've had to act very quickly on this, as you can imagine.'

Fournier settled into one of the sofas. He was a surprisingly heavy man; the springs moaned as he made himself comfortable.

'It's fine. I have nothing to fear from a microphone. Besides, we are friends, no?'

'I hope so. We certainly have a shared interest in bringing these people to justice.'

The horror of Appiah's death hit Kite suddenly; he thought of his still-warm body in a London morgue, of another wretched, pointless loss in which he was somehow complicit.

'You are OK?' Fournier asked.

'I'm fine. It's been a long day. Tell me what you know about Martha Raine.'

'What about her, please?'

'Do you think she's in danger?'

Fournier seemed to be confused by the question.

'Why? What good would it serve Duval to harm her? Why would Mavinga want her dead?'

'You said that she likes to get anybody out of her way who might damage her. And we know that she enjoys killing people.'

'She sends others to do this for her. They both do. They employ the likes of Suidani and Berida for their dirty work. The danger to Martha Raine is one of interrogation. If Cablean finds her, he will ask very professionally how to find "Lockie". If Mavinga or Duval want to use Martha to find you, their people will not be so polite.' Fournier was studying the Auerbach. 'Did you know that Cablean visited your school and asked about you?'

'He went to *Alford*?' Kite pictured the dogged Cablean, gumshoeing around in the ancient, gothic cloisters, bewildered by the sight of teenage boys walking past in tailsuits and bow ties. 'Did they tell him anything?'

'According to our most recent assessment of Cablean's progress, nothing. Alford does not have an address for you. You don't go to any of their school reunions. For this I do not blame you. It's a pointless nostalgia, no? We look at one another, try to see who has made a success of life, who is fat, who is grey.'

Kite opened the doors onto the balcony. In the distance he could see the lights of the London Eye, the Shard blinking for aircraft. He invited the Frenchman to join him. 'I steer clear of Alford,' he said. 'Not just because of work. There was an Old Alfordian from my year in Brick Street tonight. They're everywhere. Politicians. Actors. Journalists. The people I want to see from those days, I see. The ones I don't, I don't.'

'A wise strategy.'

Fournier had brought the wine and refilled their glasses. Kite turned to him.

'Who in your organisation is happy for the podcast to go ahead?'

'I don't think we should concern ourselves with this. There are bound to be those who wish to gain an advantage from an embarrassment of this kind, just as I am sure that you have enemies who would welcome your downfall. I can tell you with absolute certainty that there are individuals inside DGSE who are very angry about my investigation into one of their own. They don't care that Yves Duval allowed a war criminal to walk the streets. They don't care that he then formed a relationship with

233

that war criminal's girlfriend which has led to the deaths of French citizens and soldiers.'

'What do you mean by that?'

'Allow me to finish.' This said patiently, politely. 'They see my investigation as a betrayal of the Service. Others, like myself, the younger generation if you like, believe that in order to move into a more enlightened future the DGSE must first confront the sins of its past. The same goes for France. We are in a state of denial about our historical crimes. I include Rwanda in this, of course. But as I say, none of that is your concern. We will find who killed Eric Appiah. We will avenge him. The important thing tonight is to focus on Cablean. What can you offer him that will satisfy his famous appetite for the truth?'

'Just that,' Kite replied. 'The truth.'

'You would tell him the whole story? You would go to him?'

'Why not? This isn't a case of publish and be damned. If certain details come out, the repercussions for Martha's family would be catastrophic. My career would be over, certainly, but only because Cablean had been fed the wrong narrative.'

'I do not follow.'

'Philippe Vauban was not a paid assassin tasked by MI6 with the removal of Augustin Bagaza. He was a war correspondent with chronic PTSD who suffered a psychotic episode as a result of taking Lariam. Our intention was to kidnap Bagaza and to bring him to justice. What we didn't know was that Vauban's Tutsi girlfriend had been murdered in the genocide. Philippe opted to leave that detail out of his résumé until it was too late. In a sense he was ahead of us all the time. For him the operation was simply an opportunity to exact revenge.'

'It's a better story.'

'What do you mean?'

'I mean for Cablean. It's a great narrative. The heartbroken war correspondent with post-traumatic stress tricks British and American intelligence into supporting his plan, then betrays them by killing the target in a crime of passion. If Camus were alive, he would write it.'

'Perhaps,' Kite replied. Something had become clear in his mind. 'I propose that I approach Cablean, tell him the full story, ask that my name and the names of any active French intelligence officers be removed from the broadcast, but otherwise give Woodstein our blessing. Do you agree?'

Fournier wordlessly raised his glass of wine, halfway to a toast. Kite saw that he wasn't yet ready to seal the understanding.

'I would go even further. With your help, and with the assistance of the British authorities, we can bring Yves Duval and Grace Mavinga to justice. The incident today in New York and Berida's arrest have handed us vital ammunition. This is no longer an investigation solely into terrorist financing.'

'Duval and Muvinga are funnelling money to Islamist groups?'

'In effect, yes. They will launder and provide cover for whoever pays their 20 per cent fee. In this they are not ethical of course. Boko Haram. Allied Democratic Forces. Al-Shabaab. It doesn't matter. They are interested solely in the accumulation of money and the power which goes with it. If anything, Mavinga is even more obsessed with money and social status than Duval. She parties with Tory donors and Conservative MPs here in London, attends the sort of events that make their way into the pages of *Tatler* and *Daily Mail* online. She has blood on her hands but she also has money. The people who want that money are entirely without moral scruple. They turn a blind eye.'

'It's a modern disease,' Kite observed.

'Mavinga's relationship with Duval is perhaps the most intriguing aspect of all this. Thirty years at each other's side, enriching the other, seducing and enabling and killing. It's a love story out of Kafka.'

Kite smiled, enjoying the fact that within the space of five minutes Fournier had dropped both Camus and Kafka into conversation in a way which seemed inimitably French.

'How did it begin?'

'Their relationship?' Fournier placed his glass on the ground and looked out over the vast city. 'It began in Mali in 1995, a few weeks after you last set eyes on Mavinga. It is a tale of greed and corruption, of a spy who became a criminal mastermind, and the woman who aided and abetted him every step of the way.'

Kite picked up the glass, refilled it and handed it back.

'I would like to hear that story.'

34

Grace Mavinga – calling herself Aminata Diallo, the first of dozens of aliases she would employ across the next thirty years – had been in Bamako for six days when Yves Duval came for her.

She was sitting alone in the lobby of a modest hotel in the centre of the city reading an account of Augustin Bagaza's death in the *International Herald Tribune* which she had purloined from an American aid worker. Her English was not fluent in those days, but she was nevertheless able to understand the story and to realise that the Senegalese authorities were hunting for her. Of Peter Galvin there was no mention, only of Philippe Vauban, the French photo-journalist who had butchered Augustin and who had been shot by her 'apparently in self-defence'. Vauban himself was said to have been suffering from Post-Traumatic Stress Disorder – a psychological condition of which Grace was previously unaware – and had experienced a psychotic reaction to the malaria medication 'Lariam'.

She read on. To her fury Bagaza was described in a later paragraph as a 'war criminal' sought by the authorities in connection with the deaths of 'tens of thousands of Tutsis' during the Rwandan genocide. This enraged her. Why did nobody say the same things about the RDF thugs who had murdered countless Hutus in northern Rwanda during the civil war? Papers like the *International Herald Tribune* only ever told one side of the story. It was the West's refusal to acknowledge RDF atrocities and their total disregard for Hutu life which had caused men like Augustin Bagaza to defend themselves and to fight back against the Tutsi scum. Surely they could understand that?

'Grace?'

A white man was standing in front of her wearing pressed denim jeans and a pale linen shirt. There was a benign smile on his face, a packet of cigarettes poking out of the hip pocket of his trousers, red marks on his sneakers. Alarmed that a stranger should know her name, Mavinga stood up and attempted to leave.

'There's no need for that,' Duval told her. 'I'm here as a friend.'

'I am not Grace. My name is Aminata.'

He placed his hand gently on her arm, the very first time that he would touch her. There was something about this moment of physical contact which persuaded Grace to sit down. Duval joined her on the wide settee.

'I know a lot about you,' he began. 'I know that you lived at number 35 Rue Kennedy with Augustin Bagaza, a man you professed to love. I know that you met him in Kigali and witnessed many of the things which took place in Rwanda last year. You look alarmed, Grace. Please don't be alarmed. I am not a police officer. I am not here to arrest you. In fact, I admire you. I admire what you did in Dakar. I only wish that I could have stopped what happened. I am here to help. I can see a future for you. For us. All I want is the opportunity to talk.'

'How did you find me?'

Duval pointed upwards towards the rooms in the hotel.

'You made some telephone calls to your sister in Kinshasa. My associates are monitoring the line she uses.

238

It was easy then to pinpoint your location. I'm just glad I reached you before you moved on.'

What was strange was that, despite this revelation, Grace trusted Duval from the outset. She knew that the French government was helping *genocidaires*; it made sense that he might want to protect her. When she asked him about Peter Galvin, describing their encounter at Thiossane, it became evident that Duval had no connection with British intelligence. He told her that his team in Dakar had thwarted an attempt by the CIA and MI6 to arrest Bagaza at Rue Kennedy. He had not come across Galvin but assumed he was part of the same joint task force.

'He is not important anyway,' he assured her. 'All this belongs to your past. I want you to work for me now.'

And so she did. Two days later they travelled by aeroplane to Abidjan, checking into two separate rooms at a five-star hotel in the embassy district. Duval paid for everything. He bought her clothes and perfumes, soaps and shoes. He treated her just as Augustin had treated her, only Duval was much sharper, more distinguished, and he never pressed home his desire for her. His longing had been obvious from the first moment she had set eyes on him; Grace Mavinga was a striking woman and it was rare that a man failed to notice or comment on her beauty. Yet Duval's longing was charmingly withheld. He never threatened her or tried to blackmail her into cooperation; it was understood that she would comply with him because he was evidently her ticket to freedom. He allowed her to walk the streets of Abidjan alone, to spend time in the hotel spa; he gave her cash with which to go shopping and bought her books which he thought she might enjoy. In the evenings, over dinner, he described what was going on in northern Zaire and the horrors of the refugee camps. Duval's intention in telling her what he had witnessed was clear: instead of a bottomless future in Zaire as a Hutu pariah, she would be a free woman. Grace would not have to sell her body to the white businessmen frequenting the upmarket hotels of Abidjan. She would not need to knife a man who tried to rape her in the camps. She would avoid the cholera and the AIDS which had ravaged her sisters and brothers in other parts of Africa. She would become middle class and sophisticated.

Yves never judged Mavinga for her past nor criticised Augustin for his actions in Kigali; he understood that what the Americans and Europeans regarded as a 'genocide' was much more complicated than it seemed; there were a thousand snakes and murderers among the Tutsi population who had committed unspeakable crimes and yet would never be brought to justice. He spoke with the authority of a man who had not just read about these issues in the pages of *Le Monde* or the *International Herald Tribune*, but who had gone out and experienced the world for himself. Duval was tough, in every way braver than Augustin had been. Grace remembered Bagaza pleading for his life like a coward; she was embarrassed by the memory. Talking to Duval made her feel seen by a man for the first time; no person had ever come closer to understanding what made her tick. He was young and fit, with a self-confidence which made him even more handsome. So finally, on their fifth evening in Côte d'Ivoire, she invited him into her hotel room and they became lovers.

That night Yves told her that he had been in love from the first moment he had set eyes on her. He admitted that he had followed her around Dakar, listened to her voice on the Rue Kennedy microphones and fantasised about touching her. Grace realised that Duval must have bugged her most intimate moments with Augustin. Far from being outraged by this, she was secretly aroused. It was the first of a thousand secrets they would share.

Duval's plan took shape over the next several months. He wanted her to become an asset for the DGSE, solely under his control, answerable only to him and free to leave whenever she chose. She was to be paid a European salary every month which would afford her a good lifestyle in most African cities and leave a substantial sum available to transfer to Agnes, her sister in Kinshasa. Duval did not want to exploit Grace's beauty, though he was not naive enough to think that it could not work to her advantage. He wanted her to form a relationship with a particular minister in the Ivorian government and to report back whatever she discovered. He gave her two false passports – one Kenyan, the other Ugandan – and taught her how to work as a courier. Over time he gave further instructions in surveillance, forgery and clandestine messaging. Grace marvelled at his knowledge of this parallel world, his mastery of languages, his energy and ambition. Before long she could not imagine life without him. She knew that Duval had a wife in France and two young children, but none of that mattered to her. As long as she could be with him, learn from him and benefit from his generosity, she would be satisfied. She felt blessed by her extraordinary good fortune.

35

'So she didn't mind about Duval's wife?' Kite asked, thinking of Isobel fast asleep in Djursholm. He was standing in the kitchen waiting for a Nespresso machine to heat up. It was just before two o'clock in the morning. Fournier was seated in an armchair, still drinking the wine.

'Mind?' the Frenchman replied. 'Why should she mind? Duval left DGSE in 2002 to set himself up in the private sector. He was spending all his time in Africa. His family were still in Paris, he visited them when it suited him, but his new life was in Nairobi.'

'With Grace at his side?'

'Precisely.' Fournier was forced to stop talking as the coffee machine growled and spat, espresso materialising into a small blue cup. 'Duval's marriage survives in the way that a lot of enduring, unhappy marriages survive. They spend no time together. He moves around the world meeting clients, servicing their needs. His wife stays in Paris spending as much of his money as she can.'

Kite handed the coffee to Fournier, encouraging him to continue.

'Nobody in DGSE cared what Duval was doing. It was a crazy time. The world had too many things on its mind – Afghanistan, Iraq, al-Qaeda – to be concerned about a former French intelligence officer laundering money for despots and criminals and making himself rich in the process. The Service was aware of his relationship with Grace Mavinga, but they never connected her to Bagaza. Why would they? He had given her a completely new identity. He told colleagues that she was just a useful piece of ass. The truth of course is that he quickly turned her into a very rich and successful businesswoman with control of several hotels and restaurants in East Africa, various small businesses in France – grocery stores, petrol stations, even dry cleaners – using them for unlicensed money transmissions, false invoicing, large cash deposits and so forth. It was only when Duval started taking money from ADF, from al-Shabaab, setting up false charities and washing the money through the London property market, that we began to take notice.'

'Did Mavinga and Duval have children together?'

Kite wanted to understand more about the relationship; their business dealings were of secondary importance to him.

'She couldn't have children,' Fournier replied. 'There have been other men in her life, just as there have been many other women in Duval's. As far as I can discern, Grace was never able to conceive. It is also perfectly possible that, from her point of view, their relationship is now largely transactional. Duval is important only in as much as he can provide her with the sort of lifestyle she has come to enjoy.'

'And Duval has never been arrested? Not in thirty years?'

'Nor Grace.' Fournier was again interrupted by the growl of the machine, a thin stream of black coffee filling Kite's cup. 'There have been Suspicious Activity Reports, of course. There have been companies and organisations which have caught the attention of the authorities. There was an individual we believe was linked to Duval's network who was imprisoned for dealing narcotics, but it proved impossible to connect them in any meaningful way. He is very careful. They both are.'

Kite tested the temperature of the coffee with a knuckle and drank it as a shot.

'Much of what Duval and Mavinga have managed to achieve has been done with the assistance of a particular London law firm, Rycroft Maule, which specialises in making rich people even richer and keeping governments off their backs. I don't mean to be disrespectful to your wonderful country, Lockie, but you know as well as I do that the UK has been enabling the likes of Yves Duval and Grace Mavinga for years. Your lawyers prepare their tax returns, your PR firms polish their images and if any journalist wants to write about them, their editor knows that a seven-figure libel action is waiting just around the corner.'

'It's much worse than that,' Kite replied with an air of amused fatalism. 'Successive British governments have actively encouraged anyone with a large enough chequebook to get it out in London and start spending. Dirty money washes through the construction sector, the hospitality industry, car dealerships, football clubs, you name it. Without it, the British economy would probably go into freefall.'

Fournier grinned behind his cup of coffee, evidently pleased to be dealing with a man who seemed to share his own political outlook.

'Mavinga uses Graham Platt at Rycroft Maule,' he said. 'You may have heard of him. He was one of a number of London lawyers accused of helping Russian oligarchs hide their assets in the wake of the Ukraine invasion. Platt set up Kisenso Holdings on Mavinga's behalf, an entity of which she is the undisclosed beneficial owner. Eric was led to believe that Lindsey Berida had information about Kisenso, but as we have already discussed, he was being led into a trap.'

'Graham Platt?' Kite checked the spelling of the Christian name. 'Presumably you have eyes and ears on Rycroft Maule?'

'Sadly not,' Fournier replied. 'London is your territory. I can't get it signed off.'

'Well, you're talking to somebody who can. It's time we put the squeeze on these people.'

'That may be harder than you think.' Fournier's characteristic self-confidence had suddenly deserted him. 'Mavinga and Duval have vanished.'

36

'You don't touch me like you used to touch me,' she said. 'When I was younger, you wanted me all the time. Now I don't know what's happened. Maybe you found somebody else?'

It was a game they had started playing in these days of anxiety and doubt. The world they had built for themselves was collapsing around them. Grace Mavinga knew how Yves Duval would react to her question; it was so easy to provoke him into the correct response.

'That's not true,' he said, exactly as she had anticipated. 'You know there's nobody else.' He crossed the room to come back to her, a man of sixty-five who looked twenty years younger. His legs were tanned, his chest lean and taut – he had spent an hour in the gym every day for two decades. Duval sat on the edge of the bed and touched her, looking into her eyes. He was wearing a white hotel robe, his hair still wet from the shower. 'Do you really feel that?' he asked. 'That I don't touch you in the same way?'

Grace enjoyed the feeling of his hand. She wanted to prolong the game. It amused her; it was a distraction from Cablean. The story the American intended to tell, however biased and malign, would inevitably force the police to reopen their investigation into the killing of Philippe Vauban.

She turned away, facing the window as if in a sulk; she knew that Duval loved the sight of her long naked back. The watch he had bought her in Zurich was nestled on the bedside table next to the Cartier brooch from their holiday in Capri. The diamonds in the watch caught the morning light, clean and sharp against the white cloth. For a fleeting instant, as quick as a tiny bird which passed outside the window, Grace understood that her belongings, these beautiful jewels, were the reward for her commitment and cunning, for all the years of working alongside Yves. This moment, right now, was why she had taken the risks she had taken: jewels on a nightstand in a €1,600-a-night villa at La Duchesse de Palmar in Mauritius; Egyptian cotton sheets against her skin; a breakfast tray of freshly squeezed grapefruit juice, sliced mango and *pains aux raisins* so fresh they might have been baked in Paris that morning. Her life was a life of walk-in rain showers and soaps by Aesop and Penhaligon. Mavinga bought clothes from Alaïa, Hervé Léger, Valentino. If she wanted something by Tom Ford, she bought something by Tom Ford. She had a Chanel dress in her apartment in London which she had worn only once, on a first-class flight from Nairobi.

Now everything she had taken for granted was under threat – the Louboutins and the Lanesborough membership, the tables at Nobu and La Petite Maison, even the monogrammed Hermès Birkin Duval had given her for her fiftieth birthday. She might never see it, never use it. She was convinced that she would soon be going to prison. Her freedom was under threat from men like Jean-François Fournier and Lucian Cablean, men who knew nothing of the horrors she had endured, the sacrifices she had been forced to make in order to live this way. How dare a bureaucrat spy and a here-today-gone-tomorrow journalist try to make their names by destroying hers? How dare they think they could take on Grace Mavinga? She despised them.

'What's the matter, my love?' Duval asked.

'I'm angry.'

'You're not angry.' She felt his hand glide towards her buttocks. 'I remember how you were last night, how you were when I kissed you this morning. You don't fake with me, Grace. You don't fake with anybody.'

She continued to face the window.

'How do you know that I don't fake my pleasure?'

That made Duval laugh. Suddenly he grabbed her, turning her over, acting jealous, pretending to be angry. They made love again, the sweat between them like the first nights in Abidjan. In the aftermath of her ecstasy Grace thought again of the brooch, of the jewels. It would all be torn away from her if she did not act quickly. Yves would be arrested. These would be their last days together.

'There is something I have to tell you,' she said suddenly. 'I made the wrong choice.'

'You often do that,' Duval replied as though she was talking about something as mundane as a restaurant reservation. He was catching his breath, lying on his back against her arm, still hard, full of black coffee and Viagra.

'Appiah could trace back to us. Suidani too.'

'We know this. We've been over it.' He wiped sweat from his face and distractedly picked up a stray hair from the bed, dropping it on the floor. 'What do you mean about making the wrong choice?'

'I made you go after Cablean. I made you send Suidani.'

'He had been good for us before,' Duval replied. 'I thought he would be good for us again.'

She loved it that he refused to blame her; implicit in his answer was the understanding that they had taken the decision together.

'I don't remember things ever being so fragile,' she said pitifully.

It was not the sort of remark Duval was used to hearing from her. He stood up and put on the dressing gown. He

248

again explained that Suidani had most likely been incapacitated by 'Action Division', the black ops wing of the
DGSE; it did not follow that either of them would be
arrested as a consequence. For a start, Cablean was still
alive. What could they be accused of?

'We have to let him tell his fucking story,' Mavinga
concluded, almost spitting the words in fury. 'Maybe nobody
will care what he says. What do people worry about these
days anyway? Only themselves. Nobody thinks about the
past. Nobody cares about Africa. Maybe we will both be safe.'

'You, maybe.'

Even this was said with a kind of embattled irony; Duval
had always been possessed of tireless self-confidence. He
knew that his money and connections and his old friends
in Paris would protect him.

'And the girl who helped to take care of Appiah?'

'So they arrested her. So what? Perhaps they can place
her in Paddington at the site of Appiah's fall. So what?
The link with us is even more tenuous than the link to
Suidani. I told you already. They have no evidence.'

A tropical bird was singing in a tree somewhere outside
the window, a sound of paradise.

'I want to sell up London.' Duval sat back on the bed,
touching his lover's belly. Mavinga moved his hand away,
retreating into frustration and paranoia. 'I want to clear
out my apartment. Get rid of everything. I won't feel safe
there. I could be arrested. Even *you* don't go to London or
Paris any more. You know the dangers.' She sat up, propped
herself against the headboard and pulled a sheet over her
body to cover her breasts. 'Why else have you bought a
boat, a villa here in Mauritius? Because we could be arrested
at any moment.'

'They have no evidence, Grace,' Duval repeated, picking
up a chunk of mango from one of the breakfast trays.
'And the boat is for you. For us. We can retire.' He swallowed the fruit. 'Go to London if it makes you feel better.

Sell the apartment. You will always have enough. Do what makes you happy. But come back here.'

It was not the first time he had spoken about retirement; if she was honest, the prospect of it bored her. Mavinga knew that if she lived in a sleepy tax haven like Mauritius she would grow restless. She would miss Paris and Dubai, the trips to Venice and Capri. She would miss feeling significant.

'*Putain!*'

She leaped out of bed and walked across the room, wrapped in the sheet.

'It feels like there's no time. They know about me. They know I have properties, not just the apartment. Everything! If I don't go now, they take it all. Asset freezes. I'll be treated like a fucking Russian.'

'Then go,' said Duval. She was beginning to test his patience. 'Write to Platt. Tell him you want to organise your affairs. Kisenso is the greatest point of vulnerability. Platt will have someone he trusts who can act as a care-taker. Transfer any vulnerable assets until the dust has settled. Then, if they come after you, there is nothing to prove that you ever did anything wrong.'

She walked to a nightstand and picked up her watch.

'If it was easy to kill Appiah, then it's easy to kill this idiot bureaucrat Fournier. They are the same. Open targets.' She was allowing her anger and fear free rein. 'You have lost your strength if you won't confront Fournier. Who has he spoken to? What does he plan for us? You will let this man ruin our lives. We could go to prison. We could lose all this, and you don't care.'

She would not go back to the life she had known when she was young. She would not be ordinary. Duval followed her into the bathroom, speaking to her reflection in a vast mirror.

'Five minutes ago you said we should let Cablean say or do whatever he wants to say or do!' He knew all too well that dealing with the mercurial Grace when she was in this sort of mood was impossible. His strategy was always to remain calm and reasonable. 'Now you are saying the opposite. My love, we cannot kill Jean-François Fournier any more than we can kill everyone in the Serious Fraud Office or Companies House.'

'The British spy, then,' she said. 'Galvin. He will tell Cablean too much.'

'Who?'

'Peter Galvin. The man who spoke to us in the nightclub. The spy!' She was shocked that Duval had forgotten his name. 'Anybody who is connected to this, anybody who threatens us, they must be stopped.'

'Nobody knows who Galvin is,' Duval replied. 'He vanished years ago.'

'I don't believe that. I don't believe you have tried. All you have to do is find Martha Raine. What happened to her? You did nothing to find her either. You would not even do this simple thing for me.'

He moved towards her, taking both her hands in his.

'Martha Raine has disappeared. Nobody knows where she is. But if you want, I can very easily send a warning to Fournier. The kind he won't be able to ignore.'

'Do it then,' Mavinga replied. 'Do it quickly.'

37

With two plump DGSE files on Duval and Mavinga loaded onto his laptop, Kite was at Heathrow en route to a meeting with Lucian Cablean by seven o'clock in the morning. He had slept at the penthouse for no more than an hour, waking to Cara at the door with coffee and croissants and a plea to go with him to New York.

'I've never been. It's a gap in my CV. I ought to meet my colleagues at The Stadium, understand something about the history of BOX 88. And if by chance I have some spare time to visit the Met and go shopping on Fifth Avenue, where's the harm?'

'Nice try,' he told her. 'But I need you here in London. It's just a whistlestop visit, no more than forty-eight hours.'

Masood had turned up shortly afterwards, crisp in a suit and clean-shaven. He had put in place measures to cover the phones at Rycroft Maule.

'Let's just arrest Platt,' Cara suggested. 'He'll know where the bodies are buried. What are we waiting for?'

'We can do better than that,' Kite replied obliquely. 'Let me talk to Cablean first, get things straight.'

Kite had called Isobel on his way to the airport, telling her that he would be home by the weekend. Again, she asked him not to make promises he could not keep; then she switched the call to FaceTime so that Kite could watch Ingrid sitting on the swings in Djursholm.

'Where are you off to?' she asked, noticing that her husband was in a taxi.

'Just a meeting,' Kite replied, glad that the overnight bag at his feet was not in shot. New York meant Martha, which might lead to unnecessary tension between them. 'I'll give you a ring tonight. Kiss our little girl for me.'

By the late afternoon he was queuing at JFK Homeland Security, no fast-track diplomatic passport, no VIP channel for a trusted ally; Kite was just another British tourist travelling on an ESTA visa. Then a ninety-minute shunt through rush-hour Brooklyn and the Lincoln Tunnel before emerging into Manhattan, a place he visited as infrequently as possible. New York was a city with too many ghosts: principally of Martha and 9/11, but also of those halcyon days in 1995 when Kite had been learning his trade, before the catastrophe of Dakar and the subsequent unravelling of his personal life. So intense was Kite's aversion to the city that he tried to hold BOX 88 meetings in Washington DC or to persuade his American colleagues to make the journey across the Atlantic. But Cablean had left him no choice; Kite was the only man with the authority, not to mention the personal justification, to negotiate with him. If the existence of BOX 88 was revealed in the podcast, the consequences would be ruinous.

There was also the question of Martha's whereabouts. To Kite's frustration, The Stadium had still not been able to find her; her apartment had been watched from dawn until dusk and a member of staff had twice rung the bell but received no answer. Martha's new phone number was still being investigated, the old one having been taken offline. She had sent no emails for three days, nor had there been any transactions on her banking cards for a similar length of time. Kite was aware that BOX 88 personnel in New York had better things to do than track

253

down his ex-girlfriend, but nevertheless he berated The Stadium for not taking the task seriously enough. He was concerned; he could not discern what purpose it would serve Duval or Mavinga to have Martha killed, yet the timing of her sudden disappearance was profoundly unnerving.

He had booked into a hotel in the Meatpacking District so that he would be just a few blocks north of the apartment she shared with her husband, Jonas, and their two teenage children. Kite had not been back to that part of lower Manhattan for more than twenty-five years and found it much changed. Back in 1995, with Rudy Giuliani yet to cleanse Manhattan of its pimps and thieves, the Meatpacking District had been an ill-lit, crime-infested no-go zone not far removed from the decaying atmosphere of *Mean Streets* and *Taxi Driver*. Walking one night down West 13th Street, Kite had come across a weeping British tourist whose rental car had been smashed open and her luggage pilfered. On another occasion, with Martha, he had been offered crack at ten dollars a bag by a man whose face had been ravaged by boils and scars. Kite had loved the atmosphere of the neighbourhood at all times of day and night, the truck drivers loading flanks of beef and pork at dawn, fast-talking chefs cutting deals for the best cuts of Porterhouse. Those ten square blocks were pure theatre, insults and comedy traded on every corner, muggers lurking in the shadows, portly cops on the beat who looked as though they had walked off the set of *NYPD Blue*.

All that was now gone. Kite was aware how much New York had changed in the new century, but as he made his way south towards Martha's building on Bank Street he saw the extent to which the yuppies and hipsters had won. Just as Giuliani had become an alcohol-ravaged apologist for Trump, the Meatpacking District had been transformed into consecutive blocks of converted warehouses boasting branches of Bally, Taschen and Zadig & Voltaire; exposed

254

brick restaurants sparkled with beautiful clientele sipping ginger Cosmos and glasses of Pinot Grigio. The only concession to unruly behaviour was a perpetual smell of weed; cannabis had been legalised in the state and was now as pervasive as cigarettes had once been. Yet Kite saw no smokers. Joggers, yes; women coming back from yoga classes; but fewer bums and drunks. Nobody bothered him on the sidewalks; indeed several people even smiled as Kite passed them, an unthinkable phenomenon in the New York of old. Was it better or worse? Kite concluded that the city was rather like his own life as a married man and father: simpler and more straightforward yet shorn of both surprise and despondency.

He reached Bank Street, walking towards his past. Martha lived on the fifth floor of a building overlooking the Hudson River, roughly at the point where Sully had set down his plane more than a decade earlier. Kite did not know what he planned to do or say should he find Jonas at home; he wanted only to hear Martha's voice, to know that she was safe. Then he would be on his way.

He walked up a short flight of steps and pressed the buzzer for 10E. There was a delay. A man came out of the building with a dachshund on a lead and said nothing as he passed. Then the scratch and void of a voice coming on the line.

'Hello?'

It was a woman. Not Martha.

'Hi,' Kite responded, his heart quickening. 'Are Martha and Jonas at home?'

'You're the third person today.' The accent was Brooklyn central casting, sharp and confrontational. 'They moved out last week.'

'Any idea where they went?'

'What am I, the Yellow Pages?'

'This is apartment 10E?'

'Last time I checked.'

Kite apologised and walked away, sending a Signal to Jerry at The Cathedral asking him to look more deeply into Jonas and Martha's activities in the previous two weeks. Perhaps it was a simple clerical error: they had moved house, to a bigger place in Connecticut or Long Island, and The Stadium had failed to notice because they had not prioritised the search. But why three days without banking or emails? And why the moribund phone number?

He had one more call to make and found a cocktail bar on Washington Street. It was almost two o'clock in the morning in Senegal, but the time had been prearranged. Kite ordered a beer, found a table near a window at the back and dialled the number.

Omar Gueye picked up first ring, speaking to Kite in English.

'Right on time. How are you, old friend?'

'I'm well,' Kite replied. 'And you?'

'I'm alive. Keeping track of fourteen restaurants in five cities is taxing, but I have good people on my team. How long has it been?'

'A long time. Are you always up this late?'

'Always. You know me. I don't need much sleep. Besides, it's cooler at night.'

Kite pictured the scene: vast birds floating on thermals over the ocean; goats asleep in the half-light of dusty streets; waves lapping against the jetty at Lagon.

'Did you get the information I sent?' he asked.

'I did. And I want to thank you for it.'

The waiter in the cocktail bar called out to a colleague working the room; something about turning the music down. Rain was drumming fiercely on the sidewalks, drawing customers to the windows who gazed at the soaked streets.

'So you're interested?'

'Of course I am interested.'

'And you're in good health? No cataracts, no Covid?'

A booming laugh. 'I am not that old, Lockie. What are you now? At least fifty, no?'

'Fifty-one. And feeling every year of it.'

For a moment neither man spoke. There was just the noise of the falling rain and an image in Kite's head of fat white men falling out of Imperial at two o'clock in the morning.

'Where are you?' he asked.

'I'm in St Louis. I have a restaurant up here. But there are no tourists. The ocean is swallowing up the island. The French are digging up the roads. And nobody is eating in the restaurants. St Louis is where people have come to pray for hundreds of years. In Islam we regard it as a sacred place. So I pray, because this is where prayers are supposed to be answered. But nothing, Lockie. No tourists. No answered prayers.'

That beautiful old city, crumbling into ruin. Kite remembered a desperately thin, coughing child outside the Hôtel de la Poste, no older than three or four, dressed in rags, begging Martha to take him back to England. They had given him food, bought him medicine, not once seen a relative or even a friend caring for him.

'I have waited a long time for this,' Omar said suddenly.

Kite took a sip of beer and set the bottle down on the table. Into the crackling line he replied: 'We all have.'

257

38

Azhar Masood was done for the day and about to disappear
into the bowels of Canary Wharf station when Jerry Walters
caught up with him at the ticket barriers waving a two-page
document.

'Maz!'

Masood turned. He was on his way to watch his beloved
Arsenal play a Europa League match at the Emirates. Any
further delay would make him late for kick-off.

'Did I forget to sign something?'

A trader in a pinstriped suit murmured, 'In your own
time, mate' as he pushed past him.

'I think we may have something.' Jerry tapped the
document. 'The name "Aminata Diallo" appears in
Lockie's notes relating to Lucian Cablean and the Appiah
investigation.'

'Go on.'

'It was one of Grace Mavinga's earliest aliases. A
number traced to a cell phone in Cape Town was used
this morning to call Graham Platt, Mavinga's lawyer at
Rycroft Maule. I was told it was a male voice, local to
judge by the accent. They don't have a name yet but
they're working on the caller.'

'Show me.'

Jerry handed the transcript to Masood adding: 'Presumably it's somebody Mavinga works with closely, somebody she trusts.'

CAPE TOWN (CT): Mr Platt?

GRAHAM PLATT (GP): Speaking.

CT: I'm phoning on behalf of your client, Aminata Diallo.

GP: (hesitancy) Oh yes. How is she?

CT: Aminata has come to a decision. She'd like to sell her London properties, including the apartment in Hampstead, and to move permanently to Nairobi.

GP: I see.

CT: Also, in view of the current climate, which I believe she has spoken to you about in the recent past several times, Miss Diallo also thinks it would be wise to make significant changes to some of the financial arrangements you put in place for her.

GP: I'm afraid I can't discuss that with anyone other than Amina (sic).

CT: That's fine, Mr Platt. Easy and understood. This call is simply to arrange a meeting in London, as soon as next week if that's possible. Are you available?

GP: I'm not going anywhere. I have one or two lunches in the diary, an evening event at the Turf Club, but yes, I will be in London. I assume Miss Diallo wants to meet in person?

CT: She's prepared to sign whatever paperwork you think will be necessary. Her intention is to move her personal belongings out of the Hampstead property and to leave the UK as soon as possible.

GP: Why the sudden change of mind, might I ask? Why the rush?

CT: She can explain that when she sees you.

GP: I'm sorry to repeat myself, but my office can't prepare any contracts or paperwork of any kind without express permission from my client.

CT: Of course, Mr Platt. She will send you her instructions by courier tonight. She doesn't trust email at the moment. In the current climate.

GP: [inaudible].

CT: So can I give Aminata next Wednesday afternoon, the 11th, at 3 p.m. as a possible time?

GP: Hold on one moment, please.

CT: Of course, sir.

[break, 10 secs. CT humming, unintelligible]

GP: Yes, that's fine. Wednesday 11th, here at my office, 3 p.m. But I would ask Miss Diallo to confirm that by telephone in the usual way, please.

CT: Of course. I'll make sure she does that. In the usual way.

GP: Thank you.

CT: Goodbye, sir.

GP: Goodbye.

'She's panicking,' said Masood. 'She can feel the net closing in. Has Lockie seen this?'

'No, sir. He's in New York.'

'Tell him. And get me flight manifests for Grace Mavinga and Aminata Diallo. Cross-check with Fournier, he'll have other aliases. It's time we paid a visit to Graham Platt.'

39

Kite awoke just after dawn, ran south along the Hudson River as far as Teardrop Park then back through the West Village. There was no overnight news of Martha, instead a message from Masood revealing that metadata from a phone belonging to the woman arrested at the Moran hotel placed her in Paddington Basin on three occasions in the days leading up to Appiah's murder.

Kite ate breakfast alone in the Standard Grill, again reprimanding The Stadium for not looking more proactively for Martha. The Cathedral had arranged for him to meet Cablean in his office at Columbia University at ten o'clock. Just after nine, Cablean sent a text requesting a change of time and venue; could they instead meet at Piksers, a deli on Amsterdam Avenue, at eleven? Kite replied to say that this would be fine, wondering what had prompted the switch. Perhaps Cablean was concerned, with some justification, that his workplace was bugged. He had been told that a British intelligence officer named 'John' with first-hand knowledge of the Dakar operation had flown to New York to speak to him. Cablean had been asked to attend the meeting alone, with his cell phone switched off and placed in a Faraday bag, with no other recording devices available to him. These were conditions to which the

American agreed; he had asked to be able to write notes and London had raised no objection. Cablean knew that he was looking for a tall Caucasian man of fifty with greying hair who would be wearing a red sweater. At no point in the exchange did either party mention the names Peter Galvin, Martha Raine or 'Lachlan'.

It was raining when Kite emerged from a subway on West 86th Street shortly after 10.45 a.m. The stench of weed had followed him from Lower Manhattan; every corner of the city now seemed to smell of skunk. On the assumption that Cablean would be coming direct from Columbia, Kite walked a block north of Piksers and waited at a bus stop. The American was early too. Kite had watched several YouTube videos of Cablean and was easily able to recognise the short-legged, well-dressed man making his way south on the eastern side of the broad avenue. Beside him, sharing an umbrella, was a young woman, about the same age as Cara, with peroxide hair and face piercings wearing black leather boots over skin-tight jeans. A friend? A postgraduate student? Fifty metres short of the deli, Cablean stopped, patted the woman's jacket pocket then waved as she somewhat nervously continued south across 87th Street. She went into Piksers. Cablean then crossed Amsterdam Avenue and ducked into a grocery store. Kite was standing under an umbrella, seemingly taking an interest in the window of a CVS pharmacy and saw Cablean idly handling various pieces of exotic fruit, plainly with no interest in buying them. Meanwhile the young woman was being shown to a table in the window of the restaurant where she sat down, immediately opening the menu.

It was obvious that Cablean intended her to record their conversation or to try to take a photograph of 'John'. Under normal circumstances, such a breach of trust would have been enough for Kite immediately to cancel the meeting, but he needed to give Cablean a chance. He crossed the avenue, went into the deli and sat towards the rear with his back to the girl. He then took out his phone and dialled Cablean's number.

'Lucian?'

'John. Hi. I'm on my way, running late.' Kite could hear the till ringing inside the grocery store. 'Almost with you. Two minutes.'

'You have a friend here.'

'Excuse me?'

'A young woman. Peroxide hair. Black leather boots. She was drinking what looked like a cup of tea as I walked in.'

'I don't understand . . .'

It was evident from Cablean's abrupt, startled tone that he understood all too well.

'Could you ask her to wait outside, preferably far enough away that any Bluetooth link between you will be broken? I don't want to make a scene. It's just that it's vital, both for your security and mine, that we speak privately. As you agreed.'

A moment of silence. A man of less experience and maturity might have attempted to challenge Kite's assertion with howls of offended outrage, but Cablean was sensible enough to admit that he had been caught out.

'Sure,' he said briskly. 'I'll ask her to leave.'

Moments later, Kite heard the woman's phone ringing, followed by a brief conversation in which she said 'OK' and 'Wow' and 'You sure you'll be all right?' in various states of surprise and concern before hanging up and asking the waiter for her check. Kite did not turn, but he was aware of the woman's chair scraping back as she stood up to leave. As soon as she had gone, Kite removed his jacket to reveal the red sweater which would identify him. Two minutes later, a chastened-looking Cablean appeared beside his table.

'John?'

'Lucian.' Kite rose slightly and they shook hands.

264

He was fresher-faced than Kite had anticipated, though he was now at an age when most people he met in the course of his work were at least ten or fifteen years his junior. The American had beady, intelligent eyes, one of which was fractionally closer to his nose than the other. Kite knew from reading Cablean's work that he was an exceptionally thoughtful and well-educated man, not a natural prose stylist but nevertheless a writer with a clear moral purpose whose work was generally balanced and fair. He had located his politics somewhere to the right of Alexandria Ocasio-Cortez and well to the left of Ron De Santis; in other words, he was an old-fashioned Centrist in an increasingly polarised America. Cablean was gay, married to a long-term partner who taught mathematics at NYU and, despite the horrors uncovered by some of his investigations, seemed still to be in possession of a sense of humour. Kite doubted that the circumstances of their meeting would see Cablean revealing that side of his personality, but it was reassuring to know that he was not about to sit down with a gloomy ideological fanatic.

'Look,' he said, taking the seat opposite Kite's. 'I'm sorry for the whole thing with my friend. This story has turned up some pretty funky people. I didn't know who I was meeting, how safe I would be . . .'

'Say no more.' Kite waved away any awkwardness. 'I just happened to be across the street buying some Tylenol. I saw you coming south from Columbia, put two and two together when your friend came in ahead of you.'

Cablean looked quickly around the room, little eyes darting left and right.

'You have people here I guess?'

'You have my word that we are alone. I flew in yesterday, I fly out tonight. Now can I check that you have switched off your cell phone?'

Cablean looked slightly crestfallen as he pulled out his

phone, apologising for not yet switching it off and for failing to remember to bring a Faraday bag.

'I should be frank with you,' Kite began. 'Your communications – telephone conversations, emails, social media, even WhatsApp exchanges such as ours today which you might have believed were encrypted – are being carefully monitored by the authorities in Paris. I am not their emissary. I work for the British Foreign Office. One or two people on the other side of the Channel know that I am here with you today. We are working together on this. Does that make sense?'

'Perfect sense,' Cablean replied. His nervousness was ebbing away.

'I suggest you move the phone elsewhere in the restaurant so that we can be assured of privacy.'

Cablean stood up, headed off in the direction of the bathroom and returned moments later.

'It was low on battery anyway,' he said, accepting an offer of a glass of water from the waiter. 'They know me here. Charging it.'

Kite had been studying the restaurant's unusual wallpaper which showed horse-drawn hansom cabs being pulled along a tree-lined street on an unidentified Caribbean island. Cablean saw that he was intrigued.

'This place is a throwback,' he said. 'Twenty years ago there were delis like this all over the city. Now it's Starbucks, Joe and the Juice. You looked at the menu?'

Kite had scanned it briefly. He understood that Cablean wanted to use these early moments to assess his character, to break the ice and also to put his earlier mistakes behind him.

'It's all Greek to me,' he said, playing the befuddled Brit. 'Or should I say Russian?'

There were fish platters of sturgeon, herring and lox on offer, triple-decker sandwiches assembled with chopped liver, corned beef and tongue. Kite found that he was

266

hungry and ordered a bagel with smoked salmon and cream cheese.

'That's all you want?' Cablean had requested a black coffee.

'And a cappuccino.' Kite passed the menu to the waiter. 'Jet lag. I'm hungry every three hours. The brain has a clock. The stomach has one too.'

'Yeah, I heard that. Never eat on a plane. That's the secret.'

'Unless you're flying to New Zealand.'

There was a moment of silence. The ice-breaking was over. Kite made his first move.

'I assume you've heard the news about Eric Appiah?'

Cablean looked slightly perplexed. It was clear that he recognised the name but knew nothing of Appiah's murder.

'What about him?' He removed his jacket, hooking it around the back of the chair. 'Did something happen?'

'He was killed in London three days ago.'

The American's measured reaction gave Kite an insight into the possible danger of the Woodstein podcast: unaware of Kite's friendship with Appiah, Cablean did not offer his condolences, instead concluding immediately that he had been murdered on the orders of British intelligence.

'Your people did it?'

'Despite whatever you may have been told by an elderly woman still mourning her son and suffering from dementia, MI6 is not in the business of assassinating people. We leave that kind of thing to the SAS.'

Cablean seemed taken aback that 'John' knew about his conversations with Vauban's mother, but quickly composed himself.

'I'm not talking about MI6. I'm talking about a covert Anglo-American arms-across-the-Atlantic intelligence agency that nobody knows anything about.'

Kite conveyed to Cablean with a sympathetic smile that he was out of his depth.

'The existence of such an organisation would certainly be news to me,' he said, relieved that Cablean did not appear to be aware of the name 'BOX 88'. 'Eric Appiah was a friend of ours. We had no reason to want him dead. Others certainly did.'

'Yeah?' Cablean had arrived in a mood of polite contrition and had taken time to settle, but was now very much the sharp, sceptical reporter who believed he could tell when a person – particularly a British spy of no fixed abode or background – was lying to him. 'Others like who?'

'Does the name Grace Mavinga mean anything to you?'

'Of course it does. Bagaza's girlfriend. Disappeared after Dakar, nobody knows what happened to her. Except maybe you guys.'

'We lost sight of her too,' Kite admitted. 'There was certainly no institutional desire to prosecute her for the murder of Philippe Vauban. Shortly after Vauban and Bagaza were killed she went into business with Yves Duval.'

'She did *what?*'

'What I'm about to tell you is classified. You can act on it as you wish, on the strict understanding that the Woodstein podcast makes no mention of the name "Lockie" nor of Martha Raine. That's the quid pro quo. Do I have your agreement?'

'You know I can't promise that.'

'Believe me, it's a small price to pay in exchange for what I have been authorised to tell you.'

The two men studied one another. Kite knew that Cablean would not be able to resist the dangled carrot of a relationship between Duval and Mavinga; equally he would know that both 'Lockie' and 'Martha Raine' were likely MI6 personnel about whom it would be extraordinarily difficult to discover reliable, legally watertight information.

'Look, John,' he said. 'Just so we're clear. If you're here

268

to try to urge me not to go ahead, to play any kind of games around "official secrecy" or any of that need-to-know, plausible deniability bullshit, it's not going to wash. You can threaten me, you can push all my patriotic, Special Relationship buttons, but this is a story that deserves to come out.'

'I agree with you 100 per cent.'

'Excuse me?'

'I think you have every right to publish.'

'You do?'

Cablean's surprise was self-evident. 'You're telling me MI6 *want* this story to come out?'

'How can we stop it?' Kite opened his hands in a gesture of powerlessness. 'You have reasonably good sources. You've done the necessary legwork. You have most of the facts. All you need is someone to put them in the right order.'

There was a moment of silence.

'And you're the man to do that?'

Kite pushed a salt cellar to one side of the table, a pepper grinder to the other, making a channel between them.

'Let me tell you about Duval and Mavinga.' Cablean opened a notebook and began to take shorthand. 'Duval left the DGSE about twenty years ago. Befriended Mavinga, turned her into a highly successful business-woman with interests principally in Cape Town and Nairobi, also France and the United Kingdom. Together they're at the heart of an international money laundering operation financing, among other things, the operations of Islamic State in Africa.'

The American looked up, plainly not believing a word he had been told.

'This is bullshit, right? London's idea of diverting me from Dakar?'

'Not at all. We're just giving you Season 2. What happened next.'

269

Cablean produced a withering, don't-waste-my-time shake of the head and closed the notebook. Kite saw that the man who had gone toe to toe with veterans of the Red Brigades and Shining Path would need further convincing.

'Let me put you straight on a few things,' he said. 'Philippe Vauban was not a paid assassin. MI6 attempted to kidnap Augustin Bagaza in the autumn of 1995 in a joint operation with the CIA. The idea was simple: to put a war criminal on trial for his role in the Rwandan genocide. They might have succeeded if Vauban had not been suffering from PTSD and taken Lariam as a malarial medication.'

'Go on,' Cablean muttered, though he had not yet picked up his pen.

Kite played his final move.

'Peter Galvin was a former MI6 officer known by the nickname "Lockie" who was sent to Senegal with Martha Raine, a girlfriend oblivious to his activities as a spy.' It was as though Cablean had been shocked out of his complacency by the sudden arrival in the restaurant of a celebrity or head of state: he sat bolt upright, realising that he was at last in the presence of someone from British intelligence who could correct and corroborate almost everything he was planning to write. 'Now you and I have an agreement that Martha and "Lockie" stay out of this. You can use pseudonyms; you can say that their identities remain a closely guarded secret. You are otherwise free to ask me whatever you want. That's the level of clearance I've been given. That's how much my organisation wants to make sure you tell the truth, as opposed to a fiction cooked up by Maurice Lagarde and Brigitte Vauban.'

The waiter came over with their coffees and set them down.

'You know what, John?' Cablean reopened the notebook, picked up his pen and smiled winningly. 'I *do* have an appetite after all. Let me take another look at the menu.'

40

After his brother's murder, Omar Gueye had stepped away from the secret world, leaving Dakar to open a restaurant in Marseille. A beautiful young woman from Côte d'Ivoire had walked in one day looking for a waitressing job; six weeks later, Omar had moved her into his apartment. On Millennium New Year's Eve, while fireworks popped over Chateau d'If, he had proposed marriage. By the end of the following year, Clementine Gueye had given birth to a son, whom Omar named Naby in honour of his slain brother.

They were soon homesick for Africa. In 2002 Omar moved his family to Accra, where he made good money selling imported frozen chickens to hotels and restaurants along the coast. As his business expanded, so did Omar's desire to return home to Senegal and to take advantage of the building boom in Dakar. He purchased a plot of land on a strip of beachfront south of the King Fahd Hotel, another on the site of what would become a popular tourist hotel in Fann, riding out the financial crisis of 2008 with comparative ease. By 2014 Omar was the majority share-holder in 'Groupement Seneclem' running a property and hospitality empire valued at over $45 million.

Lachlan Kite had come knocking in the summer of 2016, passing through Dakar on his way to South America.

271

Was Omar interested in setting up and running a BOX team in West Africa? The answer was a firm no. Omar had always liked and trusted Kite; he did not blame him for what had happened in 1995, despite Kite's own feelings of responsibility for the tragedy. But he was touching sixty, still happily married and at last enjoying the fruits of his labours: there was a large house in Almadies, two BMWs in the garage, a holiday villa in Casamance as well as a second family home near Cannes. Young Naby was a talented basketball player doing well at high school, his sister a gifted painter. Why give all that up to go into battle with Boko Haram and ADF? Omar thanked Kite for the flattering offer, bought him dinner at Lagon for old times' sake, and revealed that he would only ever come back if BOX 88 managed to find out what had happened to Grace Mavinga.

'For her I come out of retirement,' he promised.

And now Kite had found her. In London, of all places, living right under the nose of British intelligence in a £3 million flat in Hampstead. When Kite had told him about Appiah's senseless death, all of Omar's old feelings of rage and disgust had reared up. He had been in St Louis visiting one of his restaurants. The operation Kite proposed had sounded straightforward enough: a British passport, transfers to and from Heathrow via Marseille, BOX 88 cover from the moment Omar touched down to the moment he left. Was he interested?

'Of course, I'm interested.'

And so it started, like passing through a time portal into his former life. Omar remembered meeting an al-Qaeda informant in a room at the Hôtel de la Residence in the spring of 1996. On the road south to Dakar, he passed the village where he had stopped for the night with a fever and woken up to find a woman going through his pockets. There had been nothing much going on in Almadies back then: no nightclubs or shopping malls, just diplomats and

CIA officers loitering around the King Fahd looking to make mischief in the salad days before 9/11. Omar would take them to beachside shacks in Ngor, treat them to grilled *capitaine* beneath the roar of the planes taking off from Yof. Now Almadies was mostly unfinished breezeblock apartment buildings and nightclubs filled with girls not much older than his daughter who would offer their bodies to strangers in exchange for the price of a dress, a pair of shoes, a fancy meal at Phares des Mamelles.

He had been instructed to go to Imperial, what Kite had referred to on Signal as 'the usual place'. A moment of melancholic nostalgia caused Omar to park his Mercedes close to the exact spot where he had left the taxi on the night of Naby's murder. He remembered sending Lockie and the crazed Vauban out into the sweltering October night, telling them the best and quickest route to Lagon via Dagorne and Marché Kermel. Omar had not been inside Imperial for more than ten years and saw that not much had changed. Out front there were the same deracinated white tourists drinking Flags and smoking Excellence cigarettes. A kid in a torn T-shirt was trying to sell them knock-off designer scarves and handbags while the traffic boomed on Place de l'Independence. As he walked inside, Omar saw two girls seated side by side at the bar, one very young in tight denim shorts, the other older wearing bright red lipstick. Neither turned as he passed; they could tell he wasn't a tourist.

Omar nodded at the waitress. He had been told that his contact would be a young white man reading a copy of the *Spectator* magazine seated in the air-conditioned section at the back of the building. Omar pushed through the swing doors into the fridge chill of the rear bar and spotted the magazine.

'Do you mind if I sit next to you?' The young man at the table was no older than thirty and already very bald.

'Not at all,' he replied. 'I was just on my way to the Novotel.'

It was the agreed exchange. As soon as Omar had sat down, his contact stood up, leaving a manila envelope on the chair beside him. Omar placed it inside the briefcase he had brought to Imperial for that purpose. The waitress came through from the main lounge and asked in Wolof what he would like to drink.

'Just a coffee,' he replied, remembering the ghosts of this place, all the conversations, the cursed night when Ackerman's decision to send Naby up to Thiossane had cost his brother his life.

'Nothing else?'

'Nothing at all.'

41

'So Mavinga and Duval were complicit in Appiah's murder?'

Kite had described what had happened at the flat in Paddington, revealing that Lindsey Berida had been accused of orchestrating the hit and was in the custody of the Metropolitan police.

'We assume so,' he told Cablean. An elderly couple had come into the dining area of Piksers and were making a fuss about where to sit. 'Martha Raine has also disappeared, her husband too.'

'I thought you didn't want me to write about her?'

'I don't. But those are the facts.'

'So what are you trying to tell me? That she's been murdered? Duval and Mavinga are taking out anyone who threatens their business arrangements, this money laundering empire you're talking about? Maybe the DGSE are trying to kill everybody? Help me out here.'

'Why on Earth would the DGSE want Appiah dead? He was helping them.' For the first time Kite sounded fractious, not because he was irritated with Cablean, but because he was concerned for Martha's well-being. He had spent days trying to work out what purpose it would serve for Mavinga or Duval to harm her. 'Taking out Appiah was a way of sending a message to anyone who was considering helping the French with their investigation. Duval doesn't want to be exposed either for Dakar in '95 or for his more recent criminal activities. The same logic applies to Mavinga. They will both target anybody who threatens their survival. Including you.'

'I can take care of myself.'

'Forgive me for saying this,' Kite replied, 'but I very much doubt that.'

It was obvious Cablean had no idea that Marianne Hette had saved his life on the subway. Fournier had asked Kite not to tell him that a DGSE team was keeping tabs on him. For the same reason Kite had remained silent about the man in an AT&T uniform who had been standing on the opposite side of Amsterdam Avenue for the previous twenty minutes keeping an eye on the restaurant. He was Hette's associate.

'Your best defence is to put out the podcast as quickly as possible. That will certainly reduce the chance that people will want to kill you.'

'I'll take that under advisement.'

Cablean was a physically unimposing man, but certainly not a coward. Taking up his pen again, he asked Kite why he had been tasked with travelling to New York to give MI6's version of the story.

'I was the only person who was qualified to do it.'

'Why so, if I may ask?'

'Because I was there.'

Their food arrived at just this moment. Kite waited while it was set down, all the time observing Cablean's mute but incredulous reaction.

'You were *there*?' He turned to stare briefly at the Caribbean island wallpaper as though he had been trans-ported to a tropical world where all his wishes had been allowed to come true.

'I was there,' Kite replied. 'I witnessed the murder of Naby Gueye. I saw Philippe Vauban hack Augustin Bagaza to death. I was less than six feet away when Grace Mavinga shot Philippe in the head. As I'm sure you've already guessed, my name isn't John.'

'Jesus,' Cablean whispered. He looked oddly humbled. 'You're the guy who was with Martha at the guest house? You're Peter Galvin. Or should I call you "Lockie"?'

Kite leaned towards him, lowering his voice.

'As we agreed, that name never passes your lips again.'

42

Graham Platt's self-belief was total. He was a man who measured success by three simple criteria: money, health and social status. By any objective standard, he was flourishing in all categories. Yearly check-ups indicated that Platt was in unusually good health for a man approaching sixty who regularly ate calorie-rich lunches at some of the best restaurants in Mayfair and Piccadilly. As a partner at Rycroft Maule, his remuneration varied according to the volume of money flowing through the firm, but he expected to earn at least £2 million a year and was rarely disappointed. He drove a Mercedes E 200 AMG Line Saloon for which he had paid just under £60,000 cash (on the same shopping spree, his wife, Marina, had been treated to a fully electric Audi Q4 e-tron which she referred to as 'my little runaround'). The two cars were parked side by side on the gravel drive of the Platt's £7.1 million residence in Virginia Water which boasted an indoor swimming pool, croquet lawn and tennis court. The Platts also owned a renovated fourteenth-century farmhouse in the Dordogne to which they repaired every August with their adult sons, Mark and Godfrey, the former an unmarried Anglican vicar, the latter a chemistry teacher at an independent girls' school who had recently become engaged to the bursar's assistant. As an investment, Platt had purchased the freehold on a three-bedroom duplex in Chelsea in the same building as a retired Conservative cabinet minister and an Oscar-winning American actress; the property was registered in Mark's name and rented to a bachelor from Oman. Platt took clients to the Turf Club tent at Cheltenham, to Twickenham for a picnic in the car park prior to matches in the Six Nations, and to the MCC for Test matches and 'a spot of real tennis'. He played golf at Wentworth, not well, but had once gone round in a tournament two groups behind the Duke of York. At his private gym, where he played squash and lifted weights, he rubbed shoulders with politicians, captains of industry and minor royalty. To anyone who questioned Platt's ethics or work practices, Rycroft Maule would point them to the Lawyer of the Year prize Platt had picked up at the 2021 Assegai Wealth Management Awards. Indeed, when his application to White's was finally accepted (as Platt anticipated it would be within the next twenty-four months), the only thing missing from his life would be an OBE for services to the legal profession.

Moments after passing White's itself on a cold spring morning, Platt collided with a middle-aged Pakistani businessman on the corner of Ryder Street and St James's. It was just after ten o'clock. He was on his way back from a breakfast meeting at The Wolseley, minding his own business, when the man bumped into him almost at full pace.

'Look where you're going!' he scolded.

The businessman had been staring at his phone, forcing Platt briefly onto the road. He noticed a three-button cuff on his shirt, a pair of polished brogues and what appeared, at first glance, to be an Audemars Piguet watch, finished in yellow gold. Platt wondered if he might have been coming from a meeting at Rycroft Maule.

'I'm so sorry,' the man said. 'I wasn't looking where I was going.'

'It's all right,' Platt replied, adopting a more conciliatory tone. 'No harm done.'

At this the businessman did a double-take. Platt saw that he had been recognised.

'Are you Graham Platt?'

'I am.'

'My name is Rehan Saleem. I wonder if we might have a little word?'

43

A woman purporting to be the personal assistant of DGSE Director Gérard Bathenay had telephoned Maurice Lagarde at his apartment in Chantecrit with a request to set up a meeting. The Service was concerned that Lagarde had sent a chapter of his memoirs to an American journalist in breach of a legal arrangement struck between the two parties at the time of Lagarde's retirement. The director was keen to find a way to satisfy the demands of a much-respected former officer who had given years of brave and loyal service to the republic. Was there a way of minimising any further damage he intended to cause so that he might avoid a likely custodial sentence?

Lagarde was bored. The sameness of his days contributed to an almost constant feeling of resentment at the way his life had turned out. Abandoned by his second wife, no longer on speaking terms with his children and possessed of few friends, he spent most of his time watching pornography on the Internet or bingeing American television series. He was sixty-three but felt and looked like a man in his late seventies. He was also vain enough to be hooked by the idea of a personal meeting with Bathenay, a man he despised. A car was to be sent to take him up to the director's summer residence on the outskirts of Limoges.

Lagarde told a neighbour that he would be going away for two nights and asked her to keep an eye on his cat, Papin, a cunning Siamese with a tendency to disappear for days on end. He also wrote a letter to his lawyer telling her that he was on his way to speak to the Director of French foreign intelligence; should anything happen to him, she would know what to do. That letter was intercepted by the DGSE in Chantecrit and immediately destroyed.

The journey north was uneventful. Lagarde spent most of the time looking out of the window and thinking of the various ways in which he intended to defy Bathenay. If the Service wanted to risk an expensive and very public trial, so be it. He would find plenty of allies among those who blamed the French government for complicity in the Rwandan genocide. They could threaten him with prison all they liked. La Santé would likely be more comfortable and certainly more intellectually stimulating than his current existence on the outskirts of Bordeaux. Lagarde had never been much of a cook so the food would certainly be better. A smile played on his lips as he considered this. No, he had nothing to live for except his reputation and the chance to humble an organisation which had treated him for years with abject contempt.

The summer residence was smaller than Lagarde had anticipated, though he noticed a modest-sized swimming pool on the long approach. His chauffeur, a man originally from Algiers called Hakim, had followed signs to Cognac-la-Forêt before turning off down a private drive with magnificent views over the surrounding countryside.

Two men, whom Lagarde did not recognise, welcomed him into the house. Hakim carried his bag inside. He was shown to a guest room on the second floor. There was a television and private bathroom; it was like booking into a small luxury hotel. Lagarde was asked to hand over his cell phone as a condition of staying and did so in the full knowledge that it would be subjected to a technical attack;

for this reason he had purposefully brought an old phone for the journey, leaving the other locked in the safe in his apartment.

The older of the two men, who introduced himself as Michel, told him that Bathenay had been unavoidably detained. Would Monsieur Lagarde like anything to eat? Would he prefer to rest or perhaps to stretch his legs in the grounds? Lagarde asked for some food to be sent to his room; it pleased him to treat the man as a waiter. Twenty minutes later, a tray was brought up by the younger man, Thierry, and Lagarde happily tucked into a plate of coq au vin served with mashed potatoes and beans followed by a selection of local cheeses. He had been offered wine but took only water, afterwards leaving the tray outside the door.

He began to feel drowsy almost as soon as he switched on the television to watch a game of tennis on Eurosport. Lagarde often had a siesta after lunch and lay down on the bed. Hakim and Thierry had been watching him on CCTV. Once he had fallen asleep they came into the bedroom and together carried him downstairs to a waiting van. Michel was at the wheel. All three men worked for Action Division, the military arm of French overseas intelligence.

Lagarde's phone was replaced in his jacket pocket. He was driven to an isolated section of the forest. As Michel checked the surrounding area for passers-by, Hakim, using a .50 gauge needle, injected the nucleoside adenosine into his left eyeball. Lagarde was dead within seconds. Opening the doors of the van, the three men took out his body and left it propped up at the foot of a tree next to a bottle of Evian and a penknife which they had used to open his wrists.

They were back in Paris by nightfall.

44

The in-flight wi-fi in Virgin Upper Class had been out of service and Kite landed at Heathrow to three missed calls from Azhar Masood and a Signal message from Fournier.

F police found ML body. Forest outside Limoges. Cause of death 'suicide'.

The French had moved without warning. Once Cablean's story went public, there would have been attention around Lagarde, journalists knocking on his door wanting the inside scoop for *Le Monde* and *Paris Match*. A dead Lagarde was a man suffering from guilt, a proud public servant who had let his country down. That was how the DGSE and their client journalists would spin it. No doubt the assassins had created an ambiguity at the scene of the crime: an empty packet of sleeping pills close to the body, high dosage in the bloodstream, but no note. A friend or neighbour would validate the assertion that Lagarde had been suffering from depression. Angry family members and social media accounts would inevitably cry foul, accusing the government of murder and cover-up, but there would never be enough hard evidence to prove foul play – and just enough suspicion around the real cause of death to put the frighteners on any other disgruntled French spooks thinking of spilling the beans to a publisher.

A BOX 88 driver was waiting for Kite in Arrivals and walked him to a Mercedes in the short-term car park. En route Kite exchanged messages with a furious Fournier, who had been blindsided by Lagarde's murder and concerned that the Action Division would now go after Duval. Kite tried to assuage his fears:

> If they take YD off the table, two of Cablean's principal players are dead within a week under suspicious circumstances. Surely Paris not that stupid? Keep the faith. Lady M still in play. That's our focus.

Fournier conceded that it would indeed be reckless of Action Division to carry out successive assassinations of two former officers so intimately tied to the Woodstein podcast. Nevertheless, he said, 'powerful figures' inside DGSE 'have always wanted the YD problem to go away'.

The exchange was interrupted by a call from Azhar Masood.

'How was your flight?'

'Bumpy,' Kite told him, opening the back door of the Mercedes. 'Branson needs to sort out his suspension. Thanks for the car, by the way.'

'So I have news of Martha.'

Kite was cheered by Masood's upbeat tone of voice. He closed the door and stepped away from the car.

'Go on.'

'Simple enough explanation. Martha filed for divorce three weeks ago, has been in the process of moving out of the family home, changing her passport, quitting her job. Her husband, Jonas Radinsky, is currently in a Colorado clinic drying out for opioid addiction. He's been stalking her, making life very difficult for a long time. Martha had employed a company to hide her whereabouts and to wipe any digital snail trail she left online. Hence we weren't seeing activity on her emails, hence her old mobile number going out of service.'

Kite was stunned, not only that Martha was getting divorced, but also that the bland, benignly industrious Radinsky had put his life in freefall. He felt that a bargain had been struck between them twenty years earlier: Jonas would look after Martha, offering her the stable family life and constancy which she had come to crave after more than a decade at Kite's side. To have turned addict and stalker was an abnegation of duty.

'So the change of passport means a change of name? Back to Raine?'

Masood hesitated. He knew enough of Kite's past to realise that what he was about to say constituted another bombshell.

'She's moving back to the UK. Rented a place in Belsize Park. Her daughter is with her. The son is staying behind in New York. He sounds like a handful. I have her number, if you'd like it?'

Kite told the driver to head for The Cathedral.

'Text it to me.' It was his way of bringing the subject to a close. 'Where are we with Mavinga?'

'Nothing. No movement. She's not in the UK. Not in France. We're relying on the French to flag her passport.'

'Fournier is pissed off. But he'll come through.' Kite explained that Maurice Lagarde had been found dead in south-west France. 'What about Platt. Is he playing ball?'

'So far. The meeting is going ahead. He understands what's at stake if he doesn't comply. The paperwork will be ready, it's just a question of the star witness showing up.'

'She'll show up.' Kite had replied with a confidence he didn't entirely feel. So much of what he had planned for Mavinga was out of his direct control; he was relying on Platt, on Masood and Omar Gueye playing their different parts. 'What about my pal from St Louis?'

'On his way. The kid in Dakar gave him the documents.'

There was a brief pause. Kite could tell that Masood was anxious about something.

'What is it, Maz?'

'Are you sure about him, Lockie? He's already worth millions. You're certain this is the right course of action?'

'It's not about the money,' Kite replied. 'This is personal for both of us.'

45

Six hours later an image from a facial recognition camera at Charles de Gaulle gave Jean-François Fournier the identity and passport number under which Grace Mavinga had travelled on an Air France flight from Cape Town. The same passport had been stamped for entry into Mauritius ten days earlier; a DGSE agent in Port Louis was immediately instructed to establish where Mavinga had stayed on the island. Fournier knew that Duval had recently purchased a plot of land on the north-east coast as well as a 41-metre luxury motor yacht, *La Belle Adjani,* registered in Reunion and valued at €10.7 million. He tended to stay in one of three hotels on Mauritius: the Constance Prince Maurice, the Four Seasons and La Duchesse de Palmar. The agent would make enquiries at each of them.

Mavinga did not stay overnight in Paris. Instead she paid cash for an economy class ticket to Heathrow, purchased a bottle of Guerlain Jardins de Bagatelle in Duty Free and dozed for half an hour on the plane. At Heathrow Terminal Five she queued for a taxi which took her to Hampstead. It was early evening by the time she got home. She had booked a masseur to come to the apartment at 7.30 p.m. and was asleep, after a light supper, by midnight.

The following morning Mavinga rose early and started packing. She took the jewels from the boxes on her dressing table, the diamonds and passports from the safe as well as various framed photographs of her sister, Agnes, and her two nieces. There was around sixty thousand dollars in cash, of various denominations, hidden around the flat; she stuffed all of it into a Waitrose Bag for Life. One large Samsonite wheeled suitcase was now full. Mavinga left it by the door, intending to take it to the meeting with Platt. In a separate, smaller case she packed five of her preferred outfits, lingerie from Desmond & Dempsey and Dora Larsen as well as three pairs of Louboutins and some Olivia von Halle pyjamas. Everything else could be couriered to Nairobi by the maid and her husband, both of whom – maddeningly – were in the Philippines for a funeral. She took no bathing suit, no books and no toiletries save for a tube of Kiehl's moisturiser and a Diptyque eau de parfum. She packed her laptop, intending to wipe the hard drive after the meeting with Platt, and took the gun from the drawer under the bed, placing it in her handbag. She would dump it en route to the airport; no sense in leaving it lying around for the removals team to find.

She put the second suitcase by the door as well as a burner phone into which she had programmed half a dozen essential contacts. Mavinga was not sentimental about her possessions: for more than twenty years she had known that she could buy whatever she wanted and replace whatever she might lose. She had survived by always being on the move. For most people, leaving the Hampstead flat after so many years would have been an emotional wrench; for Mavinga it was a business decision.

She had earlier booked a train to Edinburgh, a flight to New York, a seat on the Eurostar to Paris and a first-class flight to Nairobi. Fournier wouldn't have the resources to work out which route she was taking nor any prior knowledge of the passport on which she was intending to travel.

She would go to the meeting in Mayfair, leave for Heathrow before five and be in Kenya by morning. After that nobody would ever see her again.

Grace Mavinga was mistaken.

Parked outside her building was a Sixt self-hire van with the rear doors open and two BOX 88 Falcons roleplaying a married couple moving house. Further along the street, waiting patiently in a café on the corner of Redington Road, was a motorcycle courier – in full leathers – on secondment from MI5. With his helmet off, Cara Jannaway would have recognised him as her former team leader, Robert Vosse. At the opposite end of the road, parked in a resident's bay with a view of Mavinga's living-room window, was David Fowler, the son of Carl Fowler, Kite's point of contact in France way back in 1989.

It was Fowler who saw Mavinga bumping her suitcases down the steps just before one o'clock. A black cab was waiting for her, ordered by app. The driver got out to help with the luggage.

'All stations, this is Zero Two. LADY MACBETH moving. Navy blue blazer, red skirt. Two suitcases, black and navy blue. Brown handbag, sunglasses.'

'Copy that, Zero Two.' This from Vosse. 'Zero Three, you are mobile.'

Across the street, having loaded the last of half a dozen boxes of paperback books and kitchen utensils into the back of the Sixt van, Mary Fox took out her phone and sent a message to the team.

Black cab VRN: OVZ6 GHY. Assume destination Rycroft Maule.

46

Mavinga was early for the meeting with Platt. The cab driver helped to unload her suitcases and received a £10 tip for his trouble. He had already driven off by the time Mavinga reached the entrance to Rycroft Maule and pressed the buzzer.

'Could somebody help me with my bags, please?' she asked through the intercom.

An eager, pale-faced male intern materialised moments later and carried the suitcases into the reception area. Mavinga asked that they be kept safe. The receptionist was a middle-aged Nigerian of longstanding at the firm named Sunday; Mavinga had only ever acknowledged him in a perfunctory fashion.

'Of course, madame,' he said. He pronounced 'madame' in the French way, flattering Mavinga's sense of herself as a big shot. 'They'll be here until you need them.'

She did not thank him. There was an unsettling aroma in the building, an odd mixture of sandalwood and industrial disinfectant.

'What's that smell?' she asked, making a sour face and waving a hand in front of her nose.

Sunday and the intern glanced at one another: the intern opted to field the question.

'We've just put out a scented candle,' he said. 'Can I offer you coffee, madam? Tea? Water?'

'Water,' Mavinga replied. She was still on her feet, staring at the suitcases. 'Is Graham coming?'

'Take a seat, please,' Sunday told her. 'Mr Platt's assistant will be on her way shortly.'

'He has an assistant now?'

'Mr Platt has always had an assistant.'

Watching from the flat in Belgravia, a brisk ten-minute walk from the Rycroft Maule building, Kite was able to observe Mavinga via two CCTV cameras which had been looped into the surveillance effort. She settled into a leather sofa, picked up a recent copy of *Tatler* and began distractedly flicking through the Bystander section. On the stroke of three o'clock a young woman appeared in the lower right-hand corner of the screen.

'I'm Mr Platt's assistant,' she said. The take quality on the microphones was first-class. 'If you'd like to follow me upstairs, he's ready for you now. How was your journey today?'

Platt had a memory of the two MI6 officers laying out what would happen to him – and, by extension, to the firm – if he mishandled the meeting.

'Everything is exactly as it would be if you'd never set eyes on us,' Rehan Saleem's colleague had told him. He had introduced himself as 'John' and left it at that. 'The only difference is a name on some paperwork. You try to communicate your anxiety to Mavinga, you join her in prison. You attempt to tip her off, the police will drag you away at the same time they come for her. You do as you're told, you explain the situation, that's it. You get her to sign on the lines which are dotted. If you do that for us, Graham, then everything reverts to the way it was on Monday morning and this will all be just a bad dream. You'll still get to go to the Test match in July.

292

Your application to White's won't hit the skids. Godfrey's wedding will be the social event of the season. Do we understand one another?'

'Evidently,' Platt had replied. He was an ordinary man in everything but his fierce, quick mind. 'And I have your word that this will be the end of it? What you're doing with my client is completely unlawful and would lead to my being disbarred if it ever came out. The quid pro quo is absolute silence on your part. I can't have anybody knowing what happens here today. My livelihood depends on it.'

'Relax, Graham,' said Azhar Masood, still calling himself Rehan Saleem. 'It's not like we enjoy your company. You get this done the way John wants it done, you'll never hear from us again.'

A knock at the door. Platt's assistant, Tamsin, showed Mavinga into the room, returning moments later with a plate of fresh pastries and two bottles of mineral water, one still, one sparkling. She set them down on a wooden table in the centre of Platt's office while he exchanged welcoming small talk with his troublesome client.

'You look very well rested in the circumstances, Grace. How was your flight?'

'She asked me that,' Mavinga replied, addressing Tamsin's back as she left the room. 'It was like any flight. It was long. I slept most of the way. Now I feel like this was maybe a wasted journey.'

Hearing this on the office microphones, Kite pressed the headphones tighter, straining to pick up every word.

'Why do you feel that way?' Platt enquired.

'Maybe Yves has overreacted. Maybe this whole problem is in our heads, you know?'

A camera in a light fixture captured Mavinga tapping her temple and giving a look of bewildered exhaustion.

'Have a seat,' Platt suggested.

Tamsin returned to the office with the first of three large

cardboard boxes. She set it on the floor, took out four lever arch files and arranged them on the table next to the pastries.

'Give us two minutes will you, Tamsin?'

The assistant excused herself, but not before casting a sudden look – somewhere between nervousness and desperation – in Mavinga's direction. She was about twenty-five, pretty and bright. Was she trying to tell her something? Mavinga removed her Balmain blazer and hung it on a hook.

'Is everything OK with that girl?' she asked, settling into a chair.

'What girl?'

'Tamsin.'

Platt hesitated. Mercifully his anxiety transmitted itself as a kind of momentary confusion.

'Oh! Tamsin. She's absolutely fine. I think.' Another slight hesitation. 'Why?'

'She looked at me in a strange way.'

'Well, I'm sorry about that. She's new.'

Kite continued to observe Platt through a camera in the flatscreen television bolted to the wall facing his desk. He was doing well, but there was still a long way to go. Everything depended on the man from Rycroft Maule keeping his nerve.

'I need to be straight with you, Grace,' he began. 'There is a high degree of probability that you will be the subject of an Unexplained Wealth Order application in connection with Kisenso Holdings. The company represents about 45 per cent of your total assets. If the Serious Fraud Office can convince a judge that there's something fishy about where your money comes from and can tie it to Kisenso, you would be looking at an asset freeze potentially leading to confiscation. I don't need to tell you how serious that would be.'

Mavinga looked like someone who had just been notified of a bereavement.

'In other words,' Platt continued, 'your coming here this afternoon was very much *not* a wasted journey. There are things we need to do, and quickly, in order to get the assets out of jurisdiction and the SFO's reach. The contracts Miss Wellman has just brought in constitute the first part of a suite of transfer documents that you must sign. In a moment she'll be bringing in at least two more like that one.' Platt nodded at the box behind Mavinga's chair. 'My strong advice would be to do this today in order to protect your assets during what is inevitably going to prove to be a period of, shall we say, extreme legal turbulence.'

Mavinga stood up and walked to the table, picking up one of the contracts. She trusted Platt; if he told her that it was necessary to sign something, she would sign it. Nevertheless, she had questions to which she wanted answers.

'What happens to Kisenso? Rycroft Maule would take control of it?'

'Not directly.' Platt rose to join her, passing a framed photograph of Bruce Forsyth and the Duke of York standing next to him at Wentworth Golf Club. 'That would leave us exposed and the connection with you might be ascertainable. Ownership will be transferred to a series of shell entities in jurisdictions with little to no disclosure requirements. The ultimate controlling entity will be a brass plate company whose sole director is a solicitor practising in Winchester with whom I've done business all my life.'

'What is this person's name?'

'Rehan Saleem. We were at Oxford together.'

'Is he here today?'

'Absolutely not. It's vital that we keep as much geographical and legal distance between you as is humanly possible. Rehan is somebody over whom Rycroft exercises a certain amount of control. Does what I'm saying to you make sense?' Mavinga was accustomed to business relationships underpinned by blackmail and coercion; she assured Platt with a brisk nod that she understood what he was saying. 'He's familiar with our services and has done this sort of thing for me on several occasions, particularly in the past twelve months, not least on behalf of Russian clients who were exposed by western sanctions relating to the invasion of Ukraine.'

He's doing well, thought Kite, noting that Mavinga was behaving as though she had very little choice other than to go along with what her lawyer was proposing.

'So Saleem becomes the beneficial owner?' she asked.

'Indeed.'

She took out her phone and opened Safari.

'Are you looking him up?' Platt made a slightly panicky gesture, encouraging her to put the phone down. 'If so, can I suggest you do that on my computer, rather than yours? Just in case the authorities were ever keen to connect you . . .'

He did not need to finish the sentence. Mavinga put the phone back in her handbag and walked behind Platt's desk. He typed 'Rehan Saleem' into Google and saw, to his relief, that MI6 had created a false public profile for Saleem. In just a few clicks of a mouse, Mavinga became convinced that she was dealing with a bona fide solicitor with offices in Winchester.

'He looks . . . boring,' she observed, going back to her chair. 'And what happens if he dies? If something happens to him? How do I get my assets back?'

'A very good question, Grace!' Platt produced an extraordinarily high-pitched giggle. It was the first time Kite had ever heard him laugh. He sounded like a child who had inhaled a helium balloon at a birthday party. 'Please have no fears on that score. In anticipation of today's meeting, Rehan adjusted his Will so that Rycroft Maule now act as his executors. We would take steps to ensure that Kisenso Holdings will be returned to you.'

'When things have calmed down?'

'When things have calmed down.' Platt took a much-needed sip of water. 'What I'm proposing is really no different to the types of services Yves Duval has been offering for years. Clients and investors entrust him with their money, he takes care of it on their behalf and later returns the capital, having taken a commission. What's different in this instance is that Rehan will be paid a flat rate which will be taken out of our fees. The important thing is that we need to get these assets out of your name and to ensure, frankly, that their ownership is hidden by as many layers of anonymous companies, in as many secretive jurisdictions, as proves humanly possible. In my experience, when the authorities have a bit of this kind between their teeth, they are very reluctant indeed to let it go until they've seen some sort of result.'

There were more questions. Dozens of them. Mavinga had a detailed memory of her assets, title deeds and Anstalts; of société anonyme, of her Special Purpose Entities in the British Virgin Islands. There were complex financial instruments and shell companies within shell companies, all of which concealed and sheltered the vast wealth she had accumulated at Duval's side. In due course Tamsin brought in the rest of the paperwork. Mavinga noticed that she was studiously avoiding her gaze.

'How long have you worked here, sweetheart?' she asked.

'About four months,' Tamsin replied, her voice catching. The question seemed to have taken her by surprise.

'And you like it? Graham treats you right?'

'Mr Platt treats me very well, thank you very much for asking.'

'Intelligent girl,' Mavinga observed when Tamsin had left the room. 'Beautiful too.'

'I couldn't possibly comment,' Platt replied.

47

Just after 4 p.m. Kite received a worrying call from David Fowler. The BOX 88 Falcon had made his way back to Mavinga's Hampstead apartment and broken in.

'Safe was open,' he told Kite. 'Passports gone, ditto any firearms. No sign of a laptop.'

Fournier had told Kite that Mavinga kept a handgun in each of her properties 'just in case one day she finds herself in a tight spot and wants to shoot her way out'. It seemed likely that she had removed a gun from the safe; more likely still that she was carrying it in her handbag at Rycroft Maule.

'You don't need me to tell you that this thing can't go ahead if Lady Macbeth is armed, boss. We need to put some Closers on standby if that's the case.'

'Cara will sort it out,' Kite replied, sounding calmer than he felt. 'I'll send her a message.'

Ninety minutes later Grace Mavinga had signed away the greater part of her personal estate including nine companies entrusted to her by Yves Duval. Each contract had been witnessed by a legally oblivious eighteen-year-old public schoolboy who happened to be doing three days of work experience at Rycroft Maule because his uncle was a valued client.

'Thank you, Tom,' Platt told him as he placed the last of the transfer documents back in its box. 'Couldn't have done this without you.'

'I need to use the bathroom,' Mavinga announced, rising from the table. She did not add thanks of her own to Thomas Henry McCorquodale of 76 Drayton Gardens, London SW10, despite the fact he had uncomplainingly copied out his name and address more than seventy times for her benefit, receiving only a pat on the back for his trouble. Mavinga said: 'My wrist hurts. How long will a cab to Heathrow take at this time of day?'

She left Platt's office, having been told that she would need to leave at least an hour to reach Heathrow. Tamsin was outside, seated at a desk on the opposite side of the corridor. She shot Mavinga another look of worried complicity as she half-stood up from her chair.

'Can I help, ma'am?'

'Where's the bathroom?'

Tamsin blushed with apparent nerves, indicating that the ladies was located at the end of the passage.

'Third door on the right.'

As Mavinga walked away, she was aware of the young woman opening a drawer in her desk and taking out what appeared to be a small white envelope. She thought nothing more of it and continued along the corridor.

The ladies was empty. Mavinga checked her reflection in a mirror before entering the furthest of three cubicles. Instead of the smell of industrial disinfectant there was now a faint odour of cinnamon air freshener. As she closed the door, she heard somebody coming into the room. That person entered the cubicle next to hers, slid the lock and sat down without lifting the seat.

'Grace?'

It was Tamsin. She was whispering.

'Yes?'

'Take this.'

The young woman slid the small white envelope under the door. Mavinga, as confused as she was surprised, picked it up. The envelope was not sealed. There was a hand-written note inside on Rycroft Maule stationery.

You are about to be arrested. There are plain-clothes police officers in the lobby, two more outside. Graham knows this but is not allowed to tell you. He told me to give you this note as soon as you left his office.

'Jesus,' Mavinga whispered, but the girl had already left. She heard the swish and click of the door closing onto the passage.

The firm have moved your suitcases to our underground car park. We have a driver waiting who can take you to Farnborough airport. There is a private jet on the tarmac routing to Cairo. Your assets are now safe, everything is signed and witnessed. Graham strongly suggests you take up this offer.

To get to the car park, turn left out of the toilet, then left again. Enter the lift and press 'B'. I will meet you there with your jacket. Graham has to remain in his office or he could be accused of complicity in your disappearance. If you see anyone, do not speak to them. Please immediately flush this letter down the toilet.

The note was not signed. Mavinga was so overwhelmed by its contents that she started to moan involuntarily. She did not know if anybody else had come into the bathroom; a part of her hoped that she would be overheard and that a member of staff might come to her assistance. She screwed up the piece of paper into a tight ball and flushed it away, her body shaking.

'*Likata*,' she swore in her mother tongue. '*Likata*.'

She unlocked the door, quickly washed her hands and

was about to leave the bathroom when she remembered the gun. What if the car was stopped en route to Farnborough? How the hell was she going to get rid of it discreetly from a moving vehicle?

There was a bin near the basins with a swing lid. Grace wiped the gun down for prints, threw a small white towel into the bin and was just about to drop the weapon on top of it when she had second thoughts. She was putting the gun back in her handbag when somebody came into the bathroom behind her.

'Good afternoon.'

Mavinga turned. A white woman of about forty wearing a dark blue trouser suit greeted her with a professional smile before going into the first cubicle. She did not appear to have seen what had happened. Mavinga zipped up the handbag, pulled open the door and walked out into the corridor.

She was suddenly acutely aware of her surroundings: the oil painting of a deceased Rycroft Maule partner on the wall; a large vase of red and blue tulips on a counter halfway along the passage; the eerie silence in the building, as if every person in central London knew that Grace Mavinga was about to be arrested.

She turned left and left again, locating the lift. A tall, very handsome man approached her from the far end of a dimly lit corridor. He had the bland good looks and solid build of a policeman. He slowed as he came towards her, glancing at her figure while conveying a look of sleazy appreciation with his mouth. Mavinga lowered her eyes.

The lift opened. There was another man inside, bald and much older, standing alongside an overweight Asian woman carrying a briefcase. Both of them stepped out without acknowledging her. Mavinga felt surrounded. The mood of suffocation intensified as she stepped into the lift and pressed the button for the underground car park. Her hands were shaking.

'Come on,' she whispered as the doors closed.

A jolt as the lift descended two storeys without stopping. She was convinced that the doors would open onto a ground-floor lobby packed with armed police officers and members of the Serious Fraud Office. She unzipped the handbag and felt for the barrel of the gun. The lift kept moving. 'G' became 'B', an automated female voice announcing that Mavinga had reached the car park. Taking her hand off the gun, she stepped out into a small vestibule to find Tamsin waiting for her holding her Balmain blazer.

'Hi,' she said nervously.

Mavinga felt an astonishing surge of affection and gratitude towards this young woman who had come to her aid.

'Where do I go?' she asked.

'Just through here,' Tamsin replied, opening a door into a cold, grey concrete basement.

A black Mercedes-Benz was parked a few metres away. The driver – a prosperous, good-looking African man of about sixty-five – stepped out and touched the rim of a black chauffeur's cap.

'This man will take you to the airport,' Tamsin explained. 'He works for us. Your suitcases are in the back seat. I'm afraid you have a choice. Either you get into the front beside the driver and risk being seen as you leave, or you get into the boot for the first half mile or so of the journey. Then he can let you out.'

'The boot?' Mavinga asked.

'The trunk, the boot, this bit.' Tamsin tapped the back of the Mercedes. The driver was already back behind the wheel. 'It's the advice Graham got from our head of security. They call it a "trunk escape". Look, it's up to you, but if it was me, I would get in.'

'Help me then.'

'Give me your bag.'

Without pausing to think, Grace Mavinga handed the

bag to Tamsin, who set it on the ground. She then lifted her left leg into the boot, held Tamsin's hand for balance and climbed in.

'How long will I be in here?' she asked, looking up at the young woman from a foetal position.

'That'll be up to Omar,' Cara Jannaway replied, nodding at the driver as she slammed the boot. 'Have a safe trip.'

48

'Was there a weapon?' Fournier asked on the phone later that night.

'In the handbag,' Kite replied. 'Loaded too. We owe you.'

It was just before dawn in Mauritius. Fournier had flown out on the understanding that Yves Duval would be arrested and extradited to France within twenty-four hours. He wanted to be there to see it happen.

'So where did he take her?'

'Not to Farnborough, I can tell you.' Omar had sent Kite a simple, six-word message – **It is done. Thank you, brother** – before parking the BOX 88 Mercedes at Gatwick and boarding a late flight to Paris. The employee who had retrieved the vehicle had found no trace of Mavinga. 'My friend is on his way home. Chances are we'll never hear from him again.'

'I don't know,' Fournier ventured. 'He owns a lot more hotels and restaurants now. I would say he owes us an expensive dinner in Dakar.'

It had been arranged that Kisenso's assets, in time, would be liquidated by Groupement Seneclem, the multinational of which Omar Gueye was the majority shareholder. He intended to funnel the profits into a philanthropic trust he had set up several years earlier in his brother's name.

'What price can you put on the life of a brother or a sister?' Kite asked. 'I'd say we have done what we can for Omar. At least some good will come out of Naby's death all these years later.'

There was a problem with the encryption on Fournier's phone and he bid Kite goodnight. It was a clear, warm night in Mauritius, the bar in his hotel already closed, a lone member of staff manning the reception desk. Fournier went down to the beach and took off his shoes. He wondered if he would ever learn what had happened to Grace Mavinga. Kite had given Gueye free rein: to release her to face justice and humiliation, stripped of her wealth and protection; or to avenge his brother's murder by killing her.

A couple were walking towards him, hand in hand in the moonlight. Fournier looked along the beach. They appeared to be tourists, the man about thirty-five in chinos and a polo shirt, the woman a similar age in a summer dress. Honeymooners or Action Division? Fournier had no weapon and no meaningful way of defending himself against attack. Yet he was not a coward. He would not run. He allowed them to come to within fifty metres of his position. For months he had lived with the knowledge that his life could be taken at any moment: by allies of Duval and Mavinga; by agents of the DGSE, keen to quash his investigation; or even by Duval himself, who had surely been notified of his imminent arrest.

He could hear the couple speaking English with American accents. The man laughed at something the woman had said. They suddenly kissed passionately. Fournier turned to the ocean and stared out at the blue-black sea.

Less than three miles away, Yves Duval was sitting in the saloon of *La Belle Adjani*, his 41-metre motor yacht, smoking a hand-rolled Romeo y Julieta and enjoying a balloon of Delamain cognac in the company of a young Madagascan friend, Zora Donisa, whom he had met at a Christmas

305

party in Johannesburg and flown out for the long weekend. He had not heard from Grace, nor had he expected to. She was likely en route to Nairobi; she had told Duval that she planned to stay in Kenya for at least two weeks 'while the dust settles'. It was not unusual for the two of them to spend several weeks, even months, apart; nor was it unusual for Duval to enjoy the attentions of young African women in the interim. He had no sense that the Mauritian authorities were intending to arrest him at dawn, nor had any of his former colleagues at the DGSE informed him that Grace Mavinga had vanished in broad daylight from the headquarters of Rycroft Maule.

'Let's go out to sea!' Zora exclaimed. She had been drinking champagne all night, occasionally popping into the master bedroom for a quick line of coke. 'I've never been to sea in a boat like this. You can be my captain. I will do anything you ask.'

She was hard to resist. Lithe and beautiful, completely naked under the yellow Marc Jacobs dress Duval had given her when she arrived. It was a still night, the ocean calm; there would have been no harm in going a mile or two offshore, anchoring for the night and making love on the deck. But Duval had given the crewmen the night off. Who would untie the mooring lines and operate the anchor? What if a storm blew up and he was suddenly left alone with a drunk, stoned girl who didn't know one end of a boat from the other?

'It's too late, my darling. We're not allowed to leave the marina after ten o'clock without permission. I'm sorry.'

'What permission? A man like you needs permission?' She was animated, determined that he should submit to her will. Zora jumped up and stood behind the wheel, turning it left and right like a child until Duval had to tell her to stop in case she broke it. 'You are being boring,' she said, taunting him. 'I want to have fun. Let's go! Let's start the engine!'

'We need the crew here,' he explained, placing the cigar in an ashtray and coming up behind her. Her waist was as smooth and taut as a pipe. Duval pressed himself against her.

'Then wake them up!' she said, pushing back against him.

'At one o'clock in the morning?' He put his arm across her breasts and kissed her on the neck. 'Let them sleep. We can still have fun, you and I.'

'At least start the engine then.' Zora twisted out of his embrace, stoned eyes staring into his. 'Let me feel it. Let me hear it.'

'Fine,' Duval replied.

The keys were hanging from the instrument panel. A small model of the Eiffel Tower dangled from them.

'Cheers!' she exclaimed.

The explosion lifted *La Belle Adjani* out of the water and blew out the windows on each of the four boats moored alongside. A fireball twice the height of the palm trees lit up the night sky, crimson flames mirrored in the calm, diesel-slicked waters of the marina. Flaming debris fell onto the pontoons and neighbouring boats. A second explosion followed almost instantly, Adjani's fuel tank catching and blasting a section of engine sideways across the marina where it crashed against a low harbour wall, smashing a parked moped.

Watching the flames from a rental car on the ocean road, listening to the pounding alarms in the marina, Hakim Ziani and Michel Rousseau of Action Division concluded that Yves Duval had failed to survive the blast. Their report, filed two hours later, did not mention the presence on the yacht of Zora Donisa.

49

Martha did not attend Eric Appiah's funeral. Kite had hoped that he would see her in Dakar, but she did not come. He wondered if the same reason that had prevented her from travelling to Xavier Bonnard's funeral three years earlier was the same reason that had kept her from flying to Senegal; she did not want to be reminded of her life with Kite nor drawn back into the sadness and loss of those distant days.

Yet when he returned to London, Kite found an email from her in a long-dormant account. Martha wanted to let him know that she had moved back to London and would be living in Belsize Park for the foreseeable future with Mia, the younger of her two children. Was there an address to which she could write properly? She had heard the shocking news about Eric and wanted to express her condolences.

That was the start of it. Martha left a telephone number and Kite had rung to thank her for being in touch. He said nothing about going to her old apartment in Manhattan and deliberately failed to mention both the Woodstein podcast and the concerns he had had about her safety. They arranged to meet for dinner in Notting Hill the night before he was due to fly back to Sweden.

They had spoken only once in almost twenty years; Martha had called from New York to tell Kite the news about Xavier. The last time Kite had seen her in the flesh was three days before her wedding in 2002; they had spent one last night together, a turbulent, tearful goodbye in a hotel room in Piccadilly. Kite had been invited to the wedding but did not go, making up an excuse about 'urgent business in Afghanistan' when in fact he had been drowning his sorrows in a Paris nightclub, scanning the dance floor for someone to take his mind off what was happening. He would always think of Martha's wedding day as one of the worst moments of his life, comparable in misery to the death of his father and the loss of Billy Peele.

It was a warm spring day. Mavinga and Duval were gone. Fournier had resigned and the Woodstein podcast was making waves in Paris, at Langley and in Vauxhall Cross; according to Cara, it had already notched up almost half a million downloads worldwide. Cablean had kept his word: the young British spy in Dakar was referred to throughout each episode as 'John Roberts', a brilliant intelligence officer who had died suddenly from blood cancer at the age of forty-two. There was no mention of Omar Gueye, nor of Martha Raine. Everything else was as close to the truth as Kite had been able to recall in Piksers. Cablean had done the rest, even sending him a Signal message to say that he had tracked down Ricky Ackerman to a high school in Illinois.

'He told me to fuck off then hung up the phone.'

The prospect of seeing Martha for the first time in almost two decades had induced in Kite a kind of vertigo. He wanted to show her that he had changed; at the same time, he did not want her to think that he had lost whatever she had once found interesting about him. He knew that her beauty would have faded, just as Kite himself

309

barely resembled the man Martha had fallen in love with all those years ago in France. He needed to be forgiven for the lies he had told when they were young, the mistakes he had made; he wanted to say sorry for putting BOX 88 between them, always his work first and Martha second. Kite would reiterate, just as he had done many times before their final separation, that he had taken her for granted and wished things had been less painful for her.

The failure of the relationship had haunted him for years; until he met Isobel, Martha had been the ghost floating around in Kite's heart, an idealised, unimprovable partner who could never be replaced. Now he would see her again for the first time since the hotel room in Piccadilly, both of them with almost twenty years of life unaccounted for; children, new friendships and experiences, setbacks and triumphs. Kite told himself that he was too settled in his marriage to be changed by a reunion with his first love. Dinner would just be a catch-up between old friends. No need to make a big deal about it.

He walked into the little Italian restaurant on Kensington Park Road and saw her instantly. Martha was exactly as she had always been – a little older, of course, but the same vivid eyes, the same wise, mischievous smile. She had always dressed so beautifully, tonight in jeans and a loose blue sweater, her hair slightly silver in the light. Kite knew, in that first instant, before they had even touched or spoken, that it was not over in his heart. The realisation hit him with the force of tragedy; he did not need this and yet he had somehow expected it.

He raised his hand to greet her. There was a smattering of applause from a nearby table; somebody was celebrating a birthday. A waiter bustled towards him. Kite looked at Martha a second time, astonished that he was so elated to see her. It felt like a betrayal of Isobel and yet he was able to steel himself against any feelings of desire. He wanted only to remake the friendship, somehow to include Martha in his life without upsetting Isobel; he wanted to support and protect her now that Jonas was out of the picture. He would not allow Martha to puncture what he had built with Isobel and Ingrid; but nor could he bear to lose her a second time.

'Hello, you,' she said.

'Hello, Martha.'

They embraced for a long time, Kite inhaling her scent, the shape of her exactly as he remembered. They might have been in the hotel room again, saying goodbye for the last time.

'Sorry I'm late.'

'You're not late,' she replied. 'Let's have a drink.'

Then Kite's phone rang. He had forgotten to put it on silent. Taking it out of his pocket to reject the call, he saw that Cara was ringing from The Cathedral. He had to take it. Martha knew the apologetic look in his eyes. Business before pleasure. He said that he would be three minutes, no more.

'Take as much time as you need,' she replied, sitting down.

Kite went out onto Kensington Park Road.

'This had better be good,' he said.

'I wondered if you'd seen.' Cara sounded anxious, tentative. 'The TV. The news.'

'I'm out for dinner. What's happened?'

'There's been a shooting in Stockholm.' Kite felt the ground give way beneath him. 'In Djursholm. The gunman is still active.'

Acknowledgements

I am always amazed by the kindness of strangers. Matteo Fraschini Koffi proved an invaluable friend and guide in Senegal. Alpha Seck was similarly generous with his time. My thanks also to Esther Dakin, Paul Harrison, Aidan Hartley, Cheryl Gregory, Youcef, Dan Magnowski, Mat Doran, Tim Beard, Sam Loehnis, Bill Leslie, Laura Jeffrey, Eliseo Neuman, Michael Abbott, Jean Luc Herbulot, Thiewlé Dione, Tertia and Peter Bailey, Doudou Thiaw, Richard Brown, CG, Zack Hartwanger, Taiye Selasi, Paulette and all the staff at the Palms. I am also very grateful to Caroline Lersten Athill, Max Kaufman, Will M, Julian Fisher, Patrick Lawrence, P, Lisa Hilton, Agnes Csefalvay, Rehan Baig, Salomé Baudino and Kirsten Enrich. As ever my deepest thanks to my wife, Harriette, to Stanley and Iris, to Sarah Gabriel and Will Francis. I owe a great debt of gratitude to Julia Wisdom, Roger Cazalet, Kimberley Young, Susanna Peden, Kate Elton, Anne O'Brien, Maddy Marshall, Kathryn Cheshire, Elizabeth Burrell and Angel Belsey at Harper Collins. Your patience and understanding during a difficult period were greatly appreciated. Thanks also to Kirsty Gordon, Rachel Balcombe, Corina Brodersen and Corissa Hollenbeck at Janklow & Nesbit; to Lucinda Prain and Matilda Southern-Wilkins at Casarotto Ramsay;

and to Luisa Smith, Otto Penzler and Charles Perry at Mysterious Press.

A number of books were very useful: *Moneyland* and *Butler to the World*, both by Oliver Bullough; *Do Not Disturb* by Michela Wrong; *We Wish to Inform You That Tomorrow We Will Be Killed with Our Families* by Philip Gourevitch; *In Pursuit of Disobedient Women* by Dionne Searcey; *A Sunday at the Pool in Kigali* by Gil Courtemanche; *One of Them* by Musa Okwonga; and *The Zanzibar Chest* by Aidan Hartley.

C.C. London 2023

CHARLES CUMMING is a British writer of spy fiction. He was educated at Eton College (1985-1989) and the University of Edinburgh (1990-1994), where he graduated with 1st Class Honors in English Literature. He's been described as "the best of the new generation of British spy writers who are taking over where John le Carré and Len Deighton left off." *Kennedy 35* is the third book in his bestselling BOX 88 series.